C000294730

WINTER AT WISHINGTON BAY

MAXINE MORREY

Boldwood

First published in Great Britain in 2020 by Boldwood Books Ltd.

Copyright © Maxine Morrey, 2020

Cover Design by Debbie Clement Design

Cover Photography: Shutterstock

The moral right of Maxine Morrey to be identified as the author of this work has been asserted in accordance with the Copyright, Designs and Patents Act 1988.

All rights reserved. No part of this book may be reproduced in any form or by any electronic or mechanical means, including information storage and retrieval systems, without written permission from the author, except for the use of brief quotations in a book review.

This book is a work of fiction and, except in the case of historical fact, any resemblance to actual persons, living or dead, is purely coincidental.

Every effort has been made to obtain the necessary permissions with reference to copyright material, both illustrative and quoted. We apologise for any omissions in this respect and will be pleased to make the appropriate acknowledgements in any future edition.

A CIP catalogue record for this book is available from the British Library.

Paperback ISBN: 978-1-83889-042-1

Large Print ISBN: 978-1-83889-804-5

Ebook ISBN: 978-1-83889-043-8

Kindle ISBN: 978-1-83889-039-1

Audio CD ISBN: 978-1-83889-040-7

MP3 CD ISBN: 978-1-83889-801-4

Digital audio download ISBN: 978-1-83889-041-4

Boldwood Books Ltd
23 Bowerdean Street
London SW6 3TN
www.boldwoodbooks.com

For Uncle Jim and Auntie Jean:
Thank you for providing the inspiration for the place that
would one day become Wishington Bay, not to mention all the
happy memories.
Miss you always.

1

'Morning, Sophia!' Ernie raised a hand being kept toasty by a thick sheepskin glove. 'Bit nippy today.'

I waved back and nodded in agreement, the bobble on my woolly hat bouncing as I did so. 'Just a little!' I grinned at both him and the typically British understatements. It was absolutely bloody freezing.

Wrapping my coat a little tighter, I dug my hands into my pockets and hurried along the cobbled village streets. Now that the bulk of the tourists had gone for the winter, it was easier to do without having to negotiate round the shuffling window shoppers of summer who filled the narrow pavements during the high season. Not that Wishington Bay ever entirely closed. Its renowned beauty, and relatively sheltered position, made it popular even out of season, and of course the brilliant reputation of Ned's restaurant, where I worked as a waitress, brought people from miles away all through the year.

I took extra shifts at the restaurant whenever I could, which on many occasions was over a weekend thanks to one particular colleague, Corinne. She'd been hired by Ned as a favour to old friends and was apparently there more for the 'life experience' rather than any need to earn a decent income. The latter part was covered most indulgently by her father, allowing Corinne to be far more concerned with fitting work around her social life, rather than the other way round. My own circumstances, however, dictated that I would never turn down the opportunity to earn a little extra cash, and why I was now hurrying along the road that led towards the edge of the village.

The idea that I would ever be in a position to need to earn money at all was still one that occasionally took some getting used to but I had, in general, adjusted fairly well to this new circumstance, and thanks to Carrie and her sister-in-law, Holly, I was on my way to the first day of another new venture.

As I turned into the private lane that led down to Holly and Gabe's house, I looked across from the raised position and took in the curve of the bay, the pale sand today edged with a sea of bright turquoise. Above it, puffy white clouds chased each other quickly across the blue sky. The sun shone, although there was little warmth from it, but the rays caught the tops of the white horses as they danced across the water before breaking onto the shore. I took a deep lungful of the cold, sharp air, tasting the salt in it, and smiled to myself, realising that despite my reduced circumstances I was lucky to have ended up at Wishington Bay. Pulling my phone from my pocket, I snapped a couple of pictures of the beautiful scenery to upload onto my Instagram later before heading on down the lane towards the house.

* * *

How the world turns, I thought, not for the first time that morning, as I gave the toilet brush a thorough exploratory trip under the rim. Eighteen months ago I had never cleaned a toilet, and most certainly had never had any inclination to. Now here I was cleaning them for strangers. Well, not exactly strangers. The house belonged to Holly, and until she and Gabe had become an item over the summer he'd been renting the other side of this gorgeous Art Deco semi. Now they were both living here, in what had once been Holly's grandmother's house, and which Holly had completely renovated during her enforced sabbatical from work last year, and both were full of the joys of young love. I only hoped it stayed that way – but I'd seen the way they looked at each other so I had a good feeling about it. Love had to have a solid foundation on which to build and they, like Ned and Carrie, seemed to have been lucky enough to find the right person to help grow that love and strengthen the relationship. I'd already popped next door and given it a quick flick with the duster and vacuumed round. With the two of them off taking a long overdue holiday, Holly had asked me to keep an eye on things. And now I was back in their half of the house – the difference that Holly had made to it emphasised how outdated next door was now, making it seem more shabby than it really was. But I got the feeling it wouldn't stay that way for long.

Gigi, Holly and Ned's grandmother, had been a wonderful woman by all accounts, and from what Carrie had said her death had completely devastated Holly. It had taken her granddaughter a year to even set foot back in the house that had been almost the sole source of any happiness she'd had during their childhood. But coming back to Wishington Bay had proved to be another pivotal point in Holly's life. It was that kind of place – I knew that from experience. The people here were special and the village itself had something almost magical about it. Even if you didn't feel you belonged anywhere, even if you walked in one day with everything you owned in one bag and had no clue what your next step was going to be, all the while wondering whether you'd just taken an enormous one in the wrong direction, Wishington Bay took care of you. It wrapped its arms around you and whispered, 'It's going to be OK.' Of course, I hadn't envisioned my version of OK would include cleaning other people's toilets, but beggars can't be choosers and it would have to do for now.

If Holly had had her way, she'd already have started transforming next door but on this point Gabe had managed to get her to see that she was at risk of setting herself up for exhaustion again, exactly the situation that had forced her return to Wishington Bay in the first place. So after consideration, Holly had acquiesced and admitted that he might actually be right, agreeing to slow down with her new endeavours – for now, at least. Especially in light of the surprise Gabe had in mind.

* * *

Nate McKinley wasn't due in until this evening but I wanted to make sure everything was in place and as comforting as it could be for his stay. Ned and Carrie, and by extension their family, had been so welcoming to me that I felt personally compelled to ensure that Gabe's brother felt welcomed too. It wasn't great timing that his trip was coinciding with Gabe's surprise holiday for him and Holly but, from what I understood, it wasn't a visit his brother had been planning to make at all – at least not for a while.

The rocky marriage Nate had been struggling with for years appeared to have broken apart irreconcilably some months ago and, having spent hours on the phone and Skype to his brother, Nate had finally accepted the offer of coming to stay at the house. I wasn't sure exactly what his job was – something to do with safety and the airlines from what I could gather. Gabe had told me that Nate had been a consultant on some TV series about aviation accidents as well as a couple of big budget action films and had now been asked to write a book on the same subject. He'd negotiated the time off in order to write it, but with the deadline creeping closer, the stress of his marriage and then its complete implosion, Gabe was clearly worried about his brother. Holly's suggestion of Nate coming over and using their house as a retreat and a quiet place for him to just reset and write had seemed the perfect solution.

The timing may not have been great but at least Nate was going to have company in the form of Gabe's mostly-sausage dog, Bryan. At the moment, the pooch was lodging with Carrie and Ned, a situation they were both happy with, but Gabe had argued that, with the restaurant plus Holly's one-year-old nephew, they already had a lot to deal with, and Bryan would be good company for Nate. It was pretty hard to be sad or gloomy when you had one of the cutest dogs in the country by your side.

I finished the bathroom and then moved onto the rest of the upstairs, giving it all a dust and polish so that it was gleaming when Nate arrived. Once that was done, I moved downstairs and made sure everything was perfect there too. Labelling the last container, I checked the fridge over one more time and closed it. That should keep him going for a while, anyway. I pulled out a pad and pen from the basket I'd plonked on a kitchen chair and began writing.

Dear Nate,

Welcome to Wishington Bay. I hope you had a good flight. Everything is pretty well stocked, as per Holly and Gabe's instructions, and there are three meals in the fridge ready to be heated up to get you going, plus a couple of fresh soups. I did check with your brother if there was anything you didn't like so hopefully these will be OK.

I know Gabe has mentioned that I am happy to come in and cook for you during your time here, so once you've decided whether that's something you want to go ahead with, perhaps you could let me know. I've popped my phone number and email on the bottom of this note, and will be back next Thursday anyway to clean, if I don't hear from you before.

Good luck with the writing!

I chewed the pen for a moment, unsure how to finish off the note. I'd unwound a lot since I'd made my home in Wishington Bay, no longer feeling the need to calculate every word of everything I wrote in case someone took it the wrong way, or double checking I'd used exactly the right words and tone to ensure I was making precisely the right impression. But Gabe and Holly were my friends and I wanted his brother to feel welcome, especially as he'd been having a tough time, and so I was eager to do what I could to help.

In the end, I settled for just 'Sophia' to the note, adding a smiley face next to it, before popping the paper on the table, tucking the very corner of it under a vase of white lilies already wafting their delicious scent through the house so that Nate would see it easily upon arrival.

* * *

Nate McKinley was a man of few words. The opposite of his brother, whose open, easy manner was perfect for his career as a paediatrician, Nate's serious manner suited someone who spent his days thinking about all the ways a plane could crash. But still, a thank you text wouldn't have hurt, would it?

'I'm not sure he's going to be that thrilled to have me interrupting his day,' I said to Carrie as I popped my head into the restaurant a week later to say hi and double check my waitressing shifts.

'You're not interrupting. You're there to do a job. He knows that.'

'What's he like?' I asked.

Carrie gave a bit of a shrug as she transferred the little one to her other hip. 'Quiet. Shyer than Gabe, but he'd just stepped off a flight after a twenty-four-hour journey and his wife's flounced off with her tennis coach so it's not surprising he wasn't at his chattiest when he came to pick up Bryan.'

'You think he'll look after him OK'

She flapped a hand. 'Absolutely no question. There's no way on this earth that Gabe would have left that dog in anyone's hands he didn't trust. You know that.'

I nodded. Gabe had rescued Bryan as a tiny puppy, having found him injured and abandoned, shivering in the pouring rain on a city street. He'd stuffed him in his motorbike jacket, raced to the veterinary practice where Carrie worked and begged them to save him, whatever the cost. Bryan had been lucky to last the night but to look at him now, you'd never have known he'd had such a tough start and he and his burly, six-foot-four guardian angel had been pretty much inseparable ever since. Hopefully Nate was just as crazy about the little dog as the rest of us were.

The doorbell tune echoed round the tiled hallway. I had a key, of course, but it didn't feel right to just let myself in, especially as I still hadn't received any sort of reply to the note I'd left. I shifted my weight to the other foot, then rang again. Nothing. Slightly hesitantly, I plugged the key into the lock and turned it. No small rocket of fur and energy came flying at me and there was a stillness to the house.

'Hello?' I called out, just in case, my voice echoing a little in the entryway.

Silence.

'Mr... McKinley?' Should I call him Nate or Mr McKinley? I hadn't even thought of that.

Cautiously I moved into the kitchen and called out again but there was no reply. Well, I couldn't stand there all day. I was there to do a job and if Nate McKinley wanted to make sure he wasn't going to run into his cleaner, then so be it. That was, of course, his prerogative. I knew from past experience that some people could make a variety of assumptions about others based entirely on their jobs. I was ashamed to say that, at one point, I'd been one of them. But my eyes had now been opened to the world in a myriad of ways and I was proud to say I was no longer like that. If Nate was, then he really was different to his younger brother, and not in a good way.

'I assume you must be Sophia?'

'Holy shit!' I jumped, stumbling backwards. I steadied myself on the side of the bath as the toilet brush went skittering across the floor and stopped within millimetres of the feet of a tall, broad, very serious-looking man with a quiet but deep Australian voice.

2

The scampering of tiny feet alerted us to incoming company in the shape of a mostly-sausage dog. The love and energy wrapped up in the tiny ball of exuberance that was Bryan, with a Y, completely belied his difficult start in life. While we were all crazy for the little dog and his antics, it was hard to tell whether Nate felt the same. Glancing at his face, it was hard to tell anything much about him at all. His expression was blank and unreadable.

Bryan's eyes brightened as he got to the doorway and saw the new toy sitting at the feet of his temporary master. His tiny paws moved on the spot, desperately trying to gain traction as his snout pointed forwards and he launched himself towards it. Realising what the dog had in mind, I launched myself in the same direction, determined to grab the brush before Bryan got his jaws clamped round it. However, as I did so, Nate languidly scooped the dog up with one hand, his little paws still running in mid-air and I whisked the brush out of the way with an urgency that now seemed faintly ridiculous. I realised I was also now awkwardly close to Nate McKinley. This definitely hadn't been the introduction to my client that I'd expected or wanted. Firstly, I'd sworn at him – well, not at him – but sort of at him, and now I was half-kneeling at his feet brandishing a loo brush.

'Hi!' I said, desperately trying to act as if this was a perfectly normal introduction. I'd had a lot of practice at acting as though everything in life was just perfect, so at least I was putting some of that experience to good use. I took a step back as I did so, gaining a little more personal space between us, and saw a brief flicker cross his face. Facing him now, I yanked off my rubber glove and held out my hand to shake his. 'And yes, I'm Sophia. You must be Nate.'

He nodded briefly and shook my hand, even more briefly, as Bryan whined and wriggled under his arm.

'I expect you'll want to clean that before I put him down,' he said, nodding at the floor.

'Oh... Umm, yes. Of course,' I said, pulling my glove back on. 'I'll get on to that now.'

He nodded again. 'We'll get back out of your way.' And with that he turned and headed off downstairs, taking Bryan with him. I hadn't even had a chance to say hi properly to my little canine friend. Letting out a tight sigh, I finished scrubbing the toilet with so much vigour, powered by irritation, it was a surprise there weren't shavings of porcelain flying off. It was hard to believe this man and Gabe were even related. Gabe's open, friendly manner couldn't be more different to this man's guarded, cool one. Not one smile had passed his lips – which was a shame as it looked like it had the potential to be a very attractive mouth. Or maybe that was just as well. Who knew?

It was probably a good thing Nate McKinley was only staying temporarily because, as welcoming as Wishington Bay was, that attitude certainly wouldn't endear him to the villagers. OK, so it probably wasn't ideal that I'd flung a used loo brush in his direction, but it was an accident, and it was partly his fault for creeping up on me anyway! And I certainly wasn't happy about his insinuation that I'd been preparing to leave the floor unmopped after the toilet brush incident either! I might have been new to all this housework stuff but I'd discovered I had rather a talent for it, and even found it quite calming – gorgeous-but-moody Australian men aside. I'd even started an Instagram account to document tips and tricks I employed, along with other little moments of my days. Obviously I didn't use my real name, and never featured on it at all, but I enjoyed sharing and often picked up quite a few Likes.

I took a couple of deep breaths and calmed a little, having now moved onto the bath, the rhythmic movement of cleaning it helping me relax. I was doing this for Holly and Gabe. That's what I had to remember. Just because Nate McKinley was the unappreciative type, I wasn't going to let it spoil my day. I also reminded myself that Nate was going through some marital problems and I knew from experience that that didn't always make you the cheeriest clown in the car, so I was happy to cut him some slack on both of those accounts. But, still, manners cost nothing.

I finished mopping the floor and smiled, pleased with the shine I'd polished in. I knew Nate had no cause to doubt my cleaning duties as I'd done a trial run for Holly before she'd left and she'd been thrilled. I gathered my supplies in the little caddy and tried not to let the fact there had been no, 'Thanks for the meals you left. They were delicious!' either. Just thanks on its own would have been nice (even though I absolutely knew they were delicious).

I stood and stretched, giving one last look around the now gleaming bathroom. The toilet roll holder was full (I'd even done the pointy thing with the first sheet), and a bundle of spare rolls lazed in a wicker basket next to the wooden ladder towel rail where bright white, fluffy towels resided. A pop of bright orange was added to the white bathroom by the vase of fresh flowers I'd stood on the deep windowsill. Standing back by the door, I pulled my phone from my pocket and snapped a couple of pictures.

To be honest, it hadn't been in that bad a state considering there'd been a man living here on his own for a week. Amazingly, even the toilet seat was down! But I got a sense of satisfaction from seeing the taps shining and the modern suite clean and bright as the low winter sun beamed through the softly frosted glass of the room.

Having dusted and cleaned upstairs, I popped downstairs to fetch the homemade air freshener I'd mixed up yesterday using some white sage oil I'd picked up in the crystal shop in the village at the weekend. Not only did it smell wonderful, it was said to have cleansing properties and improve the energy of a space. I wasn't sure if I believed all that but it was a nice thought, and from my brief encounter this morning, a little less negativity round here wouldn't do any harm.

From the corner of my eye, I saw Nate sat at the lovingly worn oak dining table, a laptop in front of him. He wasn't typing, just staring at the screen, apparently engrossed. Bryan was out like a light in his bed, upside down, feet in the air, head lolling to the side and snoring gently. Nate might not be great with manners when it came to humans, but obviously Bryan had had a great time on his walk this morning so there was at least that in his favour. People who were kind to animals generally got a bit of a head start when it came to likeability in my book.

Judging by the deep furrow on his brow, writing, or rather thinking about writing things plummeting to earth at speed required a good deal of concentration. Thank goodness I'd finished downstairs while he was out this morning. I'm sure roaring round next to him with the vacuum while he was trying to work would have just about topped off the opinion he seemed to be forming of me. Putting the appliance I'd used earlier back in the cupboard, I returned the cleaning caddy and my gloves to the cabinet underneath the sink and grabbed my coat off the hook.

'I'm finished now, Mr McKinley.' After his rather frosty manner earlier, I'd decided that the formal address was the right one to go with. 'So, I'll be going.'

Bryan stirred in his bed, sleepily opened one eye and then spun round and out of his bed towards me, leaping half elegantly, half hopefully at me as he tended to do, with the innocent belief that whoever he launched himself at was going to catch him.

'Hello, my darling!' I laughed as he wriggled in my arms and snuffled his nose into my neck for cuddles. 'You obviously had a good walk!'

'Run.'

I looked up.

'He had a good run. I run and he keeps up. Astonishingly.'

I couldn't help wondering what would happen if he didn't. 'That's lucky.'

Nate gave a small head tilt, an action that reminded me of his brother. 'I would have slowed if he couldn't. Don't worry. I have no plans to abandon him on the beach.'

'I didn't think for a moment you would!' I tried to laugh it off but knew the tinge of pink on my face probably wasn't helping my cause.

'My life wouldn't be worth living if anything happened to him.'

'No, he does mean the world to Gabe, and Holly too now, of course,' I said, as I released a clearly still snoozy Bryan back to the floor whereupon he toddled back to his bed, pulled Petey Prawn closer with one paw and laid his head on him, sleepily watching us.

In response to my reply, Nate merely gave another of those short annoying nods that seemed designed to cut off all conversation and we stood there awkwardly for a second.

'Is there anything you need?' Frankly, I just wanted to leave now. Nate clearly didn't want any company other than that of the little dog, but Gabe had made me promise to keep an eye on his brother. Nate might be the eldest, but it was obvious Gabe had concerns about him, knowing he was going through a tough time.

'Need?' Nate frowned.

'Yes,' I shifted my weight and tried not to show my impatience. It wasn't exactly a hard question. 'Food, supplies, anything?'

He shook his head. 'Nope. I'm good.'

Thank you? I smiled tightly.

'Thank you,' he added, causing the pink tinge to once again flush on my cheeks. Growing up, I'd always been lauded for my peaches and cream complexion, but the truth was, it gave me away far more than I'd have liked.

For a moment I thought I saw a flicker of a smile hover on Nate McKinley's features but an instant later that impenetrable expression was back and I concluded it must have just been a trick of the light from the low sun flooding in through the wall of glass doors Holly had had fitted to make the most of the view onto the beach.

'Right. I'll be going, then. Enjoy your day.'

He gave a small shrug, nodding towards the open laptop on the table.

'Oh. I see. Well, at least you're getting out with Bryan on the beach. That's good. And there are plenty of places to explore round here, even in the off season,' I added, keeping my promise to Gabe who was worried his brother may just hunker in and write. I knew that Gabe's hope was that Nate would – at the risk of sounding a bit new agey – spend some time rediscovering himself.

From what I'd heard, his wife had been pretty high maintenance, but Nate had been well and truly smitten. But without give and take, any relationship is heading for stormy waters, and Nate gave everything according to Gabe, whose normally smiling mouth had been set in a thin line when he'd explained. But he wasn't going to discover much about himself sitting in front of a screen for the next couple of months. I had the distinct feeling that Nate really did want to be left alone but I'd made a promise to people I cared about.

Nate looked back at me.

'I mean, I can show you some if you like. Take you to some places that have become favourites for me since I moved here.'

His intense blue eyes were fixed on me for a few moments, the silence broken only by the quiet ticking of the kitchen clock and Bryan's soft snores.

And then he smiled. But it wasn't a proper smile. It was tight and awkward and the sort of smile you're given the moment before you're told you're fired. Or dumped. Admittedly, I'd not had a lot of experience of the first – at least not as the 'firee', but I'd certainly been dumped a few times and I had a strange feeling I was about to get so again. By someone I wasn't even dating!

'Sophia.'

I tilted my head in question, mirroring his earlier action.

'I'm sure you're a really nice woman...'

Where was he going with this?

'Umm... I try.'

He shifted position, and for the first time since I'd met him, he didn't look as in control or collected. Clearing his throat, he started again.

'I know my brother's been worried about me, and while I appreciate his and Holly's offer for me to come here and... any other arrangements they might have made—'

I drew myself up, feeling every muscle within me tighten, my voice cutting across his. 'They haven't made any "arrangements" with me!' I knew the colour was back in my face, but right now I didn't care. I was more concerned that Nate McKinley seemed to think I may have some sort of side business going, and I didn't particularly appreciate the suggestion.

'No, I didn't mean...' he ran a hand across the hint of dark stubble that shadowed his chin.

'Didn't mean what, exactly?'

'That you...' he faltered.

Bryan had now woken again, apparently picking up on the tension filling the room and he toddled over, stopping by Nate's thickly socked feet. He gave a little whine and Nate bent and scooped him up. 'It's all right, mate,' he said quietly, rubbing his thumb over Bryan's silky head. The little dog looked over at me, as if he wanted me to confirm this.

The distraction seemed to have given Nate time to collect, and organise, his thoughts.

'I'm just aware that Gabe knows I've been unhappy and now he's all loved up, he's in that position where he wants everyone else to be too. I'm sure you're really nice and everything, but I'm definitely not looking for... anything... to happen over here. I'm not interested in exploring or anything like that either. I just needed somewhere with peace and quiet where I can get on and write this book. Had I known my brother and Holly had other ideas, I might have made different plans.'

I stared at him for a moment, shook my head and headed towards the back door to let myself out.

'Sophia, wait.'

I didn't.

But the words were burning inside me and I'd spent a lifetime not saying what I felt. I'd made a promise I would never do that again. Sometimes it worked out, sometimes it didn't, but at least I now knew I was being true to myself. Having pulled open the door, I turned back, coming face to face with Nate who had crossed the room after he'd called. He was closer than I'd planned, which was a little unsettling. There was quite a lot of Nate McKinley – in a good way – which was inconvenient, but thanks to his superior attitude, he'd made it incredibly easy to ignore anything I might ordinarily have considered attractive about him.

'Just so you know,' I said, looking up – quite a way up – at him. 'Your brother and Holly had no such ideas as those you're suggesting. As much of a catch as you seem to think you may be, I'm certainly not looking for anyone either at the moment – and if I were... well, let's be honest, shall we? You haven't exactly endeared yourself to me so far. Gabe and Holly are just concerned about you, and everyone knows that shutting yourself away isn't good for mind or body, so a bit of exploring might not have hurt you. But clearly you're intent on staying inside your cocoon, except when Bryan forces you out of it, and that's your prerogative. People in this village care about each other. It's just the way they are. And I, for one, have been grateful for that. Obviously, it's not really your thing, and that's fair enough but it might be wise not to assume there's some hidden agenda behind everything. Sometimes people are just nice. I would have thought you'd have realised that as Gabe's your brother, but maybe not. Perhaps you should have made other plans, as you said. It sounds like a hotel room in a faceless city might have worked just as well, if not better, for what you wanted rather than somewhere people might actually care and take an interest. However, I for one won't make that mistake again. I'll be back to clean the same time next week if you want to arrange your dog walk so that I don't disturb your work.'

With that I turned back to the door, used all my willpower not to storm out and instead left in a calm and controlled – outwardly at least – manner, not waiting for Nate's reply.

3

As I stalked back up the hill towards the centre of the village and my cosy little flat above Flora's gift shop, I turned things over in my mind. I wasn't exactly thrilled I'd let off a rocket at a friend's brother but, if anything was said about it later, hopefully I'd be able to explain my actions. And I stood by what I said. From what I'd seen, the eldest McKinley brother would have been better booking into some bland chain hotel back in Australia and saved himself the airfare. Not to mention all the work Holly had put into making the house welcoming for him. When the plan to get Nate over was originally being hatched, Gabe, being a bloke, had fully intended to put his brother up in the half of the house he had rented from Gigi, and subsequently from Holly until they got together. Holly, however, had other plans, claiming the other place was too dated and not homely enough. It hadn't bothered Gabe, and possibly wouldn't have bothered Nate, especially since it appeared his plans involved him barely looking up from his computer, but Holly was adamant that he should have a warm, welcoming home to come into and had insisted he stay in theirs which, now she'd finished, was like a high-end show home. It really was stunning, and she'd added lovely little touches like a small glass bowl of what she knew to be Nate's favourite sweets on the coffee table and a couple of magazines in subjects Gabe had told her his brother was interested in. Not to mention arranging to stock the cupboards and fridge with his favourite foods. I felt a pang of sadness for Holly that all her hard work to make the man who was to be her brother-in-law feel welcome had apparently gone to waste.

Reaching my front door, I waved through the shop window at Flora, and headed in to the warmth of my flat. Collecting the post, I rifled casually through as I climbed the stairs, unlocked the interior door and headed into the kitchen, putting Nate McKinley firmly out of my mind. Opening the photo app, I added a #nofilter tag to one of the views of the bay I'd taken earlier and uploaded it. There was no location added. It was pretty unlikely anyone from my old life would ever discover my account – there were no exotic getaways, designer clothing or name drops posted on my feed, which meant it was far below the notice of the set I'd once been a part of. But I liked to make sure. I'd shut my old life away, separated myself from it entirely, and I wanted to keep it that way.

I'd deleted all of my previous social media accounts when I'd walked out on my old life and I'd been careful to keep things vague on my new Instagram. However, I happily scrolled the ones I followed and having my own again gave me an outlet to share my days beside the sea along with what filled those days.

Next, I chose the photo I'd taken of the sparkling bathroom and pressed 'Share' to my Instagram Stories. I added a cleaning gif and tagged the names of a couple of products I'd used, then pressed send. I noticed a couple of Direct Messages and opened the first, scanned it then moved on to the second, which was of a similar ilk. I'd had a few like this now and I deleted these two just as I'd deleted the others. I wasn't entirely sure if they were genuine anyway. Both of these today purported to be journalists, looking for more information on me and my account, saying how they loved what I was doing and how they'd like to feature it in their magazines. The fact that I tried to use natural and eco cleaning products, and made my own products like those used decades ago in fancy houses, seemed to be quite a large part of the appeal.

But even if these things were genuine, which I had my doubts about – it was the internet, after all – I wasn't interested. I was happy just doing my thing for me and me alone. Yes, I'd picked up quite a few followers along the way and the Likes and views did seem to be increasing but I wasn't looking for any sort of recognition, and I certainly didn't want to be featured in the media! I could just imagine my mother's face now. Even with all the Botox and surgeries, I was pretty sure she'd manage to make her displeasure obvious.

My account was just something I enjoyed. A way of keeping a record and documenting the new life I'd created here. Perhaps it was also a way of documenting the new person I'd become. A woman with new interests – interests I'd chosen myself, rather than those expected of me. A woman with a job. A woman who actually wanted to get up in the morning. But that's all it was ever meant to be – all I ever wanted it to. And all it ever would be. If these were genuine enquiries, they'd soon move on once they realised I wasn't interested. Nobody had much of an attention span these days, and for every one person like me not seeking publicity there would be a hundred others ready to bite their hands off for it.

It had been quite a revelation to find I actually enjoyed cleaning. That said, I wasn't in any great rush to take on a chambermaid job if I could help it – I'd read some real horror stories about what they had to deal with at times. But I did enjoy cleaning and tidying my little flat, making surfaces shine and everything look just so. I'd fully expected the novelty to wear off after a while, but it hadn't, and the enthusiasm had only grown. I had vague recollections from my childhood of the housekeeper using special polishes and homemade concoctions to polish this and bring a shine to that, and although I'd been fascinated, once my mother had realised I'd been spending time with the staff she'd immediately put a stop to it. I'd missed those times. Mrs B had talked to me far more in one hour as she went about her work, me trailing behind her, than my mother would in an entire week. I'd thought about Mrs B as I'd begun learning the art of housekeeping, and wished I could remember all the tips and tricks she'd shared with me. When I couldn't, I'd begun researching old methods of cleaning, reading up about products your grandmother would concoct – well, obviously not my own grandmother – but that generation. Accounts of how the grand houses kept their contents in top condition, both back in the day and now, fascinated me and I loved trying some of those techniques out in my little flat. I'd begun taking some photos documenting both my experiments and the end results of a good cleaning session, which provided a record of things that had worked (and those that hadn't!) as well as a way to remind myself of the buzz I got when the work was done, and the sense of calm and accomplishment it brought.

A notification popped up on my phone. Someone had commented on my story. I opened the app and read the message.

Looking fabulous! Told you, love, you should be getting sponsored

Flora downstairs was a big fan of my account, and having successfully put some of the tips I'd discovered into use was now convinced I should be trying to turn myself into some sort of cleaning-guru-influencer.

'Look at that Mrs Hinch,' she'd said during our last chat about it all. 'Book deals, products she uses flying off the shelves. TV appearances, too!'

My blood had chilled at the thought. I appreciated her enthusiasm but Flora didn't know the whole story – nobody did – and I was aware my excuses probably sounded a little weak and evasive. 'It's not really for me, Flora. I'm more than happy where I am.'

'Might save you some pennies,' she added.

I gave a little shrug, half in agreement. I couldn't disagree that that side didn't appeal to me, and promised I'd think about it.

A little while after our discussion, I'd been contacted by a fairly new eco cleaning brand asking me if I'd like to try their new oven cleaner. This was one household task I wasn't a huge fan of, mostly because all the products stank the place out, so their promise of natural ingredients and low odour had caught my attention. I agreed and gave them a fake name and my address, and then did a trial of it, with a short video. I didn't speak on the film, and just added captions over the Story on IG but views went up, and the company must have been pleased as they sent me some more items to try. Since then, I'd had a few more trial products and I certainly wouldn't have to spend much on any cleaning paraphernalia for the near future. So long as I kept my true identity to myself, it was a win-win situation.

My annoyance with Nate McKinley's arrogant attitude didn't last long. I'd learned to let things go far more easily since arriving in Wishington Bay over eighteen months ago. My time here had helped me discover what was truly important. I'd also discovered that when life hurled itself at you, you got a quick lesson in finding out who your real friends were. Which was why I'd ended up alone upon my arrival here. There was no one to tell where I was. They'd all picked a side – and it wasn't mine. With hindsight, I realised that had been a good thing. At last I was no longer being shaped by other people's opinions and actions. I was free to make my own choices, and although it had been hard initially, entirely terrifying in fact, it had also been incredibly freeing. Not to mention enlightening. I'd discovered a whole new world. I'd made true friends who didn't care who I was, or what I had – the latter being very little. And the former wasn't important. They knew who I was now, not who I'd once been. In the back of my mind, I did feel bad that I wasn't being entirely honest with the people I'd come to call real friends. They were open with me and although I had begun to learn to trust and open up more since settling here, I still couldn't bring myself to reveal everything. Not yet.

* * *

'Penny for them?' Eloise, my friend and fellow waitress, asked after she finished taking a booking on the phone. I was standing with my back to the restaurant floor, smoothing my apron distractedly.

'Huh? Oh,' I shook my head. 'Nothing in particular,' I said, hoping my pink cheeks wouldn't give me away.

I couldn't deny I'd been a little stung by the fact Gabe's brother clearly thought I looked in need of setting up on a date but the brisk, chilly walk home that day had helped cool both my face and my annoyance. By the time I'd reached the top and passed by the garden at the top of the hill, still beautiful even in the depths of winter, I'd resolved to push the encounter, and Nate, firmly out of my mind until I had to return for the next scheduled clean.

Unfortunately, Nate McKinley had just put a big dent in my perfect plan. He was currently sitting by the window in Ned's restaurant, gazing out towards the sea, watching as pewter waves reared and crashed onto the beach. Last night's storm had lingered into the morning and, although the worst of it had now passed, the winds were still near gale force, bending the palms outside with a vigour that made me wonder at their resilience.

Eloise appeared to accept my explanation, nodding her head instead towards the tables.

'Hottie at nine o'clock,' she winked as she nudged me aside so she could write the reservation in the book. Ned and Carrie still favoured the old-fashioned way of booking, and I liked that. It was simple and it worked. Why make it more complicated than it needed to be? A pretty good mantra for life, now I thought about it. I smiled to myself and wondered if I'd spent too long in the crystal shop in the village.

I glanced up, then looked back, watching her write. 'That's not a hottie. That's Nate McKinley. Gabe's brother.'

Eloise finished her task and raised her head, sneaking another glance at Nate as she did so.

'Really?' she replied, smiling.

'Uh-huh.'

'The one you're housekeeping for?'

'Yes.'

'I hope you've got a frilly apron and feather duster then.'

I shook my head, smiling, and she chuckled.

'We didn't exactly hit it off. Besides, he's so wrapped up in his work and whatever else, I'm not sure he'd even notice.'

Eloise gave me a look. 'Believe me. He'd notice.' She glanced over again. 'Oh, if I were twenty years younger...' Eloise winked.

'He might like older women,' I grinned back.

'That's true. Although we both know he'd never measure up to my Bob in real life.'

I gave her a little squeeze. Bob had retired from a stressful but exceptionally well paid job a couple of years ago and they'd moved down from London permanently to the little fisherman's cottage they'd bought decades ago as a peaceful bolthole away from the city. Eloise had always been the sociable type and loved to mix with people, so now worked at the restaurant a couple of times a week. Bob walked her there, and met her again at the end of the shift. Every time. The love in both their eyes was evident and I'd have given everything to have had someone look at me like that after four months, let alone coming up to forty years married. Even four weeks might have been nice.

'You'd better get over there. He's already glanced this way a couple of times.'

'Right.' Grabbing my pad and pen, I smoothed my long apron once more, pushed my shoulders back and walked over with a purposeful, confident air and tried to ignore the fact we hadn't exactly parted on the friendliest of terms.

4

'Good afternoon.'

Nate's gaze swung from the stormy sea to me. Dark grey shadows under his eyes contrasted with the blue gaze and his skin was pale and drawn. He looked exhausted.

'Hi.' It looked like I'd been right on my previous assessment as I took in the faint smile hovering uncertainly around what was definitely an undeniably attractive mouth. 'I didn't realise you worked here as well as doing the housekeeping.'

I kept my expression fixed and tried not to bristle.

He dragged a hand across an unshaven jaw. 'Judging by that look you're trying not to show, I think I may have just put my foot in it. Again.'

'Not at all.'

Crap. My 'really not bothered' face was way too rusty!

He quirked an eyebrow in disbelief.

'I'm smiling!'

'Yep. And it looks like it's hiding a desire to write "lace with arsenic" on that order pad.'

I burst out laughing, feeling my face relax as I did so.

'Actually, I was only going to put "sprinkle". You weren't quite bad enough to deserve "lace".'

He looked at me, that smile still in shadow. 'You sure about that?'

I shrugged. 'We all have bad days.'

Nate studied me for a moment. 'I guess so. And thank you. I wanted to apologise anyway, though.'

I waved my pad. 'Nothing to apologise for. Now, what can I get you?'

'I think there is,' he said, ignoring my question. 'I'm pretty sure I was unforgivably rude.'

'Well as I've forgiven you, that can't exactly have been the case, can it?'

'I think that just means I'm exceptionally lucky.'

'That too,' I grinned.

And then he smiled back. Behind me I heard Eloise drop the glass she was drying and I wasn't surprised. Nate McKinley's smile was one of those that could make a lot of women drop a lot of things. It was beautiful and unexpected and a tiny bit crooked which made it perfect.

'I am sorry for being such an arse the other day.'

'It's fine. Really.'

'It isn't. And I think you were right.'

'About what?'

'Taking advantage of the place. If I'd wanted to stay inside I could have stayed in a hotel at home, like you said. I know Holly went to a lot of trouble to make the place welcoming and comfortable for me, and I didn't really appreciate that until you tore me off a strip about it.'

I felt the colour creep onto my chest and was thankful for the high-necked top I'd chosen to wear today. Of course, that couldn't hide my cheeks, which also felt decidedly pink.

'Don't be embarrassed, please,' he said, his dark brow furrowing as my colour deepened. 'I deserved it. And I probably needed it.'

I shrugged. 'Gabe said you'd been going through a stressful time. We're not always ourselves in those situations.'

He turned his gaze back to the window. 'I'm not sure I even know who I am these days.' His voice was quiet and I wasn't sure if he realised he'd spoken aloud. He turned back and looked up, the palest imitation of the earlier smile on his face. I smiled back, but as I met his eyes I saw nothing but sadness. I recognised that same sadness. Had felt it myself for too many years. My resolve was set. I couldn't fix Nate's relationship but I could do my best to make sure this break refreshed him and maybe he'd be able to find himself again. I knew what it was like to feel lost and I hated to think of someone else going through that. Gabe and Holly had been incredibly kind to me and I would do what I could to pay that forward.

'So, is today your first foray out into the big wide world of Wishington Bay?'

A hint of the smile returned. 'It is. Gabe said that Ned had promised to keep a table available for me, which I know is a really kind offer bearing in mind those Michelin stars on the door.'

'Ned and Carrie are big on family.'

'But I'm not family.'

'Family doesn't always mean those you share the same blood with. You make your own family. And Gabe is a part of theirs – so that extends to you.'

He shook his head a little as if he were having trouble understanding the whole concept.

'I should thank him.'

'He's not here at the moment but I'll pass it on. You can catch him another time. If you're brave enough to keep up this actually leaving the house for a purpose other than dog walking, of course.'

The smile widened a little more. 'Did you just challenge an Aussie bloke?'

I shrugged.

'Holly might have mentioned that Gabe has a competitive streak he blames partly on his heritage and partly on his gender.'

'Sneaky.'

'Whatever works.'

He laughed then. Softly. As though he was testing something out, an unfamiliar action. I once again felt that wash of sadness and quickly covered it with a smile, hoping this time that Nate didn't see straight through it.

He pulled the menu towards him. 'What do you recommend?'

'Honestly? Anything. It's all delicious.'

'Is the fish caught locally?' he asked, nodding towards the fishing boats moored further up the bay.

'Yes. Every day. Which is why there's a couple of things off the menu today. Those with the stars.' I pointed them out with the end of my pencil. 'The storm was too bad for the boats to go out last night.'

'I'm not surprised. The waves in the night were huge.'

I tilted my head. 'Were you up?'

He screwed his nose up a little. 'I don't always sleep brilliantly.'

'You do look a little tired.'

The shadowy smile was back. 'I look knackered and I know it.'

'No! Not... that bad.'

He gave me that look again.

'OK. Yes. You look shattered. There. Happy now? You can complain to my boss that I've been insulting the customers.'

Nate shook his head. 'Not at all,' he said, pointing to his choice on the menu. 'Actually, your honesty is very refreshing.'

'Oh... OK. Good choice, by the way. Would you like a drink while you wait? I'll bring you some water anyway.'

'Water's good, thanks.'

'Right. I'll go and put this through. Wave if you need anything else.'

Nate nodded and I turned to leave.

'Oh! Sophia?'

I glanced round.

'Thank you for all the food in the fridge and freezer. The meals, I mean. That was really kind of you. I should have replied to your note. I'm sorry.'

Instinctively, I leant over and touched his arm briefly. 'You're very welcome.' With that I hurried across the restaurant and into the kitchen. Making a show of checking my order, I knew that the sudden flush on my cheeks wasn't only from the whoosh of heat as I entered the bustling, steamy room but from the electric charge I'd felt race through my body as I'd leant towards Nate.

Taking a deep breath, I inwardly gave myself a head shake. Honestly? What was wrong with me? I'd stood there a few days ago and told him to his face that I wasn't looking for a man. And I wasn't! So why on earth had I gone momentarily gooey the second I'd brushed my fingers across his wrist? I tore off the page from my order pad and handed it over to Ned's second in command.

'Thanks, Anton.'

'Anything for my favourite waitress,' he grinned, and I shook my head. Anton had been teasing me like that since the day I'd started. I hadn't had a clue what I'd been doing, having never worked at anything before, let alone as a waitress. His dark brow and Gallic flourishes had slightly terrified me to begin with, aware of the fierce reputation some chefs had. But I needn't have worried. Ned didn't stand for any of that nonsense in his kitchen and Anton was really a teddy bear. I just wasn't looking for him to be my teddy bear. We'd had a couple of drinks together as friends and those evenings had only confirmed that the required spark wasn't there. But we'd laughed a lot, cementing our friendship further. Annoyingly, that spark I'd been avoiding had now arrived like a bolt of lightning from the most unexpected, and most inconvenient, source. Perfect.

* * *

A short while later, having seated various other customers and dropped off several more orders with Anton, the device hooked on my apron string gave a buzz and I headed back to the kitchen to collect my order. Picking it up, I gave myself another mental shake to clear my head and pushed through the double doors from the kitchen back out into the restaurant. It was busier now and the noise level had risen, giving the place a great, buzzy vibe. Outside it might still be howling with horizontal rain but in here everyone could forget the weather and just enjoy themselves and the food. Most of the other restaurants in the village closed for the off season, but Ned's was always busy, his reputation ensuring that the booking ledger was constantly full.

'Here we are,' I said, placing the plate expertly in front of Nate.

'That looks great, thanks.'

I smiled. 'Enjoy!'

He nodded, but there was something in it that seemed... off.

'Is there something wrong? If you've changed your mind, I'm sure we can see about sorting something else out.' Ned had been explicit in giving us all instructions to ensure that Gabe's brother was to be treated as though nothing was too much trouble. I had an idea that Corinne would be thrilled to act on this instruction once she got a look at the man himself.

'No! Please,' he held up a hand. 'It really does look delicious.'

'But?'

He looked up at me through his lashes. 'You don't miss much, do you?'

I waggled my head. 'I've got pretty good at reading people since I've been working here. So, what is it?'

'Really. It's nothing.'

Clearly it was a lot more than nothing.

'Well, I don't believe that for a moment.'

Nate picked up his knife and fork.

'You know, I can just sit here and wait until you tell me.'

That shadowy smile flitted over his face. 'If I didn't think that might get you fired, I might take you up on that,' he said, taking a forkful of smoked haddock and dauphinoise potatoes. 'God, that's good.'

'I'll pass that on to the chef, thank you.'

Nate met my eyes briefly and nodded. I could see that was the last I was going to get out of him. His expression had closed down and was now back to the unreadable one he'd worn when I'd first met him.

'I'll leave you to enjoy your food.'

He nodded again, his gaze barely meeting mine before returning to his plate.

The rest of my tables kept me busy for the next hour and I'd had a brief conversation with Nate about puddings and coffee but that had been it. He'd stayed distant and I couldn't help thinking over his comment about him considering the option of taking me up on my offer to be annoying and sit at his table. Although he'd admitted that perhaps seeing something other than the four walls of the house might be a good idea, I still hadn't got the impression that company was high on his priority list. In fact, he'd been fairly clear that it wasn't. I glanced over my section, pushing the conversation to the back of my mind as I checked whether anyone needed attending to. Seeing Nate's plate empty and his wallet on the table, apparently poised for payment, I headed over.

'How was everything?' I asked, taking the card Nate offered and putting it into the portable payment machine.

'Amazing. Really. I'd love to thank Ned personally when he's got a moment.'

'He's here tomorrow if you want to drop by. I'm sure he'd be thrilled to meet you. Him and Gabe are as close as brothers, and I know he's looking forward to meeting Gabe's real one.'

Nate gave another of those nods, not quite meeting my eyes.

'Did I say something wrong?' I asked, as I handed the machine over.

'No. How do I put a tip on here?'

'Oh. I skipped that screen.'

He handed the machine back to me. 'Then please unskip it.'

'You don't have to. Like I said, Ned's all about—'

'Family. I know. But you and I are not family and I'd like to tip you.'

I reluctantly pressed a couple of buttons and took the programme back to the required screen, then handed it back. Nate took it without looking at me, pressing buttons when prompted.

'I don't know a lot about waiting tables but I'm pretty sure you're not supposed to put customers off trying to tip you.'

He handed the machine back and this time met my gaze with a direct one of his own.

'I don't... usually.'

'I don't want anyone going to extra trouble.'

I shrugged. 'Too bad. I'm afraid you don't get a say in that.'

He shook his head and made a sound that might have been a laugh. 'Is that so?'

'Yes. It's all been agreed.'

'I see.'

The machine churned out the receipt and I tore it off and handed his copy to him. 'Thank you.' I gestured to the copy I held. 'And you shouldn't have done, really.' The tip Nate had put on was way more than generous.

'Yes,' he said, softly. 'I should.'

I smiled and felt that traitorous blush begin to creep.

5

'So, what are your plans for the rest of the day?' I asked, handing him the expensive cashmere overcoat he pointed to on the rack and trying not to notice just how nicely it fitted his broad shoulders. 'More writing?'

'Yep,' he said, pulling the collar up against the weather and layering a scarf before pulling out a pair of what looked to be buttery soft, dark brown leather gloves. 'I'll get Bryan out for another scoot about the beach before it gets dark and then crack on with the book.'

'How's it going?'

He shrugged. I waited for more but it quickly became apparent that that was the full extent of his answer. I pondered on whether to say what was in my head. Nate did the head tilt.

'What is it?'

'How do you do that?'

'You're pretty easy to read.'

'I am not. I've had a lifetime of training to prevent that!'

Oh. Bugger.

'Really?' he asked, interest in his tone.

'Obviously it didn't work!' I laughed, but even to my own ears, it sounded a little off. 'Anyway,' I said, still unsure whether to wade in, but desperate to change the subject. 'I was just going to suggest that you might want to take it easy this afternoon. Maybe.'

'Do you advise that to all your clientele?'

'Only those who look like they might fall face first into their warm chocolate pudding.'

Nate dragged a hand across his jaw. 'That obvious, eh?'

He looked like he needed to sleep for a week but I thought telling him that might be overstepping the mark just a little. 'No, you just look a little tired today.' *And the last time I saw you.*

'Yeah. Like I said, I'm not sleeping too great, so you're probably right.'

'Is there something wrong with the bed? I can get you different pillows, if you have a preference, or if—'

He held up his hand and caught mine within it briefly. 'The pillows are fine. Thank you. Everything is perfect. It's just me.'

'Oh,' I said, eloquently, as I tried to ignore the tingles shooting through me from his touch.

From what I'd heard, the separation hadn't been Nate's idea. And here I was getting sparks off a man who was clearly still in love with his estranged wife. Jeez, I really could pick them.

'Don't get blown away walking back,' I said, escorting him to the door.

'I'll try not to.'

'I don't know how I'd explain that one to Gabe, so probably best.'

He gave me a little salute before putting his head down and heading out into the gale. I watched the tall, broad figure covering the ground briskly with long, strong strides until he turned out of sight.

* * *

'Thanks for coming today,' Carrie said as Eloise and I settled alongside her at the table. Set up in front of us was an array of leaves, berries, wire and baubles along with a wire wreath frame.

'It's a pleasure,' Eloise said, picking up and putting down some of the leaves, before inspecting the decorations. 'Although I've never really been the creative type so you might have to display my wreath as far out of sight of the customers as possible.'

Carrie laughed, patting Eloise's hand. 'I'm sure it's going to be lovely. Have you ever done anything like this, Soph?' she asked.

I shook my head. 'Not at all, but I'm excited to try. Although, again I can't guarantee I'm going to produce anything worthy of display in a fancy restaurant like Ned's. Maybe Burger King?'

We giggled together as the glass of complimentary champagne went to our heads and shushed each other as a small group of men came in, all dressed in green jumpers with the name of the hotel embroidered on the upper left chest. An older gentleman with a cheerful face that looked like it had spent many a season outdoors stepped to the fore.

'Afternoon, ladies,' he glanced over at the sole chap who had come in with his wife shortly after us. 'And gentleman.' There was a murmur of laughter, fuelled somewhat by the bubbles. 'I'm Doug, the head gardener,' he held up his hand. 'And no, I'm not making it up. That really is my name.' Behind him, his colleagues grinned. One to his left, a tall, good looking outdoorsy type with slightly ruddy cheeks and sandy blonde hair caught my eye and held the grin. I smiled back as I took another sip of my drink and pondered over the wisdom of us skipping lunch today in order to get here in time.

'Looks like Soph has pulled already,' Eloise stage whispered to Carrie, as up in front Doug demonstrated how to begin with our wreath making.

'Oh, I have not,' I said, giggling along with them. I really shouldn't drink at lunchtime. Free or not, I was way too out of practice.

'Perhaps he'll be able to give her some hands-on demonstrations.' Eloise widened her eyes and Carrie stifled a snorted laugh. Doug glanced over, gave a patient look with a hint of smile and continued. The other gardener caught my eye and grinned again, giving a quick eyebrow raise as he did so.

'Sorry,' I mouthed.

He shook his head and gave a surreptitious 'OK' signal with his thumb and forefinger. I nudged the others and tried not to laugh again. Missing lunch definitely hadn't been a good idea.

As the demonstration came to a close, Doug introduced his helpers, advising that one would be coming over to each table to assist in any further supplies or advice.

'I wonder which one will take this table?' Eloise asked, looking pointedly at me.

'Oh, shush,' I said and busied myself in collecting the leaves from the centre that I planned to start my wreath with.

'Afternoon, ladies.' The deep voice had a soft West Country lilt and I looked up to see that the sandy-haired gardener who'd grinned across at us earlier now stood in front of our table. 'I'm Billy and I'm here to cater to your every whim.' He winked at an older lady opposite me who flapped her hand at him. 'Wreath wise, of course.'

'We've got a cheeky one, here,' the lady said, chuckling.

'So, who do we have?' Billy asked.

'I'm Gloria, and this is my friend Barb.' Barbara raised her hand in a little wave, which Billy returned.

'I'm Carrie.'

'Eloise.' They both turned to me as did Billy's gaze.

'Sophia,' I said, looking up and seeing the green eyes of the gardener hover on me a little longer.

'It's a pleasure to meet you all, ladies. Now, does anyone need any help?'

Gloria immediately commandeered Billy to help her get started while Barb already seemed to be charging ahead. I got the idea she'd done this before. On our side of the table, the three of us were desperately trying to remember what Doug had said and making slow, albeit steady progress.

'These are looking great,' Billy said as he finally managed to pry himself away from Gloria's chattiness and attend to his other guests.

'Flattery will get you everywhere,' Eloise teased him. 'Won't it, Soph?' she added. I gave her a look, but she just beamed back at me.

'Do you need any more eucalyptus?' Billy asked, coming round to crouch next to me as he studied my creation.

I looked round at him blankly. His expression was open and friendly and he read my thoughts.

'This one,' he said, lifting up a sprig of a type I'd been winding round my frame to start off with, the supply of which on the table had dwindled.

'Oh! I'm so sorry. I had no idea what is was called.'

'No reason why you should,' he replied in a languid manner. 'Back in a jiffy. Anyone else need anything else?'

A couple of requests were put in and Billy disappeared off to the front of the room where large buckets were stuffed with extra supplies.

'I think you have an admirer there, ducky,' Gloria chuckled across the table.

'See,' Carrie added, 'I knew it wasn't just us. He's definitely got his eye on her, right?'

'Absolutely,' Gloria winked. 'Lucky girl.'

'Oh, he does not. He's obviously just chatty to everyone. It's all PR. They want people to return.' I shrugged it off.

'Well, I certainly think he wants you to return.' Gloria wasn't giving up and Carrie and Eloise weren't helping, egging her on.

'Ssh! He's coming back,' I whispered.

'Here we go,' Billy said, laying the eucalyptus sprigs in front of me and popping some more holly that Barb had asked for in front of her.

'Thanks, love,' she said, barely looking up as she continued work on what was looking to be a very professional wreath.

'I think you've done this before, Barb,' Billy said, pursuing the conversation.

'I do the church flowers every Saturday and I've done a few of these in my time, I suppose.' She smiled up briefly before beavering on.

'I just dragged her along for company really,' Gloria laughed. 'Although I should have known she'd show me up.'

Barb patted her friend's hand, clearly not so absorbed in her work as to miss the comment. 'Yours is looking lovely, dear. Don't be silly.'

'And where are you putting your wreaths, ladies?' Billy asked, turning to us three.

'They're for a restaurant.'

'Oh, great! Any particular one?'

'Yes, Ned's over in Washington Bay.'

'Wow! Wreaths for a Michelin starred restaurant. No pressure!' He laughed again, something that seemed to come easily to him, his whole manner relaxed.

'No pressure, really. I just thought it'd be nice to make our own this year.'

Billy cocked his head. 'You're from the restaurant?'

'Yes. I own it along with my husband, Ned.'

'And you're all making wreaths for there?'

'Yes. Eloise and Sophia are both part of the team and kindly agreed to come today.'

'Do you need any more?' Billy asked. 'We're trained on these the first Christmas we get here and I've been here nearly ten years now so I've knocked up a few in my time. We had a couple of last minute cancellations so there's some frames spare.' He shrugged.

'It would be great back up if Soph and I make a mess of ours,' Eloise giggled at me.

'Those are going up whatever,' Carrie pointed at the creations in front of us both. 'But if you're sure that's OK? I don't want to get you into trouble.'

'Nah, it's fine.' Billy waved away her concern.

'I can put a tag on it, that it's from here, if that helps.'

'You really don't have to but if it makes you feel better, that'd be great.'

'It would. Deal,' Carrie smiled.

'Deal.' Billy returned it and pulled a chair from the stack behind us. 'Mind if I join you properly?'

There was much shaking of heads and assent given as Billy placed the chair next to mine. I shuffled along a little more towards Eloise, who didn't budge. I nudged her gently and she looked up.

'What?' she asked innocently.

'It's a bit of a squeeze at the moment,' I whispered.

'I think a bit of a squeeze would do you the world of good.'

I widened my eyes at her. 'You were trying to get me together with Nate the other day.'

'I know. And you wouldn't go for him, so maybe the outdoorsy type is more up your street. You know, you with that accent and him… It's all a bit *Lady Chatterley's Lover*.' Eloise leant round me, still without moving her chair. 'Billy, what's your surname? I don't suppose it's Mellors?'

'Oh, my God,' I mumbled, tipping the last dregs of my champagne down my throat, and desperately hoping he didn't get the reference.

'No, Eloise. Sorry to disappoint you. It's Myers.'

'Close enough,' Eloise smiled before finally moving her chair and allowing me to give Billy a little more room.

As we both shuffled our chairs round the table, from the corner of my eye, I saw him smile at Eloise and shake his head good naturedly. Oh God, he totally got the reference.

'So, what do you do at the restaurant?' Billy asked, his voice quieter.

'I'm a waitress.'

'Do you like it?' he asked, his fingers expertly winding foliage round the frame in front of him, his eyes not entirely on the job.

'More than I thought I would, to be honest. You meet a lot of different sorts of people.'

'Although only those that can afford to eat at such a restaurant.' He gave me a look.

'Actually, Ned's always been pretty good about having a wide range on his menu. He's not into all that snobbery that a lot of chefs are. Thank goodness.' I knew I'd have enjoyed my job a lot less if I'd merely swapped one world of snootiness for another. 'You should come. Bring your partner. I'm sure they'd love it.'

'They probably would if I had one.'

'Oh. Right. Well. Then come anyway. We have plenty of people who come on their own to eat for one reason or another.'

'I'm a little more social than that.'

I flicked my glance to him and laughed. 'Yes, I rather got that impression.'

'I'd like to take you though. Assuming you aren't otherwise engaged.' He glanced at my left hand. 'Figuratively speaking. And, of course, wouldn't mind eating where you work.'

Typically, Carrie and Eloise's in depth conversation had momentarily lulled just as Billy asked the question.

6

'Oh! I... um...'

Billy leant over a little more, aware that we now had an audience. 'No rush. I'll have to drop these round anyway as I won't get them both finished today. Maybe you can let me know then?'

I looked round at him, the features of his face gentle, his expression understanding, and nodded.

'Sorry. I'm always told I go for things a bit quickly.' He frowned. 'Not that you're a thing. I mean—'

'I know what you mean.' I frowned at the smooth and shiny gold bauble I was trying to affix to my wreath. 'What I don't know is why this won't stay where I want it to.'

Billy peered across and gently laid his hands over mine to turn the wreath over and inspect it. 'If you move it just along here a little...' he pointed, having let go, allowing me to make the adjustment myself, rather than taking it over, which I appreciated, 'you can wrap the wire round that bit there...' He waited while I did so. 'There. Perfect. It's just got a bit more to hang onto there and gives it more stability.'

I held up the wreath in front of me.

'That looks great, Sophia,' Billy said.

'Thanks for the help,' I said, smiling, pleased with my creation.

'Any time,' he replied as Carrie and Eloise exchanged a look and I pointedly ignored them.

* * *

'Let's have a picture before we go, shall we, Barb?' Gloria bustled her friend into place. Barb didn't look thrilled at this but she had seemed to enjoy herself, if quietly. 'Come on, Billy. We need evidence that we've spent the afternoon with a big, strapping lad, don't we?' Barb blushed, although I was sure I detected a small smile. Gloria winked at us three as we watched. 'Got to give the WI something to talk about, eh?' she added, making us all giggle.

'Mind if I take one to put on the hotel's socials? They love evidence of people having enjoyed things like this.'

'Of course not. Just remember to get my good side!' Gloria laughed, giving Billy a big squeeze for the camera.

'How about one of you three?' he asked, having extricated himself from Gloria.

'Oh, that'd be lovely, thanks,' Carrie said, handing him her phone as we bunched together and held our wreaths. Billy snapped a couple before returning the phone.

'Can I get one of the three of you to add to our collection too?'

'Sure!' Eloise answered as I made what I hoped was a subtle step away. I had no wish to be on the hotel's social media feed anyway but this was five star, with an excellent reputation. Exactly the sort of place that I might have stayed in previously and exactly the sort of place those from my old life would still stay in. Plenty of people scanned social media for more info on a place before booking these days and although I knew the likelihood of anyone I knew seeing it was low, it was still too much of a risk.

'Where are you going?' Carrie asked. 'Come on, get in the shot.'

'I'm just not really comfortable with being on social media. But you three look great. Do you want me to take it for you?' I asked, desperately trying to divert the attention.

'What do you mean? You're always snapping pics for your Insta,' Carrie said as Billy waited with Eloise, his phone resting loosely in his hand.

'Yes, but not of this,' I whispered to Carrie, pointing to my face as I gently steered her backwards to join the other two.

'I don't know why you worry. You're hardly the back of a bus!'

'It's not that. It's... complicated,' I said, feeling uncomfortable now. Things really would have been easier if I'd just told everyone the truth when I'd moved to Wishington Bay. Or at least those I'd grown close to. I'd just been so determined to separate my old life from my new one and now... now there just never seemed like a good time. But I would. One day, I definitely would.

'It's fine,' Billy broke the ripple of tension. 'Plenty of people don't like it. It's why I always ask first. If Eloise and Carrie don't mind though?' He looked to them for an answer before handing his phone to me, catching my eye as he did so. I took the photos and we all began gathering our things.

'You OK?' Billy's voice was quiet as he came to stand next to me. 'I'm sorry if I made things awkward.'

'No, not at all,' I said, trying to dismiss it. 'I'm just a bit funny about things like that. I didn't mean to seem like a diva.'

'You didn't at all. Although...' he paused and I looked up, meeting the laughing eyes. 'It'd be nice to have a picture of all of you. Us.'

I nodded. 'You're right, it would.' I dug my phone from my

bag. 'Here. You've probably got the longest arms. You take it,' I said, as I gathered Carrie and Eloise around me Billy squeezed in and took the selfie before showing it to the rest of us.

'Aah, that's lovely,' Eloise smiled. 'You'll have to send that one on.'

'We could put it up in the restaurant,' Carrie said, a tentative look on her face.

'Yes, that'd be great,' I smiled back. There was a board in the restaurant where Carrie and Ned pinned up various photos of the staff, great food shots, pictures of the fishermen hauling a catch destined for the restaurant on to the beach as faint swathes of dawn colour streaked the sky behind them. I loved this board. And I loved that Ned and Carrie did it. As we'd explained to Billy, Ned's restaurant might be award winning but it was first and foremost a family restaurant. And I was part of that family. Which made me feel even worse about the fact I was keeping a secret from them.

'Will you send that to me?' Billy asked. 'I promise not to post it anywhere.'

'It's just the corporate stuff I'm a bit hesitant about.' I had no concerns that any of my old friends would be following a gardener. Unless they were on television, of course. Although even that didn't make any difference to some. The fact that someone got their hands dirty for a living was enough for them to decide they 'weren't our sort of people'. Having spent the afternoon in Billy's company, I realised now how much they – and I – had missed out on by taking this attitude.

'So?'

'Oh! Yes, right. I... I guess I need your number?'

'Nicely done,' Carrie nudged him and winked in a very unsubtle manner.

I shook my head at her, laughing as I handed my phone over for Billy to enter his number.

When I took it back, I found the photo, pressed share and then searched my WhatsApp contacts for the new addition. Finding him, I pressed send and a moment later a small chime rang out. Billy opened the message.

'Perfect. Thanks.'

'It's been so lovely to meet you, Billy,' Carrie said as she and Eloise both hugged him. 'Thanks for making it such a brilliant time.'

'You're very welcome. I've had a great time too.'

'And you must stay and eat when you drop those off,' Carrie said, checking her watch as she did so. 'I've already told Ned about it when I rang him to tell him to come and collect us and he completely agreed. On the house, of course.'

Billy's ruddy cheeks coloured more. 'Oh, Carrie. You can't do that.'

'Already done.'

He inclined his head in a thank you.

'And a guest, of course. If you want.' Again, the look she slid across to me was not understated.

'I'm working on that part.' He grinned back and I felt my cheeks begin to colour, almost matching his own outdoor complexion.

'Looks like Ned's here,' I said, recognising the car as I turned away a little and glanced through the leaded casement window.

'Saved by the bell.' Billy looked down at me and I met the gaze, shaking my head a little.

'When's a good time to drop those extra wreaths off?'

'Oh, anytime. And the offer to eat is an open invitation – just take it when you're ready.'

'Thanks. That'd be great. You think it'd be quiet here in the winter but we're actually pretty busy at the moment and have a couple of people out with flu.'

'It might give you more time to decide who you'd like to bring, too?' Carrie said. If she'd have pointed at me with a huge foam finger, it would have been less obvious.

Billy gave us all another quick hug before heading out towards the front entrance of the hotel. Ned was waiting in the car and Carrie popped the boot, allowing us all to lay our creations inside. The baby seat was in the front with their son sleeping happily, tucked cosily inside it. The three of us climbed in the back seat and strapped in, before giving Billy one last wave as Ned drove away.

'Good time?' Ned asked as he pulled out on to the main road.

'Very,' Carrie said, leaning forward and tucking the blanket round the baby a little more. 'Quite... productive.'

Ned glanced back momentarily in the rear view mirror. 'Sounds like there's a story there.'

'And we're all eagerly awaiting the next chapter.' Eloise joined in the tease.

'Billy that I told you about on the phone?' Carrie continued. 'He's dropping off the wreaths he's making for us in the next few days. We're hoping it gives him time to work on who to bring for his free dinner.'

'Sounds fair enough. So what am I missing?' he asked, looking round as he stopped at a set of red traffic lights.

'He took rather a shine to our Sophia, here.'

'Oh, did he now?' Ned's eyes lit up with mischief.

I pointed my finger at him. 'Don't you start.'

Ned laughed as the lights changed and we headed home towards the bay.

* * *

The wind had blown the previous day's heavy cloud through by the next morning but from my window I could see people walking their dogs on the beach, wrapped up with hats, scarves and mittens. Standing in my cosy flat with the winter sunshine streaming in, I could imagine it was glorious out there. Well, glorious in a freeze your bits off kind of way. Checking the clock, I guessed that it should be a good time to go in and clean Holly's house. Nate had mentioned he usually took Bryan out in the morning, and by the state of the little dog last time they obviously spent a fair bit of time on their walk. Nate had been friendlier at the restaurant than at our initial meeting – until he'd shut down again – but I wasn't about to assume that made me or the noise of me vacuuming any more welcome in his space. Best to stick to my original plan of keeping out of his way as much as possible. I felt the tingle of colour on my face as I remembered the fizz I'd felt at his touch. Yes. Definitely a good idea to keep out of his way. Ramming my woolly hat with its oversized bobble down onto my head so that my eyes just about peeked out, I finished bundling up against the cold, grabbed my bag and jogged down the stairs, hoping to start building up some warmth. As I stepped outside, the crisp, sharp air made me gasp a little as I turned back to lock the front door. I gave another gasp as I turned towards the street and bumped my forehead straight into a strong, broad chest that definitely hadn't been there a minute ago.

7

'Oh, I'm so sorry. I—' I looked up and stopped. The chest belonged to Nate McKinley and he was now standing there, looking down at me. Worst of all, he was smiling. I mean, as he was going through a difficult patch, it was great to actually see him smiling. It's just that it was such a good smile that, from my perspective, it made it really, really bad.

'My fault. Narrow pavements. Big guy. I don't fit very well.'

Actually, I thought he fitted in pretty damn perfectly, looking at him now with his beanie hat pulled down over his ears, an expensive-looking down jacket keeping him cosy, long, solid jeans-clad legs and hiking boots. Clearly, I needed to get a grip.

'It's fine. Are you off for a walk?' I asked, distracting myself from the unexpected smile by bending down to play with Bryan who was decked out in a coat that looked to be made by the same brand as Nate was wearing.

'Have you got a new coat?' I said, giggling as Bryan rested his paws on my knee and snuggled his head into my neck for a cuddle, his whole body whipping to and fro with excitement. From the corner of my eye, I saw an elderly couple approaching us on the pavement. Scooping Bryan up, I moved all three of us into the quiet road for a moment to let them pass.

'Bit chilly today, Soph!' the chap called, making a 'brrr' motion as they passed, his wife giving me a wide smile and patting my arm with her gloved hand as she passed.

'Certainly is, Albert. Keep wrapped up!' He waved a hand in agreement and carried on.

I stepped back onto the pavement, pulling at Nate's sleeve to get him to follow me as a car appeared round the corner.

'I've not seen this before,' I smiled, cuddling Bryan to me, his lead hanging in a loose loop from Nate's wrist. 'Have you been treating him?'

'I didn't want him to get cold. How do you live like this?'

I rolled my eyes at him. 'Don't be such a drama queen. It's not that cold.' As I said this, a funnel of wind shot out of one of the alleys and wrapped itself round me, producing an involuntary shiver.

'Nah. Positively balmy.'

I gave him a look and tried not to smile.

'You did realise it would be winter when you came here, right?'

'Yes. Of course. I'm just not sure I thought it through properly.'

'Well. I'm afraid I can't do much to fix the temperature,' I said, bending down to place Bryan back on the floor, much to his disgust, judging by the look he gave me and the fact that he was now attempting to climb back up my boot. 'But I can make sure you have a clean, tidy and warm house to reside in. By the time you finish your walk, I should be done. I've got some homemade soup to put in the fridge for you to heat up for lunch too so hopefully that will help.'

'We've done our walk. I just strolled up to the restaurant to see if I could catch Ned as you'd said he'd be in this morning.'

'Oh. I thought you... I...'

Nate adjusted his beanie and tilted his head slightly, waiting for me to finish.

'Did you catch him?' I changed tack, having lost my original direction.

'Yeah. Really nice guy. I think my brother's got a really good friend there.'

'He has, and I know Ned feels the same about Gabe.'

Nate nodded and the shadow from yesterday flitted across his face again.

'You'll always be his big brother though,' I ventured, tentatively.

'Yeah. Whether he likes it or not.' He smiled but there was no heart in it.

I moved us off of the pavement again briefly to let more pedestrians through before stepping back up.

'What's that supposed to mean? Do you think Gabe would have gone to any of this trouble to get you over if he didn't want to? I mean, I know he's pretty easy-going but he's no pushover.'

'My mum can be pretty persuasive, and I know she's been worried about me. Gabe feels a bit guilty he's over here so anything he can do that might please Mum, he's going to do it.'

I stared at him for a moment, then gave an eyeroll that was so big I could practically hear my eyeballs rattle in my skull and then turned away, in the opposite direction to Nate's house. Two seconds later, a large hand caught my arm.

'Where are you going and what was the massive eyeroll for?'

'One, I'm going to do a bit of shopping. I'll come and clean when you take your walk later if you can give me a time. And two, the eyeroll was because what you said was total and absolute rubbish, and the fact that a clearly intelligent man like you can't see that just makes it even more ridiculous.'

'Is that right?'

'Yes,' I said, meeting his eyes defiantly. 'It is. Gabe was desperate to be here with you but he said you'd made it clear you wanted to be on your own and would only agree to come when he was on holiday. You also made the same thing perfectly clear to me the first day I met you. So your brother did the next best thing. He gave you his home to be alone in and made sure you were surrounded by people that love him, and ergo, care about you. I'm not entirely sure what your problem is, but your brother not loving you definitely isn't one of them!'

He watched me for a moment.

'Ergo?'

I felt my mouth drop open and quickly closed it as cold air raced down my throat.

'Seriously? All that and the only thing you took from it was "ergo"?'

'No. Not the only thing.'

'Well, that's a relief.' My mother had always told me that 'sarcasm was not attractive, dear'. But right now I wasn't trying to be attractive – especially not when I was freezing my arse off. Nate McKinley was, undoubtedly, gorgeous. But he was also hard work, complicated, and only here for a short time.

I made another attempt to head off in the direction I'd turned to when the large, gloved hand caught hold of me again.

'I feel like a bloody yoyo. Will you stop doing that?'

'Well, stop going in the wrong direction then.'

'I'm not.'

'You are. The house is that way.' He pointed down the bay, in the opposite direction to the way I myself was pointed.

'Yes. And I'll go there this afternoon. As I said. In the meantime, you can work in peace and I can go and get my shopping.'

'What about my lunch?'

'Excuse me?'

'You said there was soup for lunch. If you don't come until later, it'll be too late.'

I stared at him for a moment. 'How are you and Gabe even related?' I said, wrestling the tub from my bag and thrusting it at him. 'There. There's your soup. You're welcome.'

Bryan's lead tightened a little and we both looked down to see him trying to snuggle across Nate's boots so that, even despite his posh new warm coat, he could lay down with the least amount of tummy on the cold pavement.

'You should get him home before he gets too cold. What time shall I come to clean?' All the friendliness of yesterday had evaporated and I felt a knot in my stomach. I knew I'd made a promise that I'd try and cheer Nate up while he was here in order to repay Gabe and Holly for their friendship, but it was just too damn hard. Nate was clearly used to people waiting on him, having the best things in life, and not appreciating any of it. Stupidly I, like many I suspected, had been taken in by that smile. He might have some sadness still darkening his mood, but looking like he did, there was no way he'd be lonely for long. So long as the woman in question wasn't terribly bothered about manners...

'Now.'

'Pardon?'

'You were on your way when I bumped into you, weren't you?'

'Yes. But that was when I thought you were going to be out.'

He moved to shift his weight and then stopped as he noticed Bryan resting comfortably across the top of his boots. He lifted his gaze from the dog to me. 'I'll lift my feet up when you vacuum and everything. I promise. And I make a mean hot chocolate. I think we'll both need a bit of thawing out by the time we get there.'

See? I wish he wouldn't do that. Just when I was wholly convinced he was a total arse, he'd go and say something endearing. It was really, really annoying. I lifted my head. The arrogance was gone, replaced by that sense of... almost as though he were unsure. Out of his depth. But how could that be right?

'You made it quite clear that you'd prefer me to do the house-keeping when you were out the last time I was there.'

'Actually, no. You put those terms in place. Not me.'

'You didn't argue.'

'You didn't give me a chance. You're kind of formidable when you're riled up.'

'I was not riled up!'

'Yeah. You were. Kind of like you are now. And when you shoved this at me.' He held up the soup container.

'Well, you're rude! And unappreciative.'

Oh, my God. I was stood on the pavement having an argument with a man I barely knew, hurling insults at him. I could hear my mother's voice now – 'like a common fishwife!'

'Nothing I haven't been called before but I'd like to apologise this time, because I never meant to be either.' He removed his hat, ran a hand over the short, dark hair and yanked it back on. 'Please come back to the house with me. I don't care if you clean or not but I'd really like to share this with you.' He nodded at the container.

The sincerity in his voice and eyes took all my bluster away.

'I made it for you.'

He grinned. Almost laughed. Almost. 'I've got a pretty healthy appetite but this looks like it could feed a whole family. Please?' he asked again.

I felt a pull inside me and nodded.

'Thank you.'

I shook my head and hoiked my bag higher onto my shoulder.

'Let me take that,' Nate said, reaching for it.

'No, really. It's fine.'

'I'll swap you for Bryan?' he gave me a slight eyebrow raise. Without waiting for an answer, he slipped the lead off his wrist and over my own in the same swift motion as relieving me of the bag. Opening it momentarily, he placed the soup tub back in.

'Something else in there smells really good!'

'It's a clementine cake.'

'And what lucky villager is getting that?'

I fiddled with my hat for a moment as I watched Bryan's little tail dance about in happiness as he scooted along, his toenails making a satisfying, soothing tappity-tap in the quiet of the morning.

'Actually, that was for you too.'

I felt him looking at me but refused to turn.

'You know there's a supermarket a few miles away, and I have Holly's car. You don't need to do all this. I'm sure Gabe didn't mean for you to go overboard—'

'It's just a cake.'

'And soup. And dinners. All of which I can buy pre-prepared if I wish.'

'True. But they're not as good for you as the ones I make, and I'm happy to do it.'

'Why?'

'Why what?'

'Why are you happy to do it for someone who's rude and unappreciative?'

I let out a sigh, flicked my gaze to his momentarily and then looked away again. 'I enjoy cooking. Holly and I have baking sessions together sometimes.'

'Not Carrie? I met her when I met Ned and I've heard Gabe talk about her loads. She helped save this little dude, didn't she?' he asked, pointing at Bryan.

'She did, yes. And she's lovely. But she doesn't cook. She comes along too though and is our chief taste-tester. It's nice.'

'It sounds it.'

We walked along in silence for a few minutes. Gulls wheeled and screeched above us, and to our right, the sea swooshed gently, a calm, blue pool today in contrast with the steely grey fierceness of yesterday.

'I'm not great with people, Sophia. As you'll have noticed. I don't have Gabe's easy manner and I usually sit in an office, mostly on my own to do my work. Meetings are not social occasions. I say my bit but I can't do all that chit chat stuff. My wife was the outgoing one. When she's there, it's her people want to talk to and be with, and that's always suited me. Gabe and I have always been close but it got harder when I married Serena. Her and Gabe rubbed each other the wrong way. I think because he didn't fall under her spell like most men do. But he's my brother. And he's a pretty good judge of character, as it turns out.'

I wasn't entirely sure what to say. It was the most words he'd ever said to me in one go and a part of me didn't want to break the spell. In my previous life I'd often been told I was a good listener, although I'd always thought myself a bit of a fraud when I felt the only reason I was good at listening was because most of the time I just had nothing to contribute to the conversation. Friends and relatives would be sitting there getting worked up at what, to me, seemed entirely insubstantial topics of absolutely no consequence and yet the fact that Melanie Farquar's three-year-old had turned up at the gymkhana with the same colour ribbons in her hair as Cornelia's little darling, having been specifically told what Cornelia's ensemble was going to be, did not seem the end of the world to me. So I'd sit there, mostly listening. Making the right noises and nodding where I thought it appropriate, while all the time making sure to neither agree or disagree. This was their fight and I didn't have the energy or inclination to get involved in something so petty and inconsequential.

Initially when they'd all begun turning to me to vent about every little moment of unfairness levelled at their darling child, I'd wondered at their lack of sensitivity. But they were just too wrapped up in their own world of privilege and one-upmanship. Eventually, as I'd begun to see the world I lived in with clearer and clearer vision, I stopped blaming them and just accepted that they weren't doing it to be cruel. It just hadn't occurred to them to think that knowing I would never be a mother myself might make it hard to listen to them banging on about the latest imagined infraction against their toddler.

But for now I was happy to listen. More than happy, actually. Nate's voice was low, and smooth and the melodic quality to his accent made it all a very pleasant experience. Obviously I wasn't happy that the subject was clearly one painful to him. He'd stopped and I looked up at him as we walked along in the chilly, crisp winter air.

'Go on.'

The small part of his face that wasn't wrapped up against the cold hinted at an embarrassed smile.

'Nah. I've waffled on enough. I must be boring you to tears. I'm surprised you haven't turned round already and left me to clean my own place.'

'Don't be so silly. It's good to talk. And as you said, we got off on the wrong foot, so it's nice to start again. And people generally get to know one another by talking, so I think you're doing just fine.'

He gave a waggle of his head. 'Maybe. I'm not sure they start by pouring their deepest, darkest secrets out in the first proper conversation they have with someone, though.'

Laughing, I bumped lightly against his arm. 'If they're your darkest secrets, I really don't think you have anything to worry about.'

'Oh?' he asked, turning to me. 'That makes it sound like you have something far more interesting to share.'

I glanced up briefly before focusing my attention back on Bryan's slinky little body scuttling along, intent on getting back to a warm house that held a cosy dog bed, and a fireplace to snuggle down next to.

'Hardly,' I said, adjusting my scarf with one hand and hoping that the slight flush I felt on my skin could be put down to the cold rather than anything else. After all, I wasn't exactly lying about anything. I just hadn't given everyone – or anyone – all the facts about my life prior to Wishington Bay. To me, it was a different life. An unhappier life, and a separate one. And that's how I wanted it to stay. It had nothing to do with who I was now and I didn't want people looking at, or treating me, differently. I liked who I was now. I felt a part of things here and I was worried that might change if they knew the whole truth.

8

'So, what's your story?' Nate's deep tones interrupted my thoughts.

'Huh?' I squeaked, caught off guard. Thankfully a sudden gust of wind took my words and washed them out to sea, so any guilt that might have been interpreted in my tone at not having been entirely honest about my background was taken with it.

'I said, what's your story? How'd you end up in Wishington Bay?' he asked again as he unlocked the door to the house and then stood back for Bryan and me to enter first.

'Oh,' I said, bending down to unfasten the little coat the dog had been tucked into. Bryan wriggled out and zoomed off to his water bowl and began lapping quietly. 'Fancied a change. Got in the car. Stopped when I ran out of petrol. You know, the usual sort of thing.' I repeated a story I'd told plenty of times now, and it was true. That was exactly what had happened. There'd just been a lot more drama and emotion wrapped up in the original exit than the casual tone applied to the tale suggested.

Nate stepped closer and began helping me off with my coat.

'No need to look quite so surprised,' he said, that hint of smile flitting across his face. 'I know you think I'm an obnoxious grouch, but I was brought up with manners. Honestly.'

'That's not what I think at all,' I replied, letting the coat slide from my arms, watching as he carefully hung it on a hook in the hallway.

'Fibber,' he grinned this time, as brief as a shooting star, his face lighting up in delight at the tease.

'I'm not!'

'OK.' He didn't look up from where he was now sat unlacing his boots, but I could tell from his tone that he didn't believe me.

I pulled off my own and snagged the bag Nate had been carrying across the hall towards me. Fishing out my indoor flat shoes, I pulled them on, ready to get started on work. But his reply was bothering me.

'I really don't think you're a grouch.'

He sat up, his bright blue eyes fixing on me, and for a moment I lost the ability to think entirely.

God. Did he have to be quite so 'good looking with a hint of vulnerable'? It really was quite inconvenient.

Nate tilted his head. 'You planning to let me in on that conversation any time soon?'

I stuck my head in the under sink cupboard, ostensibly to grab the cleaning caddy that held all the paraphernalia I would need. The other benefit was that it took me out of the sightline of Nate for a moment while I got my head around the fact that he kept doing what he'd just done. I'd been married for over fifteen years and not once had my husband seemed to have a clue what was in my head. Admittedly, some of that had been my fault. After a while, I hadn't wanted him to know. But with Nate I didn't seem to have a choice. It was like the words were being projected on my forehead for him to read. And I wasn't sure how I felt about that.

'Are you sure you don't mind me cleaning while you're here?'

'Yes. I'm sure. And full points for the swift change of subject.'

Bloody hell. This bloke didn't miss a trick. Clearly denial wasn't going to work so I just went with it.

'Thanks.'

He gave me a look that leaned towards exasperation, but there was a hint of smile – if you looked hard enough.

* * *

'I'm just going to pop some soup on to cook for tomorrow and then I'll be upstairs, out of your way for a while.'

'You're not in my way. And you don't need to keep feeding me. I'm pretty sure that wasn't in your contract.'

'Actually, I'm being cheeky and borrowing the soup maker to make some lunches for myself. As for the rest? Yes, it sort of was.'

His dark brows knitted together. 'So Gabe thinks I've completely lost the ability to look after myself?'

'Oh, stop being so paranoid,' I said, flicking him with a duster as I passed. 'If it had been left to Gabe, you'd have been next door completely fending for yourself. It's Holly you have to thank for all the extra touches.'

He said nothing and I headed off into the beautiful, bright kitchen area. As I piled some carrots, potatoes and coriander on to the worktop, Nate appeared and lounged against the doorjamb.

'I've barely met Holly. Just sort of in passing on Skype. She's been very tactful and left me and Gabe to it.'

I glanced up momentarily from peeling the carrots. 'She's lovely. She and Gabe have been wonderful for each other.'

'So I hear.'

I gave another glance and stopped.

'Planning to let me in on that conversation anytime soon?' I asked, repeating his own phrase back at him. He rewarded me with a smile that was more than his usual ghost of one.

'I don't know. Usually these things are reciprocal.'

I waved the knife in my hand before setting about chopping the carrots into chunks. 'Believe me, you're not missing out on anything in here.' I rolled my eyes back in my head in an attempt to point at my own brain. The action seemed to amuse him and as smile lines crinkled round his eyes, his whole face changed. I was surprised at how pleased I was to see the transformation. Although as it only added to his attractiveness, another, more rational part of me was flapping about, blowing a panic whistle so hard that the pea shot out!

'I'm not so sure about that.'

'I am. So, what are those thoughts swirling round in your brain? They look far more interesting.'

He smiled again, then pushed himself away from the doorway and pulled out a stool from the worktop opposite where I was working.

'I'm just a little surprised someone would go to all this effort for a person she hardly knows.'

I frowned at him briefly as I chopped the potato and added it to the soup maker. 'You're going to be her brother-in-law.'

'Still...'

I shook my head as I measured the stock to add. 'Remember what I said about Ned, and family?'

He nodded.

'Holly's the same. Even more so because you're going to be actual legal family. Of course she's going to want to make sure you're comfortable. Plus she knows what it's like to be unhappy,' I added, pouring in the stock and setting the machine going. 'Wishington Bay helped change her life for the better. I think she's hoping it will work its magic on you too, and anything she can do to help that along, she will.'

He hadn't replied and as I turned round from where the machine was plugged in, I saw his expression had closed off.

'And you can knock that off too.'

His head snapped up. 'Excuse me?'

'That mean and moody, silent tough guy look. I've had enough of that. You have a lovely smile and you're not such an arse when you're being yourself so do us all a favour and be that chap.'

Silence.

I used to be pretty good at keeping everything in. Not saying what I thought. It wasn't the done thing where I grew up. But since moving here, starting again, I'd rather lost the knack. It had been a relief to be honest. I was always careful to try to be tactful but occasionally my mouth ran ahead of my brain.

'You're big on honesty, aren't you?'

I blushed, not just because Nate was studying me intensely. He was right. I was big on honesty, but I also knew I hadn't been entirely honest with him – or anyone in Wishington Bay. And at his comment, the guilt of that gave me a good nip on the backside.

'When it's possible, yes.'

'Are there times it isn't possible?'

'Occasionally.'

'Such as?'

I swallowed, avoiding his eyes as I cleared up the detritus from the soup preparation. 'Well, you always have to consider the situation, don't you? People's feelings, etcetera.'

'And did you consider my feelings when you just called me a grumpy sod?'

Wiping the counter off, I gave a brief glance. 'Those weren't my words and you know it.'

'No. In fact, you called me an arse.'

I shrugged. I had, so there was hardly any point in denying it now.

'But I offset that but saying that you have a lovely smile. Which you do.'

'And you reckon that makes it even.'

'Pretty much.'

I risked a glance. His gaze locked onto mine. My confidence was wavering but I wasn't about to show him that. 'Don't you think?'

Nate seemed to be considering the possibility.

'It's a long time since anyone's said anything like that to me.'

'What? Called you an arse?' I raised my eyebrows. 'Not being rude, but I kind of find that hard to believe.'

He considered me for a moment. 'OK. Kind of rude, actually, but point taken, and I'm sure you're right. I don't suffer fools gladly and that can sometimes translate as being an arse, depending on who you speak to.'

'That's probably accurate but it doesn't mean they're right.'

'True. But I was actually referring to the other part of your comment.'

I thought back. 'The compliment part?'

'Yes.'

I smiled. 'Oh, come on. You do possess a mirror, right?'

He shook his head, but the expression remained. It was hard to define exactly, but as much as he tried to bluff, it was impossible to hide the sadness in those striking eyes.

'You're serious.' My words were quiet and a statement, not a question.

He shrugged, the shadowy smile hovering round a mouth

that was far too dangerous for me to concentrate on for too long. I met his eyes.

'Nate...'

He waved a hand and pushed himself away from the counter. 'It's fine. It's not even something I think about. Blokes don't really, do they?'

I wasn't entirely sure about that. Some of the men I'd met thrived on compliments. Often fishing for and revelling in them.

'You just took me by surprise. Even if you were just trying to balance out the insult.' He gave the briefest of grins as he turned away.

'I wasn't!'

He turned back, the force of tone taking us both a little by surprise. His brows raised minutely.

'I... wasn't,' I repeated, trying to make it a little more casual this time, although I think we both knew that ship had sailed.

His Adam's apple bobbed and I could practically see the cogs in his brain working. Trying to compute. What had happened to this man to think he wasn't worthy of the simplest of compliments? Or at least for him to have found himself in such a position that he no longer knew how it felt to receive one? Whatever had gone on between him and his wife, she'd clearly done a pretty thorough job.

'Thank you.'

I smiled. 'You're very welcome.' He fidgeted for a moment and I moved the conversation on quickly. 'So, that should be ready in about twenty minutes. I'll pop down and sort it out when it beeps. In the meantime, I'm going to make a start on the upstairs.'

'I guess I should get on with some work.'

'Your enthusiasm does you credit.'

He smirked at the sarcasm. 'I know. Bad, eh?'

'Not going well?'

'I'm undecided at the moment. Some days I read it back and it seems OK. Other days I feel like I may as well just chuck it all in the ocean.'

'Well, don't do that. We're very proud of our Blue Flag award so adding pollution won't be appreciated.'

'Duly noted.'

'Is this the first book you've written?' I asked, mounting the bottom stairs as he followed me out to the hallway.

'No. I've written a few textbooks before. This is the first time I've ever had to try and make one entertaining, though.'

'What's it about?'

'Air crashes.'

'Oh. Not exactly the jolliest of subjects.'

'No. Not really.'

'So that's what you do all day?' I asked, climbing the stairs as I noted Nate following behind me. 'Study air crashes?'

'Sort of. More study the best way to try to prevent them.'

'That sounds like a pretty important job.' I caught his shrug. 'What's that for?'

'My wife used to say I should have been a pilot or something because it was more glamorous and exciting.'

I placed the caddy on the hall console and picked out an organic polish spray and cloth. 'Glamour isn't everything. Plus, I think airline pilots are overrated. I've dated one or two in my time.'

His mouth twitched.

'I assume in your job you generally got to go home to her every night, unlike a pilot? That seems like a pretty good benefit to me,' I said, giving the dresser in the master bedroom a quick spritz as Nate took a seat by the window and looked out at the sea, the sunlight making the wave crests sparkle as they broke on the sand.

'Actually, I think that was one of the many downsides for her.' His tone was laced with sarcasm.

I looked round and met his gaze. 'Sorry. I didn't mean to bring up bad memories.'

Nate shook his head and gave that pretend smile. 'You didn't.' He made no attempt to move but I got the impression that a change of subject might be appreciated.

'You know Holly meant for you to sleep in here as your trips clashed?' I said, motioning to the room that had remained untouched since he'd arrived.

'I know. I just felt a bit weird and the guest room is really nice. Certainly more homely than my apartment. Or a hotel room.'

I smiled without looking up, catching the reference I'd made in my little speech the first time we'd met about him being better off in some faceless hotel chain room.

'She worked really hard on the whole house, so you're right. Every room is lovely.'

'Yeah, Gabe said something about her having transformed this place.'

'Totally. I only came here a couple of times before Gigi passed away and it was really nice. Holly had had the bathroom and kitchen updated for her but the rest was stuck in a little bit of a time warp.'

Nate turned away from the window and back to me. 'You'd never think so now.'

'No. She really seemed to find her niche. She's quite in demand for her interior design services now.'

'Gabe worries about her working too hard.'

I gave a little head waggle. 'It's understandable. She was a total workaholic when she came back here. The only reason she finally returned was because her boss put her on an enforced sabbatical after she had a major panic attack in his office.'

'Really?'

'Yes. Ned and Carrie were really worried about her but I think she was in denial about it all,' I said, dusting the deep windowsill next to where Nate was sat. 'And of course, once Gabe witnessed her having one, all his "doctory" instincts kicked in.'

'Plus the fact he had the total hots for her.'

I grinned. 'Yes. I think that certainly contributed to his attentions. He told you that, huh?'

'He was gushing. It was pathetic.'

I flicked him with the duster. 'I think the word you're looking for is romantic.'

'If you say so.'

I rolled my eyes at him and continued with my work. 'Anyway, he just gets a little protective, knowing she has this tendency to be a workaholic. But she does love what she's doing now. I think she'll be OK. Holly doesn't want to ever go back to how she was, and she's an intelligent woman. She pulls back when she needs to.'

'That's good to hear. I'm looking forward to getting to know her better.'

'She'll be thrilled to hear that.'

'To be fair, she doesn't know I'm an arse yet.'

'Oh God, you're not going to let me forget that, are you?'

He gave a small headshake. 'Nope.'

I straightened the bedclothes and decorative cushions and dusted the bedsides.

'So, what's wrong with next door?'

'Huh?'

'Earlier, you said if it'd been up to Gabe I'd have been next door and fending for myself. Isn't that where Gabe was living before? He never said that there was anything wrong with it.'

'There isn't. It's just not had the Holly touch yet.'

'So that's still in the time warp?'

'Very much so.'

'What are they planning to do with it? Holly owns it too, right?'

'Yes,' I said, shooing him out of the room now that I'd finished. 'I don't think they've decided yet. She bought some paint and just plans to decorate it throughout to start with and then go from there. Whether they keep it or sell, it's still going to need painting. Once that's done, she might have a clearer idea of what to do with it.'

'It must be hard. I mean, I know this was her grandmother's house, and Gabe said her gran was kind of everything to her.'

'Yes. She was. She lost her mum young and, from what I understand, their dad didn't cope so well.'

'Difficult situation.'

I nodded, agreeing as I entered the guest room. The bed was already made, as always.

'I feel weird you cleaning up after me.'

'I'm employed to do it. And if you feel weird, don't watch,' I teased.

I picked up a sweatshirt from the chair, preparing to fold it, but Nate whipped it out of my hands.

'I can do that.'

I gave him a look and took the clothing back.

'Don't you have a book to write?'

'I have writer's block.' He shrugged before turning. 'What's that beeping noise?'

I finished straightening the room as I answered. 'The soup maker. I'll be down in a minute to sort it out. You can heat up the one I brought earlier for your lunch, though,' I said, glancing at the clock.

'What about your lunch?'

'I'll grab something when I get back home.'

'It looked like there was quite a lot in that tub.'

'Enough to keep you going for a few days. Nothing like some warming soup to comfort a body on a chilly day like this.'

'And what about comforting your body?'

9

My head snapped round and for once it was Nate's turn to blush. 'That came out very differently to how it sounded in my head.'

'I imagine so.'

'Let me start again. Can I reiterate my request of earlier and ask you to join me for lunch? There's obviously plenty.'

I took a step down the stairs and glanced back up.

'There's really no need for you to do that.'

'I know. But... I'd really like it if you would. I mean, if you have time of course. Sorry. I didn't think. You probably have plans. I—'

'No. I don't. I just... It was unexpected.'

Nate gave me a glance as we got to the bottom of the stairs. 'Wow. I really am that bad, huh?'

'No! Don't take it like that. I just know you like your peace and quiet and your own company.'

He followed me through to the kitchen and watched as I unplugged the soup maker and removed the lid, releasing a waft of delicious smelling steam into the bright room.

'That smells good.'

'It does, rather, doesn't it? It's one of my favourite recipes. It's the same as the one I've brought you, so I hope you like it. It's just so much quicker to make in the soup maker. I must treat myself to one of these at some point,' I said, as I unplugged the machine and took a couple of empty tubs out ready to decant the steaming liquid into. Beside me, Nate emptied the container I'd brought with me into a pan and began gently heating it through on the hob.

'I'm sure I will. Everything of yours I've had the pleasure of tasting has been amazing. Even if I haven't been gracious enough to tell you until now.' He grabbed a second bowl and put it down alongside the one I'd prepared earlier, his eyes meeting mine in a silent question.

'Are you sure?' I asked.

'Very.'

'Then that would be lovely, thank you.'

And there was that laugh again. Unexpected and rumbling and incredibly sexy. 'That's generously polite considering our rocky start.'

I smiled, trying to push the sound of his laughter away from regions it had no business affecting.

'It's never too late for a new start.'

'Do you believe that?'

I placed the now full bowls on the counter in front of the breakfast bar stools and motioned for him to take a place as I grabbed the fresh bread I'd seen sat in a bag from the local bakery on the side.

'I do,' I said, placing a spoon beside his bowl as he busied himself tearing off a couple of hunks of bread and placing them on the side plates I'd added.

''Scuse fingers.'

'No problem.'

'Don't you?' I asked, referring back to his question. 'I mean, new starts and all that?'

'You were right. This is delicious.'

'I know. And stop changing the subject.'

He gave the briefest of grins round his mouthful before swallowing.

'You caught that, huh?'

'Yes. So spill.'

'Probably not the best thing to say to a man with a full bowl of bright orange soup in front of him.'

'Oh, you seem the together type. I bet you've never dropped anything on an expensive tie in your life.'

He continued eating but gave a small shake of his head.

'See? Together.'

'Or boring. Depending on how you want to look at it.'

'What's boring about coordination?'

He shrugged. 'Everything. Nothing. I don't know. Just a bit... dull, I guess. And you're this vibrant, sparky woman that I'm expecting to be entertained by having lunch with possibly the most straight-laced man you ever met.'

Ha! If only he knew. Next to some of the men I'd met, Nate was positively a party animal. But I couldn't really explain that, without explaining other things I wasn't ready to. Instead I fixed him with a look for a moment, then reached across and tore off another piece of the soft, white bread. 'Let me know when you're done with that pity party over there and we can get on with having an interesting conversation.'

He drew up a little beside me. 'Pity party?'

'Uh-huh,' I nodded, my mouth full of bread.

'I am not having a pity party!' He actually sounded quite affronted.

'Oh, of course you—' As I looked up, I saw it. I saw the look in his eyes. And I realised he wasn't at all. He believed it. Believed that he was boring and had nothing of value to offer anyone in conversation. My thoughts went back to what he'd said on the walk home, about his wife being the chatty one, his job being fairly solitary and obviously quite a sober one. And then, of course, there was the fact that she'd left him. Is that the impression he had of himself? That she'd moved on because he was boring? I hardly knew him and yes, he was serious but I'd seen flashes of something else too. And I'd heard that laugh – a laugh that still felt unfamiliar. As though it had escaped in a moment when his concentration had drifted for a second. But then it got reined in and put back where it belonged. I could see there was far more to Nate McKinley than he was currently showing. And far more than he believed there was.

'I'm sorry,' I said, wanting the tension now obvious in his shoulders to loosen as it had earlier.

'It's fine.'

Clearly it wasn't.

'No, it isn't. I was... mistaken. And I'm trying to apologise. Sometimes people say things for attention. I should have known you're not the type to do that.'

Nate continued eating. 'You hardly know me. Easy mistake to make.'

'I'd like to change that. I mean about knowing you. If you'd let me.' He slid his glance to me briefly. 'You know, just so I don't mess up again and we're not left sitting here so rigid that I think I might actually snap. Kind of like we are now.'

He gave a brief nod of agreement as he finished his soup. I reached over to the pan and poured a little more out into his bowl.

'I'm fine.'

'You're too lean.'

It was his turn to give me a look. 'I'm twice your size.'

'I'm small boned. Eat.'

'I don't know about small boned. Bossy, though, I could agree with.'

'Oh, shush and eat or I'll put a sea slug in your bed.'

'I make my own bed.'

'And you think that'll stop me?'

He slid his gaze across again but this time I could see a glimmer of humour. 'Probably not.'

'You're not boring, Nate. Don't let anyone make you feel you are.'

'It's not others. It's me,' he answered, too fast for me to believe the truth in his words. It was like a defence. An automatic answer, and my mind went back to what he'd said earlier about Gabe being a good judge of character. I already knew from Holly that Gabe and his family had done their best to like Nate's choice of wife but it's hard to watch someone you love change and be manipulated. But there's also nothing you can do when that person is so head over heels they don't see any faults. It's an impossible situation. And one that often doesn't end well – one way or another.

Nate cleared the bowls and held out a hand when I made to dismount the breakfast stool. 'Coffee? Or would you prefer tea?'

'Tea. Please.'

'Thought so.' There was a hint of amusement in his tone and I frowned.

'What does that mean?'

He turned and leaned on the counter as the kettle behind him boiled, his long legs crossed loosely at the ankles, cosy thick socks on his feet.

'That accent. It couldn't get more upper-class English. I kind of feel like I should be in a butler's uniform waiting on you.'

I swallowed.

If only he knew…

'I just went to a good school. They were up on that sort of thing. I guess it stuck.' That was true, at least. 'And in case you haven't noticed, I'm not wearing a uniform.'

'Maybe I should have had Gabe put that in the contract.'

I threw him a look but felt my traitorous cheeks try to colour.

'I didn't think women blushed any more. It's kind of endearing.' He moved and took two mugs from the cupboard, setting them alongside the kettle.

'And men aren't supposed to make comments about frilly maids' uniforms! So, we're even.'

His laugh rumbled clearly this time, and when he turned it was like a different person. Now the resemblance to his brother, despite the difference in colouring, was clear. His eyes crinkled the same way, the smile was almost the same, but a little more off kilter which made it all his own, but the joy that Gabe tended to radiate, even more so since meeting Holly, was there. I'd met their parents a few times when they were over earlier in the year and we'd chatted on and off when they'd come to the restaurant. They were warm and welcoming and relaxed, and for the first time, Nate seemed a part of them.

'I'm not sure why you're laughing but as you've been wound like a spring since you got here, I'm at least relieved to see you relaxing a little more.'

'I'm laughing because I hadn't mentioned anything about the maid's uniforms being frilly. That was all you!'

'Oh pfft!' I said, trying not to blush again as I swept crumbs from the breakfast bar with the side of my hand.

'True. I was thinking more of a lab coat style.'

'Oh, you were.' My tone was disbelieving.

'Yep.'

He had such a brilliant straight face that I literally had no idea if he was now telling the truth or not.

'Right... well. Anyway. This is going to have to do when it comes to uniforms and just because I speak a little differently from you—'

'A lot differently from me.'

'Whatever. I'm still good at my job.'

'That was never in dispute. I'm just curious as to how you ended up in Wishington Bay, waiting tables and cleaning grumpy blokes' houses.'

'You're saying I don't seem the type?' It wasn't the first time I'd been questioned in a similar vein.

'Something like that, maybe.'

'Never judge a book by its cover and all that.'

'I'm not judging. I'm curious. Two very different things.'

'What did you do to that dog?' I asked, stepping over Bryan's basket as Nate dragged it into a pool of sunlight, while the dog remained unmoving inside it, upside down, feet in the air, snoring softly. 'Are you putting rum in his dog treats or something?'

Nate grinned. 'Nope. Just having fun. It's a long time since I've had a dog to play with.'

'I don't suppose your lifestyle really allows for one.'

'Not really, no. But probably more so than Gabe's did at the time he got Bry and he still made it work. And my wife was at home most of the time so it wouldn't have been out of the question.'

'Sometimes we mean to do things and never get round to them.'

'Serena wasn't keen.'

'Oh.'

'Yes. And you told me off for changing the subject earlier, now you're doing the same.'

I stood up from loading the dishwasher and left the soup machine soaking with some hot soapy water inside to deal with later.

'There's not a lot to tell really. Marriage. Divorce. Time to start again.'

'And you what? Got in the car, pointed it in a direction and kept going until it was running on fumes?'

I was surprised that he'd remembered my explanation of how I got here. 'Pretty much,' I said, pulling a face.

'And you stayed?'

My smile was soft as I looked out of the window up the bay. 'Wouldn't you?'

When he replied, his voice was just as soft. 'If only it were that easy.'

I turned back and gave him a smile, understanding that sometimes things were a lot more complicated, even when we didn't want them to be.

'I should get on with my work, otherwise I'm still going to be here at dinnertime.'

Nate handed me the tea he'd made. 'I don't think Bryan would complain about having some different company. I'm pretty sure I've exhausted everything we have in common.'

'But he is a great listener.'

'He is that.'

We both looked towards the dog. Still snoring.

'Better when he's awake, though, as a general rule.'

'Yep.'

'Thanks for this,' I said, gulping the hot liquid down and tidying the kitchen a bit as I did, killing two birds with one stone.

'You don't need to scald your throat. No rush. But I'll get out of your way.'

'Thank you for lunch. It was lovely.'

'That was all down to you.'

'The company wasn't, and nor was the offer. So, thank you. Just accept the damn gratitude, will you?' I laughed.

He gave the briefest head tilt of acceptance. 'OK. Thank you. It was lovely. And novel. I can't remember the last time I had lunch without my eyes being focused on a document or screen.'

'Really? And you still manage not to drop anything on your tie. I'm impressed. I can't always manage that even when I'm concentrating. Much to my mother's eternal shame.'

'I can't imagine anyone ever being ashamed of you.'

How little he knew…

'That's sweet of you, thanks. But you really should take time out to eat lunch properly.'

'Actually, eating lunch at all is a bit of a novelty unless it's a business one. The one at Ned's the other day was my first experience of sitting down to lunch as an exercise in itself, for no other reason than to actually eat lunch, in as long as I can remember. And that was only after being castigated by you that I wasn't taking advantage of my surroundings.'

'It was?'

'Yes. Why do you think I looked so much like a fish out of water?'

'You didn't.'

'I kind of asked you to join me then, except obviously I knew it was impossible as you were on duty. I felt so odd.'

'You looked fine. Nobody thinks anything of people eating on their own. Especially these days. Everyone is so wrapped up in themselves or have their faces stuck to their phones. It's habit.

Getting comfortable in your own company? It's a good thing to work on.'

'You're saying I'm likely to be that way for some time so get used to it?'

'No!' I replied, my mouth in a horrified 'O' shape. 'That's not what I meant at all!'

And then I saw the merest twinkle in his eye.

'You're teasing me.'

'Only partly.'

'Hmm. Well, I'll let you off. One time deal though.'

'I'll remember that. Thanks.'

'Right. I'm going to finish off upstairs.'

'I'd better go and do some writing before the pooch wakes up and wants another walk.'

We looked down.

'No danger of that any time soon,' I grinned. 'You could always follow his lead. No pun intended.'

Nate's brows knitted together.

'Take a nap.'

'Now? It's the afternoon.'

'I know. That's generally why they're called afternoon naps. I was reading an article just the other day – very good for helping lower blood pressure according to the latest research.'

'Is that so?'

'Yes. And it wouldn't surprise me to learn yours was high.'

Nate didn't reply which, in my head, only confirmed my diagnosis.

'Anyway. Think about it. I can always nip back and do the vacuuming tomorrow.'

'It's fine. I'm going to go and write. Or at least try to.'

'OK. Good luck.'

'Thanks. I'm likely to need it.'

I headed back upstairs and began tackling the bathroom, then pulled the vacuum out of the cupboard. After Holly had tripped carrying the cleaner upstairs one time, Gabe had insisted on having a machine for upstairs and one for downstairs, and a mini one for the stairs themselves. Holly had objected but not for long. She knew that Gabe's stints in A&E had brought him into contact with plenty of accident victims, including those who'd been performing apparently simple tasks. But even simple tasks could go wrong and change a person's life forever. Or even worse. Holly stood her ground when she wanted to, but there were certain things she knew weren't the battles to pick. This arrangement made her fiancé happier and more relaxed and that was a good enough reason for her.

Having cleaned everywhere apart from the area Nate was now working in, tucked at one end of the table, I did my best to work round him. His fingers moved swiftly over the keyboard and the screen moved gradually as more and more words filled the page in front of him. It seemed the block he'd mentioned earlier had passed. Either that or he'd just been procrastinating before. Occasionally he'd stop, one hand moving to stroke Bryan who had now migrated from the dog bed to his temporary master's lap. I vacuumed through and packed everything away, rinsed the soup maker out and put it back in the cupboard.

'Sorry to disturb you, Nate. I just thought I'd tell you I was off.'

'You're done?'

'Yes.'

'Oh.'

'Is there something wrong?'

'No... it's just... nothing.'

I raised an eyebrow. 'It's what?'

'Nice.'

'Having someone clean round you?'

'No. Just having someone around.' Immediately a shy, embarrassed smile ghosted on his face. 'That sounds so sad and dopey. Forget I said that.'

'No, it doesn't. And actually, I know exactly what you mean.'

He nodded.

'How's the book?'

'Good, actually. Surprisingly. You're obviously a lucky charm.'

'Maybe it's more to do with you allowing yourself to take a break from things from time to time. You have to give your body and mind time to recharge.'

His gaze stayed focused on me for a moment, before swinging round to the view beyond the window.

'Maybe,' he said.

'Is there anything more I can do before I leave?'

He looked back at me, gave that ghost of a smile again and shook his head. 'No. Thanks. You've done more than enough.'

'OK. Well, have a good evening. Don't work too late.' I turned to go.

'Wait.'

I turned as I heard the sound of the chair move, immediately followed by the excited revving up of Bryan's little paws, unwilling to miss out on any possible excitement, trying to get a purchase on the wooden floor. He got his front paws to the corner of a thick rug and propelled himself towards Nate.

'What's wrong?' I hesitated, one hand on the door handle.

'Nothing,' Nate said, grabbing his coat off the hook at the same time as shoving his feet into his boots. 'I'll walk you home.'

Bryan picked up on the magic W word in the sentence and began racing round even faster.

'You don't need to do that.'

'I know,' Nate replied, before looking down and meeting my glance square on. 'But I'd like to.'

10

Did he really have to add 'interesting and friendly' to those gorgeous looks? Could he not have stayed the arrogant, rude man I'd initially thought he was? Honestly, him turning in to what was on the verge of 'a really nice guy' was pretty inconvenient, especially when teamed with those striking blue eyes that now looked out at me from under the beanie he'd pulled down low. See? Even a beanie, the one item of head gear guaranteed to reduce most people to looking like they'd raided their gran's tea cosy stash to keep their head warm, looked good on him.

'Sophia?'

I snapped to. 'Huh?'

'You OK?'

'Yes. Absolutely.'

He frowned and pulled at the hat a bit. 'I know it looks kind of ridiculous.'

I suddenly realised I'd been staring at him and, it would seem, he'd completely misinterpreted the reason. That in itself, was kind of adorable. And judging by the uncomfortable look on his face, this was no false modesty. I felt my heart squeeze and tried to ignore it, along with all the other feelings Nate McKinley was awakening. Automatically I reached up and caught his hands, gently pulling them away from his head.

'It looks fine.'

So much more than fine...

Nate didn't say anything, but his gaze drifted down to where I was still holding his hands. I dropped them suddenly – and inelegantly.

'Sorry.'

He gave an almost imperceptible shake of his head.

'I just meant... you need to have more confidence in yourself.'

His blue eyes focused momentarily on mine before looking away.

'No one looks good in a beanie. But I'm afraid comfort is winning over style.'

'See, that's the thing. Ordinarily I'd agree with you. That's kind of why I was staring.'

Mostly.

'Because you seem to be the exception to the rule.'

His expression was one of embarrassed disbelief as I settled my bobble hat over my own ears.

'Come on Bry, mate,' Nate said, turning away and quickly ensconcing the little dog in his new coat and clipping the lead to his collar.

'Ready?'

He nodded and I opened the door, a sharp chill rushing into the house as I did so.

'Bloody hell,' Nate frowned as we stepped out. I waited, fussing with Bryan for a moment as Nate locked the door behind us.

'Wishing you were back home?'

He turned back, his gaze settling on my face. For a moment he said nothing, then he glanced down at the dog who was dancing around, snapping at the cold air rushing up off the sea before looking back up.

'Nope,' he said, then made a gesture, indicating I should lead the way along the path that led up away from the beach and through the village.

* * *

We walked in silence for a little while, but it was companionable, rather than awkward. The sound of the sea washing the beach filled the air as twilight settled around us. We walked past a house with a beautifully tended garden, artfully lit, and I told Nate about the lovely older couple that lived there, and how they had created the garden from scratch over the many years they'd lived here.

'It must be nice to have something like that,' he said, throwing another glance back at it as we walked on.

'A garden?'

'Yeah. Well, one like that. Something that's grown with you. Changed.' He shook his head. 'I don't know. I know what I mean, but I... it's sounding stupid.'

'No,' I reached out, resting my gloved hand on his arm momentarily. 'It isn't. I know exactly what you mean. There's a story in that garden. The plants that have been there from the start, like anchors to the place. The ones they bought on a special trip or were gifts from others. It's got a history.'

He looked at me for a moment. 'Yeah. That's it. That's it, exactly.'

'Why are you looking at me so suspiciously?' I asked, laughing.

He paused, gave a brief hint at a smile and didn't answer.

We walked on a bit longer until Nate stopped at a lamppost, which Bryan duly watered.

'What's this?' Nate asked, pointing to the poster that had been stuck on there. 'Is that here?'

'Yes, the Christmas Victorian Fayre. The village holds it every year. It's been going as long as anyone can remember.'

'Since Victorian times?'

I smiled and shrugged. 'Maybe! I kind of hope so. That would be wonderful, wouldn't it?'

He nodded. 'Back to the whole thing about having a story I guess.'

'Exactly!' I grinned.

'So, what happens then? At this fayre?'

'Well, the whole village gets involved. All the shops are open, and lots of other traders come and set up little stalls selling food and gifts, plus mulled cider and wine, of course. There's music, and best of all, everyone dresses up in Victorian costumes. I've only been to one, last year, but there were times when I glanced round and you really could have been back in Victorian times.'

'Would you have liked that?'

'What?'

'Being back in history.'

'Oh.' I tilted my head one way, then the other. My mother used to chide me on this habit, telling me I didn't need to get my brain to roll around in my skull to produce a simple answer. I begged to differ. That hadn't gone down well either. 'I don't know. Sometimes I think that things were a lot simpler back then. Life's so complicated these days, don't you think?'

'Seems to be.'

'But then I sit in a hot bubble bath, in a warm, cosy flat and consider that things aren't so bad after all.'

'Pros and cons.'

'Exactly.' We turned the corner into my road and strolled on. 'What about you? Do you think you'd have liked living back in Victorian times?'

'I think it was probably easier for blokes. There were a lot fewer restrictions on them than there were on women.'

'That's true.'

'But bearing in mind my job, I'd be a bit stuck for an occupation, I think.'

'How did you get into it? I mean, presumably you didn't just wake up one day and decide you wanted to study plane crashes?'

'No. Not really. I think, like a lot of positions, it just kind of happened. I have an engineering background in aviation and, of course, I was always interested in ways to make air travel safer. A position arose, I was offered it and I just continued in the same vein.'

'Gabe didn't explain exactly but I got the impression you're pretty high up in it all now.'

Nate glanced away, and I took that as a yes.

'Do you like it?'

'It's interesting.'

I studied him for a moment. 'Forgive me for saying this, but you don't seem terribly enthusiastic.'

He lifted a hand, pulling his collar closer to his neck as a breeze whipped down the street. 'It's not exactly a subject people like to hear about.'

'Says who?'

'My wife... ex...' What to call her for the moment seemed to confuse him. 'Anyway. She felt that it freaks people out, hearing about that sort of thing, so...' he shrugged. 'She probably had a point.'

I was beginning to see where Nate's self-belief and confidence had gone. Crushed up in the apparently highly manicured nails of his estranged wife.

'I somehow doubt you'd stand there and start quoting hideous facts and statistics if someone enquired what you did for a living.'

'No,' he shook his head. 'By now everyone knows that air travel has a very good statistical safety record.'

'That's what I mean. And you've advised on films and TV programmes, haven't you? That's impressive. People love to hear about anything like that. I don't know why she'd want you not to talk about any of that. I'd be interested to hear it if I were at a party with you.'

He looked down at me. 'Is that so?'

'Definitely. And believe me, I've been to far too many skull-numbingly boring parties in my time, so I know what I'm talking about.'

'How come? I mean, how come all the parties?'

'Umm… oh, my ex-husband was into all that stuff. Social gatherings and so on.' Nate's gaze lingered on me for a moment and I tried to act casual. I was aware that my answer had been vague but I hadn't had time to prepare and I wasn't a natural liar. He looked back up the street and let it go. Hopefully, he was just assuming that I didn't want to talk about my ex and that was enough explanation for the wishy-washy nature of my response.

'Then I wish I'd met you at one of these parties.'

I looked up, smiling. 'I wish you had too.'

We slowed as we came to Flora's shop and the door to my flat next to it. 'Honestly, you have an interesting job. Don't hide your talent under a bushel.'

'I thought it was light.'

'What?'

'Light. I thought it was don't hide your light under a bushel. Whatever a bushel is.'

'It's a wooden bucket that was used for measuring dry goods. And it is. I was just simplifying things.'

'For the dopey Aussie?' There was a flicker of humour in his eyes, but I got the feeling there was some truth in the question.

I gave him a head tilt and raised my brows, my face serious. 'No.'

He held the look for a few moments then glanced away, the briefest of nods his acceptance.

'How do you know that?'

'What?'

'What the hell a bushel is?'

I shrugged. 'My brain is full useless information.' Half of which I'd learned at one of the last finishing schools to be still running in Switzerland. Although quite where I'd picked up what a bushel was, I had no idea.

'Thanks for walking me back.'

'Pleasure. Thanks for the company. And the soup. And the cleaning.'

'I get paid for the last two.'

'They paid you to cook for me every day? Blimey, Gabe really doesn't think I can cope by myself, does he?'

'It's not that. I think it's more that he thinks you've been alone enough.'

'Well, that makes me sound a right sap.' He squinted as he looked away, and unnecessarily adjusted his hat.

I let out a sigh. 'No. It doesn't. Nobody thinks that, except perhaps you, and if that's the case, then you need to start listening to someone else.'

Nate looked back. 'Like you?'

I drew myself up. 'Maybe. If it's a choice between demoralising thoughts like that and positive ones, then fine. I'm up for the job.' I followed this with a salute. I've no idea why, having never done this once before in my life. My mother definitely wouldn't have approved. And now I'd chosen to do it in front of the most gorgeous man I'd ever met. Of course I had. Why wouldn't I?

On the plus side, that man was now smiling and if it took me making a bit of an idiot of myself to bring out that incredible smile, it might just be worth it.

'Thanks, Sophia. It's been a good day. Rocky start, but worked out well I think.'

I thought back to when I'd stood here earlier today, shoving the tub of homemade soup at him and tearing him off a strip for being arrogant and rude. The flush warmed my cheeks despite the chill of the late afternoon.

'Yes, I think it did.'

'I should let you get in out of the cold.'

'Do you... do you want to come in for a coffee or something?' I asked.

He shook his head. 'No, but thank you. Maybe another time?'

'Yes, sure. Of course.' I was going for casual and hoping I'd nailed it.

'I'm going to scoot back with this monster and get some more words down while I still feel inspired. It's the first time it's happened for a while so I'm trying to make sure I take advantage of it.'

'That's great! I'm really pleased to hear it.' And I was. There was a little less tension in his face and the chill of the day, combined with our brisk pace, had brought some colour to his cheeks, and both suited him.

I bent and gave Bryan a big fuss then stood back. I'd become a bit of a hugger since I'd moved to Wishington Bay, but I quickly decided that might be a bit much for Nate right now. I settled instead for a brief laying of my hand on his arm and a wave before unlocking the door and disappearing inside my flat.

I'd been delighted to find out I enjoyed hugging. My mother had always thought it common and we'd been fervently discouraged as children. On the odd occasion an acquaintance hadn't got the telepathic message that hugs were not the done thing, she'd stand there rigid as a fire poker until the whole, ghastly experience was over, then walk away. It had seemed normal to me at the time but now when I thought back on those occasions, I felt mortified for the other person who must have been either completely confused, or embarrassed, or possibly both by the sequence of events. It would have horrified my mother to think I had now become 'one of those ghastly huggers'. I smiled at the thought and made my way up the stairs to my flat.

11

The following weekend I was off shift and making the most of the situation by catching up on some chores early before taking some time out for myself. I glanced over at my phone as it buzzed.

Pop down for a coffee if you're not busy?

I'd cleaned the flat, nipped out to the bakers for a fresh loaf, in order to make some toast, bought a jar of locally made marmalade and was now sat on the sofa, feet up, reading a book. Outside the sky was leaden and held the promise of early snow, so although I knew I ought to get out for a walk, my cosy surroundings and novel were much more appealing at the moment. But it would be nice to have a catch up with Flora so I put the book down, stuffed my feet into trainers and jogged down the stairs. Scooting out of my front door, I raced out of the cold into her warm shop. There were a couple of customers browsing as I made my way to the till and gave Flora a hug.

'Hello, love. I didn't disturb you, did I?'

'No, not at all. How are you?'

'Not bad.'

'Been busy?'

'It's starting to get busier now everyone's beginning to shop in earnest for Christmas. I'm just trying to summon up the energy to start decorating the shop actually.'

'Want some help?'

'Do you mind? Aren't you due at the restaurant today?'

'No. Weekend off. Much to Corinne's disgust.' I winked and Flora smirked.

'Goodness knows you've covered enough of hers since you started. I don't know why you do it.'

I shrugged. 'It's extra money and it's not like I have a lot of other plans. Unlike Corinne.'

'I think she finds work an inconvenience,' Flora said. 'Spoilt from the day she was born, that one. And now she uses her looks to get away with more. I don't know why Ned puts up with it. She never seems to do as much running around as the other waiting staff whenever we've been in there.'

'Carrie's not exactly a fan either but she said Ned's known Corinne's family since he was a kid. I guess it can be tricky when business and pleasure mix. Anyway, the important thing is I'm off today, so what can I do to help?'

'Are you sure you don't mind?' Flora's hopeful expression would have changed my mind even if I had.

'Not at all.'

'Oh! That'd be lovely, Sophia. Thanks ever so much. I feel bad taking up your weekend.'

'No need. I enjoy doing things like this.' That had been another new discovery. Last year was the first time I'd ever decorated for Christmas. I'd bought the biggest tree that would fit in my flat and still allow me access – which unfortunately meant it was pretty small – plus a bulging basket full of decorations and several strings of white fairy lights. I'd then spent a very happy afternoon decorating the tree and pinning up decorations and strings of soft white fairy lights round the place. The set I'd fitted in my kitchen looked so adorable that I'd left them up permanently. Of course, it wasn't that my previous houses hadn't been decorated for the festive season – in fact, the last house had four trees. And, of course, two more in the London flat. It's just that they were done by the staff.

I'd always been a bit jealous when I watched Hallmark movies (in secret, obviously, as these most definitely wouldn't have been approved of) and saw families decorating trees together. Even some of my friends kept at least one tree for decorating with their family. But my mother had never been into all that. It was a job for other people, and then she could enjoy the fruits of their efforts. And my husband wasn't at home half the time anyway so he probably wouldn't even have noticed if the trees were there or not, let alone ever have the inclination to decorate one.

As the customers she had been serving left, Flora studied me for a moment, an expectant look on her face.

'What?'

'OK, as you're obviously not going to tell me outright, I'm forced to ask. Who was that extremely gorgeous man walking you to your door the other day? And was that Bryan he had with him?'

'It was, yes. That's Nate, Gabe's brother. He's over here house and dog sitting while they're away.'

Flora looked at me expectantly. 'And?'

'And what?'

'Oh, come on, love. I've been around the block enough to recognise when there are sparks between people.'

'Oh, Flora, there aren't any sparks,' I said, laughing. 'Have you been sniffing those Christmas candles again?'

'Well, you looked good together so there definitely should be,' she replied. She tilted her head. 'Are you absolutely sure?'

'Yes. I mean, yes, really there aren't.'

'Well, that sounds like a waste.'

'He's not here for anything like that. And neither am I,' I added quickly.

'But he walked you home.'

'Bryan needed a walk.'

'And the swathe of sandy beach right in front of the house would never do for that,' she grinned.

'Oh, shush.' I waved a hand. 'He's been going through a difficult patch and is just looking for some peace and quiet.'

Flora frowned for a moment. 'Is he married?'

'Separated.'

'Likely to reunite?'

I shrugged, feeling a little uncomfortable about discussing Nate's private life behind his back. I knew Flora wasn't the type to gossip to others but even so. It was Nate's business and no one else's.

Flora rested her head in her hands. 'Well, I can see I'm not going to get anything juicy out of you. Spoilsport.'

I laughed and gave Flora a squeeze round the shoulders. 'There's nothing juicy to tell. Honestly. I'd been down to clean the house and Nate had been in front of the computer screen for a while, writing. Bryan was due a walk and it was a good opportunity for Nate to take a break too so he walked with me into the village. He wasn't walking me home; he was just walking with me in the same direction.'

Exactly.

'Right,' Flora said, the look in her eye saying a whole lot more.

I smiled and shook my head. 'Come on, show me where these decorations are before I change my mind.'

Flora jumped up, laughing, and headed out the back. 'Mind the shop for me for a minute. I'll be back in two shakes.'

I'd served a couple of customers and was just wrapping up a beautiful china figurine when Flora re-emerged a short time later carrying one box and pushing another along with her feet.

'Wait a minute, Flora. I'll help you with that.' Flora was long past retirement but seemed to have more energy than most people half her age, and there was nothing she wouldn't have a go at. But her current method of moving things still looked like an accident waiting to happen. She paused, considered, caught the look in my eye and bent to put the box down.

I rang the sale through, handed the customer her receipt and gave her and the little girl a wave as they closed the door behind them, sealing out the biting wind that practically blasted each customer into the shop every time it opened. Going over to Flora, I picked up the boxes and set them on the table, then dived in for a rummage.

'These look like tree decorations. Is there a tree back there?'

'No, I need to pop down to Greg at the grocer's and collect the one he's put aside for me. He normally drops it off but he's put his back out at the moment.'

'I can do that. I assume it's not too big?'

'No, it's only a little one as it's going to go in that corner over there so can't take up too much space. It's usually all bound up so shouldn't be too unwieldy. Are you sure you don't mind?'

'Not at all. Do you want me to go and get that now or get on with the rest of the shop?'

Flora tapped a well-manicured nail against her lip for a moment. 'If you could grab the tree, then one of us could be doing that while the other one decorates the actual shop. It'll get done in half the time then.'

I nodded. 'Good plan. I'll just nip back up and get my coat and then head down to Greg's now.'

* * *

'You sure you're going to be all right with that, Soph? I can ask my son to drop it round to Flora later, if you like.' Greg was watching as I endeavoured to find the best way to carry the tree, which I had a feeling was bigger than Flora was anticipating,

'Yes, I'll be fine. It's just a case of getting it in the right position, I think.' I jiggled it again and tentatively moved. Right, this could be it. I gave it one last jiggle and headed away from the grocer's back up the street towards Flora's shop. My arms were wrapped tightly round as much of the tree as I could reach, which had proved the best way of carrying it. The only slight downside with this method was the tiny fact that all I could see was tree so I had to rely on others giving way to me. I bounced off something and apologised as I hoiked the tree back up from where it was slowly slipping down my body. Tentatively I peered round it and realised I'd just apologised to a lamppost. As I gave the tree another jostle, the string holding the top few branches together rolled further up and let loose its captives, one of which pinged out and smacked me in the face.

'Ow!' I said, trying to overcome the urge to drop the tree where I stood and give it a good kicking. 'No good deed goes unpunished,' I grumbled as I tightened my grip on the foliage and set off again. It seemed a lot longer back to Flora's shop than it had been in the other direction. I could feel the damn thing slipping and heading slowly for the pavement. Doing my best to grab hold of it, I tried to speed up, reasoning that I might be able to beat its descent to the floor. In reality, all this did was hasten the tree's slide to the ground. As the trunk made contact with the pavement, it acted as a form of brake – something I hadn't accounted for, and having sped up my pace, now had no time to prepare for. Momentum carried me on, into the tree until we were both sprawled on the pavement.

'Sophia?'

I kept my face in the tree for a moment, trying to pretend I wasn't lying astride a Christmas tree in the middle of the pavement. If I ignored it, maybe it wasn't happening.

'Sophia?' the voice came again. OK. So it was definitely happening. 'Are you OK?'

I turned my head to where Nate had now crouched down level with it. 'Hello.' I added a casual inflection as if to convey this was a normal, everyday occurrence. His face assured me that was not the case.

'What are you doing?'

Humping a Christmas tree in the middle of the village, obviously.

Suddenly two large hands were on my upper arms and I was quickly upright. So quickly I got a momentary headrush and staggered a little. Nate's hands once again steadied me. Looking up, I saw his face was creased with concern.

'I'm all right. Really.'

He dropped his hands to his sides and it was then I realised Bryan was tucked into the front of his coat, peering out at the world from this new, advantageous position. His head wiggled as he tried to say hello.

'Keep still, little mate.' Nate adjusted his coat and I gave Bryan a quick scratch behind the ears to satisfy him.

'Sure you're OK?' Nate asked.

'Fine. Honestly.' So long as you didn't count mortification. I focused my attention back on the tree and began to bend down to start my next round of Christmas tree rodeo.

'Wait.' Nate put a hand on my arm and I stood. Reaching into his coat, he lifted out Bryan, who didn't seem too thrilled with this development and handed him to me, whereupon the little dog seemed to forgive his temporary master. Nate bent and scooped up the tree, jostled it so that it leant against one shoulder, handily enabling him to also see where he was going, something I'd lacked the benefit of, and turned towards me.

'Where do you need this?'

'It's for Flora's shop. The little gift shop next to my flat. But you don't have to do that. I was fine. I just needed to put it down and get a better purchase on it, that's all.'

Nate began walking. 'I think you'd handled the putting it down bit quite well. Might need to work on the other part.'

'That better not be a smile on your face.'

'Not at all.' He turned, the gorgeous, shy smile lighting his face.

'Glad to hear it,' I grinned back.

We reached the shop far quicker with Nate carrying the tree with long strides as opposed to my Geisha style shuffling.

'Here we are.' I scooted across in front of him and opened the door to the gift shop, catching the raised eyebrow that Flora shot me.

'I met Nate part way and he offered to carry the tree for me.'

'How kind of you, Nate. I'm Flora.' She held out her hand and Nate shook it.

'Pleasure to meet you. You've got a lovely shop here.'

'Thank you. So, you just happened to run into Sophia?' she asked, now fussing Bryan who had been transferred to her arms while I ducked under the counter to find some scissors to cut the remaining ties of the tree.

'More tripped over. She was causing a bit of an obstruction.'

Flora looked round and I narrowed my eyes at Nate which brought the smile from his eyes to his mouth and suddenly I didn't mind any more.

'I was taking a short rest.'

'While lying on top of the tree in the middle of the pavement,' Nate filled in helpfully.

Flora let out a giggle before hastily covering it. 'Oh, Soph. Are you OK?' Popping Bryan down to explore the shop, she came over to me, squinting as she put a hand to my face. 'You've got a red mark, there.' Her hand was cool as it touched my cheekbone.

'The tree got loose from its top tie and sort of smacked me in the face. It's fine.'

'Was this before or after you mounted it in the street?' The giggle was given free rein this time.

I gave her a look and bent to find the next line of string. Sliding the scissor blade underneath, I closed them, making a satisfying snip. Less satisfying was the branches pinging out, a fact I hadn't accounted for in my distraction, mostly by Flora but admittedly a little by Nate who was now answering Flora's chatty questions as best he could.

'Oh, for crying out loud.' I slapped a hand over my eye as it watered, tears streaming down my cheek. My mother definitely wouldn't have approved of some of the phrases I'd picked up but at least it was free of swear words which, considering how much it had stung, was a miracle in itself.

'Sophia?' Nate crossed the little shop in about two strides. 'What happened?'

'Really? Again?' Flora asked, coming to stand beside him, and coming up to about his elbow. Bustling in, she took my hand away from my eye – she really was stronger than she looked. 'Look up,' she said and I did so. 'Down... left... right.' Doesn't look like you've got anything in there but go upstairs and bathe it with some cotton wool.'

'It's fine, Flora.'

'Nate, my dear. Would you accompany her?'

'I said I'm fine.'

Flora looked unmoved and Nate looked awkward.

'Fine,' I said and turned towards the door. 'But don't go trying to move that while I'm gone.'

'Wouldn't dream of it. Besides, Nate's just offered to help us pot it up when you're done so it's all sorted.'

I glanced at Nate who shrugged. Flora was the kind of woman who could get anyone to do anything, but never used her powers for evil. Although I wasn't entirely sure this example counted as using them for good. There was a twinkle in her eye that had me suspicious. I only hoped that Nate hadn't noticed.

12

I knew my flat was compact but it had never seemed more so than it did now with Nate McKinley occupying what felt like at least half of it.

'This is nice,' he said, looking around.

'It's a little small, I know.'

'But it's welcoming. That's the main thing. Like Holly's place. It feels like a home.'

'Thank you.' I headed into the bathroom and grabbed some cotton wool pads from a jar and headed back into the kitchen to boil some water. Once it began to warm, I flicked off the kettle and poured some in a bowl. Dipping a pad in, I squeezed out the excess. As I lifted it to my eye, Nate's hands closed over mine. 'Here, let me do that. Just sit with your head back.'

'It's really not that bad.'

'I don't think Flora is the kind of woman to take no for an answer, no matter how sweet she looks.'

He might be the strong, silent type but he was certainly observant. I did as he said and he laid the cotton pad gently on my eye, his hands brushing my cheek as he did so.

'How's that?'

'Fine. Thanks.'

'Is it still stinging?'

'A little.'

'OK, just rest for a bit. Is Bryan all right exploring round here?'

'Yeah. He's had the odd sleepover here so he's familiar with it all.'

'I think he's asleep on your bed.'

'Well, that makes a change, having a man in my bedroom,' I said, without thinking then immediately wished I could dunk my entire head in the bowl of water before me.

'I mean...' Literally I had no idea what I meant or where I was going with that sentence, so I shut up. Momentarily.

'So, doesn't your house feel like a home?' Smooth, Soph. Almost seamless. Thankfully Nate complied with my obvious wish to change the subject.

'No. Not really. It's very on trend, apparently, not that I'd know. But it certainly doesn't have that sense of warmth that this place has, or Holly and Gabe's. I felt that the moment I walked in there. It was really nice.'

'Better than a soulless hotel room after all then?' I removed the pad and winked. At least I tried to wink but, thanks to my sore eye, it came out a lot more lecherous than I intended. 'Ouch.'

'Probably best not to try winking for a bit.' Nate said, gently laying a hand on my shoulder to get me to sit back as he placed a fresh damp cotton pad on my eye.

'It was a bit sore.'

'And a little terrifying.'

'Thanks.'

'You're welcome.'

I smiled and closed my other eye for a moment, breathing in the woody scent of his aftershave.

'You don't have to help with the tree, you know.' I opened the other eye again. His expression was back to that unreadable one he'd had the first time I'd met him. 'I mean, it's very kind of you but I know you've got a deadline and stuff, and Flora is ever so good at talking people into doing things they might not want to do and then they realise when it's all a bit late that they've agreed—'

'I'd like to,' he interrupted, thankfully, as by now I was aware I'd begun to ramble but was struggling to find a way to stop the torrent.

'Oh.'

'If that's OK with you?'

'Yes!' Oops. Bit too enthusiastic. 'I mean, of course. That'd be lovely. So long as you're sure.'

'Yeah, it'd be nice I think.'

I stole a glance at him and definitely agreed it would be nice.

'I think this is OK now,' I said, lifting the cotton pad. 'We can head back down now if you like. Unless you'd like a coffee or something first?'

'That'd be great. But show me where things are and let me do it.'

'I'm fine, really. Stop fussing,' I smiled at him.

He conceded but I could see the hint of reluctance. 'Not that I don't appreciate it,' I said, gently. Which was true. I couldn't remember the last time I'd had someone showing concern like this and I had to admit it felt nice. No point getting used to it though.

I pushed myself up and headed to the kitchen. 'What would you like?'

'Whatever's going.'

I pulled a couple of mugs out of the cupboard, plopped some coffee powder into them and flicked the kettle on to boil.

'There might be some biscuits hiding in here somewhere,' I said, opening a couple of cupboards before spying a packet lurking on the top shelf. 'Can you reach those?' I asked, as Nate easily snagged them.

'Yep,' he said, handing them to me.

We took the coffee and biscuits through to the lounge and sat back on the sofa.

'How's the book going?'

'Good, I think. I need to thank you for giving me a kick in the pants about getting out and about more. Since I stopped moping, I've actually been more productive.'

'I never said you were moping. I know you've been through the mill. I'm not entirely unfeeling, you know.'

'No, I know. I didn't mean it like that. But I am appreciative.'

'Well, then, you're welcome.'

We sat chatting for a little longer before checking on Bryan who had now wriggled himself into the top of my bed and was looking very comfortable under my duvet with his head poking out, and gentle, contented snores drifting from him

'We can leave him there. I can nip up and check on him again in a bit.'

With that, we headed back down the stairs and into Flora's shop, ready to get the tree in place and decorated.

'Better?' Flora asked in a voice loaded with all sorts of questions.

'Fine, thanks,' I smiled innocently.

She gave me a head shake, and a gentle push over to where Nate was already hefting the tree into the metal pail Flora had placed beside it.

Together we settled the tree in its pot and moved it in to the space Flora had set aside for it.

'Thanks.'

'My pleasure. Are you going to decorate it?'

'Uh-huh,' I said, bending down and lifting the box of decorations onto a nearby stool.

Nate shifted his weight as he gave a short nod.

'You're more than welcome to stay and help, although I don't want to distract you from your work.'

'I'm on course to hit my deadline. I was up early today and got my word count in so I'm happy to stay and help if I can be useful.'

I'd seen a few female customers browsing the shop, all the while throwing apparently casual glances over at Nate, so I had an idea that Flora would be more than happy to have him stay longer, even forgetting the fact that she was clearly doing her best to set me up with him.

'That'd be lovely, then,' I replied, and a watched as he relaxed his shoulders, the smile brief but striking. 'Still not sleeping too well?' I asked as I passed him the lights to wrap round his side of the tree.

He gave a shrug. 'It's better than it was, which is something.'

I stole a glance as he passed the lights back round to me. The dark shadows under his eyes remained but they were less than they had been that first week I'd met him.

'All these walks and sea air, you'll soon be sleeping like a log.'

'I look forward to it.'

I smiled and handed him the second set of lights. 'So, what did you have planned for today before being roped into doing this?'

'I volunteered. And nothing much. I was just getting a little stir crazy earlier so thought Bry and I could do with some fresh air. I was just wandering aimlessly really when I came across you sprawled on the pavement hugging a tree.'

I leant around the tree and stuck my tongue out.

He laughed. 'I'm glad I did though. This is nice.'

I returned the gentle expression. 'It is.'

Nate passed the end of the light string back to me, our fingers brushing as he did so. The touch sent ripples throughout my body and I turned away as I felt warmth flush my face. Sticking my head practically inside the decoration box and making vague rummaging sounds, I waited for my heart rate to settle before emerging.

'You OK?' Nate asked, concern creasing his face when I did.

'Uh-huh!' I said, lightly. Clearly he wasn't affected in the same way as I was, which I supposed was good. He had enough to think about without me complicating matters. Although it would have been nice if he'd shown some sort of reaction. I'd had far too many years feeling like I was incapable of stirring any sort of response from a man so it would have been nice if the universe gave me a break occasionally and show that I wasn't the sexless being my husband had made me believe I was. I stole another glance at Nate and smiled to myself, at the same time as giving myself a pep talk. Just because my husband hadn't seen it, perhaps because he'd been too busy looking at every other woman but me, didn't mean I wasn't attractive. Nate might not see it either but those were the breaks. He had more than enough on his mind right now, but at least he was giving me something pretty to look at this winter.

'You're quiet.' He looked across at me and raised a brow.

'I didn't realise I was usually noisy,' I grinned. I'd thought about another wink but my eye was still stinging and I didn't want to send him running for the hills in fear.

'You know what I mean.'

'What would you like to talk about?'

He gave a shy look under his lashes as he reached into the box and grabbed a handful of baubles.

'Nothing. I was just wondering if you wouldn't rather be doing this on your own.'

I took one of the baubles he was holding and placed it on the tree, then repeated the action.

'Absolutely not. It's nice.' I bumped my arm against his. 'You're nowhere near as bad company as you seem to think you are.'

'I've not got Gabe's easy manner. I feel like that's a minus point.'

I looked up at him and shrugged. 'That's because you're not Gabe. You're you. And you have your own ways and manner, which doesn't make someone else's better or worse.' I stretched up to hook another bauble on a branch. Nate gently took it from me and placed it where I wanted it. 'Thanks.' Without thinking, I wrapped my arms round one of Nate's and gave a quick squeeze. 'It wouldn't do for us all to be the same, and there's nothing wrong with you.'

Nate looked down at me hesitantly, a hint of colour showing through his light tan. 'Thank you.'

'You're welcome,' I replied quietly, meeting the intense blue gaze and trying to ignore the fizzing I felt in my stomach as I did.

'Oh, that's looking beautiful!' Flora exclaimed, clapping her hands as she came around the tree to where we were standing. I let go of Nate's arm and he stood back, straighter. For a moment there was nothing but Michael Bublé crooning about being home for Christmas to break the silence.

Flora opened her mouth and I gave a miniscule head shake to warn her not to say the words that were currently making her eyes twinkle. I knew whatever it was would only be a tease, but Nate's confidence was fragile and I didn't want Flora's well-meaning words making him uncomfortable just as we seemed to be making a little progress.

'Beautiful,' she said again, looking at the tree and giving Nate a gentle pat on the arm before sending a private wink my way.

* * *

Having finished decorating Flora's shop, we said goodbye and headed back upstairs to see Bryan. From his yawning squeaks and stretches, it was apparent he'd only woken up when I'd placed the key in the lock.

'Lazy bones,' Nate smiled at him as he scooped him up, the little dog wriggling with happiness as he nuzzled into his neck. 'I guess I'd better get him back for his dinner.'

I nodded, surprised at how much I wanted them both to stay.

'Thanks for today, Sophia. I had a good time.'

'You're welcome. Feel free to volunteer to be put to use any time you like. I'm sure we can find you some chores.'

'I think I'd like that.'

'I was joking!' I laughed.

'I wasn't,' he shrugged. 'It's nice to feel a part of something. It's a long time since I felt that way.'

'Well, if that's what you want, then you've definitely come to the right place.'

He turned to go and I followed, bouncing off his back as he stopped suddenly and turned, his arm shooting out to steady me as I pinged backwards.

'Sorry. I just had a thought.'

'That's enough to make anyone stop in their tracks,' I grinned up at him. He gave me a patient look then smiled. It really was a waste it wasn't seen more often.

'Funny. I was wondering whether Holly and Gabe have a tree hiding away somewhere, and decorations?'

'Holly had a fresh one last year but there should be a box of decorations somewhere.' He nodded. 'And I'm sure Greg at the grocer's will be able to provide you with a tree. That's where I picked Flora's up from and he seemed to have plenty left. You sound like you have plans.'

He gave a small shrug. 'I guess you've put me in a bit of a Christmassy mood and I thought it might be nice to have the house decorated too.'

'That's a great idea, Nate.'

'I'm speaking to them later on video. I'll check if they mind then.'

'I'm sure they won't.'

'No, you're probably right but it feels best to check. Plus I can ask where the decorations are, and if there's anything she'd prefer me not to use. You know, something that was her gran's maybe.'

'Honestly, Holly was so excited about you coming over. I know she was upset your trips clashed but really, with Holly, that house and everything in it is to be used. Remember—'

'Family,' he interrupted.

'Exactly.'

'Thanks for today,' he said again.

'You're welcome.' This time I went in for the hug but feeling the rigidity of his body as I did so, I suddenly realised that might have been too presumptuous. And then he relaxed, his arms wrapped around me and gave a gentle squeeze. One more of the bricks in his wall had come down.

I smiled as he pulled back, gave Bryan a little fuss and waved them off.

13

'Nobody told me there were going to be gorgeous men at that wreath making thing,' Corinne pouted as she looked at the pin board and the picture Carrie had printed from my phone.

'That was just good luck,' Eloise said, coming to stand next to us. Looking past Corinne who was sizing up Billy in the photo, she winked. 'He was quite taken with our Soph here.'

'Really?' Corinne said, unable to cover the surprise in her voice as she moved on to inspecting her false nails.

I gave my throat a small clear and did my best not to rise to the bait.

'Yes. Quite enamoured, he was. Be nice to see him again when he drops off the wreaths, won't it, Soph? Maybe you can set that date he was asking for then.' I knew Eloise was rubbing it in for Corinne but I wasn't used to discussing my love life – any of my life – with too many people. And especially not with my frosty colleague.

'He actually asked you out?' Corinne's heavily but perfectly made up eyes widened.

'I don't know why you're so surprised?' Eloise's voice was prickly now. 'Sophia's a gorgeous looking woman.'

Corinne pulled a face that suggested she didn't exactly agree but was deigning to give me the benefit of the doubt, for the moment. 'But she's like forty!' She might as well have said four thousand.

'I am not forty!' I said, a little more vehemently than I planned. That particular number was certainly becoming clearer on the horizon but in the meantime I was going to hold on to my thirties. Especially in the face of smug twenty-two-year-olds.

Corinne gave a disbelieving flick of her high definition eyebrows. 'Whatever. Anyway, it's probably his job to flirt with middle aged women. Make people like you book up in the hope you might actually see him again. By then, of course, he'll be on to the next lonely looking prospect.'

'Corinne!' Eloise snapped, but I shook my head at her as Corinne gave Billy's photo another once over before sauntering off. She got to the window and began taking selfies, angling her phone just right, pouting her cosmetically enhanced lips and tossing her hair.

'You all right, love?'

'Of course. She's just put out because she thinks she might have missed out on something.'

'She was invited.' This was true although we all knew Carrie had secretly been relieved when Corinne had said no. And she wasn't the only one.

I wasn't sure what it was exactly about me that Corinne had taken a dislike to but, from the moment I started at Ned's, she'd made little snipes and digs at every opportunity. To be fair, she didn't seem to be all that friendly to anyone except Carrie and Ned, because it suited her purposes for the most part. Keeping this job was the deal she'd made with her mother that would ensure her father kept her allowance nicely topped up. Doing the job well was obviously not part of that deal. Carrie, I knew, wasn't keen on the arrangement but Ned was a lovely guy and in a tricky situation having known her family for years, so unless Corinne screwed up in a major way we all had to deal with her. There were, of course, a few people who got the full benefit of her charms.

The lunch shift at the restaurant was heaving but I couldn't help notice Nate tucked away at a table for two by the window, his face turned towards the plate glass, watching the sea wash the beach. It was a cold and clear day, the promenade area outside busy with people walking along, wrapped up against the chill, noses and cheeks red, as dogs played fetch or ran around with other four-legged pals, skidding and dancing on the exposed sand.

'I'll give you my entire day's wages if you let me take over that table,' Corinne said in a low whisper, pulling me furtively to the side by my elbow.

'Huh?'

She nodded not terribly subtly in Nate's direction.

'Him. He's gorgeous and I already checked – there's no wedding ring.'

'You know that doesn't always mean someone isn't married.'

'No, I know. But please, Sophia?'

'What's going on?' Eloise bustled up, hooking the pager on her apron as she did so.

'I'm taking one of Sophia's tables to help her out,' Corinne explained, airily.

Eloise gave us both a look. 'That's not like you to not keep up, Soph. You OK?'

Great, now it looked like I was bad at my job. Thanks, Corinne. And I hadn't actually agreed to anything yet, but my fellow waitress was young and pretty and used to getting her way.

I didn't answer. Suddenly my pager went off and I headed back towards the kitchen to collect my order. Coming back out, laden with plates, I wound my way through to the table next to Nate's. Corinne was already at his side, smiling, with her wide, heavily lashed eyes focused entirely on him. I handed out the order, checking that my table had everything they needed and making a note to bring two more glasses of house white before turning away. As I did, Nate looked past Corinne and caught my eye. I returned his smile, gave him a brief wave and headed over to the bar to get the drinks. As I poured the second one, Corinne appeared at my side, snatching a bottle of some locally brewed beer from the fridge.

'What are you doing?' she hissed at me.

I turned, her tone surprising me. 'Sorry?'

'What are you doing?'

'Umm, pouring wine.'

She gave an exaggerated huff, the kind girls her age excelled in, and then looked at me.

'I saw you. At the table. I told you – he's mine.'

I didn't have time for her petulance today. The restaurant was busy and she'd already made it look like I couldn't keep up with my job. Also, I'd never actually agreed to her taking Nate's table despite it being in my section. She'd just assumed. I'd let that go but I was in no mood to put up with her spoilt childishness.

'Actually, you said nothing of the sort and I don't think you can just go around claiming strangers for your own. I also don't appreciate you telling Eloise that you were doing it because I couldn't keep up. That doesn't exactly make me look good.'

Corinne inspected her fingernails, either unbothered, or not listening, or possibly both.

I gave up. Grabbing the glasses, I stood them on a bar tray and made to leave.

'Sophia?' Her voice was softer now. Maybe there was hope after all.

'Yes?'

'Can you open this beer for me? I don't want to break my nails.'

Hope evaporated. I opened the beer, picked up my tray and walked off.

'Hi,' Nate said as I turned, having handed over the wine to the table next to him.

'Hi,' I replied. 'How are you?'

'Good thanks. Busy in here today.'

'Yes. Sunday always pulls the crowds.'

He nodded. 'I was sort of hoping you might be serving me.'

I smiled but said nothing.

'I just... thought that maybe I could ask—'

'Here we are!' Corinne appeared, placing herself purposefully between me and Nate, and putting his beer down in front of him with a flourish. I noticed she bent a bit lower than she needed to, and an extra button on her blouse was now undone. Nate glanced up to thank her and got an eyeful of pert, twenty-two-year-old cleavage. He sat back a little. Corinne gave me a brief triumphant look, completely missing Nate's discomfort and positioned herself so that I was out of sight completely. I looked up to see another diner trying to catch my eye and headed over to the table.

'Hi. Can I help?'

'Yes, we've been trying to get our waitress's attention for a while but she seems to have disappeared.' The table was in Corinne's section, the other side of the restaurant. This was exactly why we had sections and why we didn't mess around with them, no matter how gorgeous the clientele.

'I'm ever so sorry about that. What can I get you?'

They placed an order for four of Ned's special sticky toffee puddings.

'Great choice. And would you like to follow those up with tea or coffee, which of course will be on the house to apologise for you having to wait?'

They took up the offer and I headed back to place it with the kitchen. As I came out, Eloise caught me.

'What's all this with Corinne and Gabe's brother?'

'She doesn't know who he is. I didn't get a chance to say much.'

'Ned won't be thrilled at her messing about with the sections so she can chat up a customer. Did you see she's undone her blouse even more than usual? Honestly. I know Ned's known her for years but I think she's taking the pee with it all. She always wants to cover tables when there's a celebrity here and then flirts like mad, and now this.'

'I know. I don't think Nate quite knew what to do with himself.'

'She's too young for him anyway. What is she thinking?'

'I guess she clocked the cashmere coat, and expensive watch, added it to the rest of him and that was enough.'

'Are you bothered?' Eloise asked quietly.

I shrugged. 'I don't like to think he's uncomfortable but he's a chap and she's young and pretty. He looked a bit taken aback to start with, but they all seem to come around soon enough, don't they?'

Eloise raised a slim brow. 'Spoken from experience, it would seem.'

I busied myself with my notepad and gave a small shrug. 'Anyway, I'd better go and get these puddings. I've already had to give table nine four free coffees as they'd been trying to catch Corinne's eye while she was busy trying to catch Nate.'

'Oh God, really?'

'Better that than unhappy customers.'

'Absolutely. I'll have a word with her when I can.'

I didn't think it would do much good, but Eloise was welcome to try.

'What are you doing?' Corinne snapped again as I dropped off the sticky toffee puddings and headed back to the wait station to check on the rest of the bookings. I'd hardly stopped, had been on my feet for hours and had ended up covering half of Corinne's tables as she spent more and more time loitering beside Nate's.

I glanced up briefly from the booking ledger.

'You've taken half my tips!'

I held her furious gaze for a moment while I tried to work out if she was actually serious. Realising she was, I let out a half disbelieving laugh and began walking away. My shift was nearly done and I was quite ready to go home and put my feet up with a bucket sized mug of tea. Corinne caught my arm.

'I want those tips.'

'Corinne. First of all, you can let go of my arm. Secondly, despite the fact that your deal for taking that table was your "entire day's wages", I still didn't take your tips. I covered several of your tables because you were too busy trying to chat up one particular customer to notice that they'd been trying to get your attention for ages. I don't think the restaurant deserves to get a bad reputation just because you can't be arsed to do your job properly when a pretty face enters the room.'

'You're just jealous because he was interested in me and not you!'

'Right. If you say so.'

'He's taking me out next Friday night.'

I stopped. I'd said to Eloise that they all came around eventually, but stupidly I'd had the thought that maybe Nate was different. He hadn't seemed as bowled over by Corinne as some male customers were, but I guess he'd relaxed into it after all.

'Cat got your tongue?' she asked.

I dug into my apron, pulled out the money I'd put in the side pocket for Corinne's tables and placed it on the booking ledger.

'There's your tips.' And with that I walked away. I couldn't wait for this shift to be over.

As I stacked the chairs, Eloise mopped the floor while Corinne pretended to be stacking chairs on the other side of the restaurant but in reality did very little but keep checking her phone.

'I've about had it with her,' Eloise said, glancing up again from her chore, and waving through the window to Bob who was stood chatting to someone. He raised a hand. 'She always wriggles out of any clear up.'

Eloise had a point, but Corinne always had an excuse or was sure to mention how close friends her family was with Ned which meant nothing was ever said to him. And, of course, when he or Carrie were on the floor, she was as hard working as the rest of us.

'Corinne. You know my rules about phones on shift.' Ned had appeared from nowhere and Corinne flushed beetroot at being caught.

'Oh, sorry, Ned, but my grandmother's not very well and I just wanted to check how she was.'

Eloise's groan was audible. Corinne flashed her a look.

'Is that right?' Ned asked.

'Yes, she thinks it might be flu and you know how dangerous that can be for the elderly.' She flashed Eloise a look as she said this, and I could practically hear my friend's blood boiling in her veins.

'Cheeky cow,' she muttered at me, under her breath.

Ned leant on the wall. 'That's funny because I just ran into your gran earlier on the beach and she seemed absolutely fine. In fact, she'd just been out for a dip with the sea swimming group.'

'Oh! I... meant my other gran.'

'The one that died four years ago?' His tone was casual but there was no mistaking that Ned was annoyed at being lied to.

Corinne opened her mouth and then closed it again.

'Don't let me see it happening again. And give the girls a hand clearing up. You're all paid the same to do the same things. No one is above it.'

'We've finished now,' Eloise stated, in return for the dig about her age.

Corinne flashed her a look of daggers, which Eloise shrugged off. Having put away the cleaning gear, we walked over to where our coats hung, and got ready to leave.

'Thanks for that,' Corinne snapped.

'No one to blame but yourself, love,' Eloise said, holding the door open for me. Corinne followed behind.

'Hello, love. Good shift?' Bob asked, kissing his wife. 'Hi Soph, Corinne.'

'Hello, Bob. You're looking well,' I replied. Corinne gave him a thin smile before looking back at her phone.

The man he was talking to turned round. Nate.

14

'Hi,' he said. 'I thought as I was already here, I could maybe walk you home?'

'Oh, that would be lovely!' Corinne gushed, a sharp elbow hastening me to the side.

Nate fiddled with his hat for a moment. 'I... er... sorry. I meant...'

'He meant Sophia, Corinne. They already know each other,' Eloise explained, a tad too joyfully.

Corinne looked from me to Nate, and then back again. 'Really?'

Again with surprise? Wow. Thanks.

'Well, I guess I'll just see you next Friday then, Nate,' she said, looking up at him from under her thick, false lashes, before turning and strutting off up the harbour.

We all watched her go for a moment then turned back to face Nate.

'I literally don't know what she's on about.' He looked genuinely confused.

'She made a point of saying earlier that you had asked her out.'

He shook his head. 'I didn't. I don't know...' He let out a sigh and dragged one large hand across a freshly shaven jaw. 'She said something about there being a ceremony for the Christmas lights being turned on in the village next Friday. She was going on about it and I just wanted to get on with my dinner. I couldn't get her to leave so I said something inane about maybe seeing her there, hoping she would get the hint and go. I guess she's got the wrong idea.'

'No, she's just trying to make sure other people get the wrong idea, I think, love,' Eloise said, glancing at me.

'Do I need to say something?' he asked, frown lines creasing his already serious face.

'Not at all. You're grand. And I'm Eloise by the way.' She held out her hand and Nate shook it.

'Nate McKinley.'

'The lovely Gabe's brother.'

'Yes. He seems pretty popular in these parts.'

'You're pretty popular yourself, by the looks of it,' Bob chuckled. Nate didn't answer, instead busying himself pulling up his collar.

'Go on then, take this girl home. That's the least you can do after she's been run ragged covering tables while Corinne was busy lusting over you.' Eloise winked to soften the tease.

Nate shook Bob's hand and I gave them both a hug before we parted ways and headed home.

'I'm sorry if I caused a problem,' he said as soon as they were out of hearing.

'Oh, don't be daft,' I said, 'Eloise is just teasing you. And you can't help looking like you do.'

He glanced away towards the sea.

'You really don't like compliments, do you?'

He gave me a quick glance. 'It's not that.'

'What is it, then?'

He shrugged. 'I don't know. Just feels odd.'

'Why?'

'Was she really trying to chat me up?'

I grinned. 'Uh-huh.'

'I'm about twenty odd years her senior.'

'True, but you're kind of nice looking.'

He slid me a glance.

'You know. If you like the obvious drop-dead gorgeous, body of a god thing.'

And then he laughed. Really laughed, and I watched the stress fall away from his face.

I smiled, happy to see this change. 'Laugh all you want, but you can't argue with facts.'

He gave me a look. 'The fact that my wife ran off with her tennis coach would suggest otherwise.'

'No,' I said truthfully, hating the flash of pain in his eyes, however much he tried to cover it. 'Some people don't realise what they've got. But that's their loss.'

'I don't think she sees it as a loss.'

'I would.'

Whoops!

The blue gaze locked onto mine. 'I mean, anyone with any sense would. You've got a mirror. And you're decent, solvent and when you let yourself, have a good sense of humour. Who wouldn't see that as a loss?' I added, aiming desperately for casual.

The flicker of a smile crossed that very tempting mouth before he looked back the way we were going.

'Thanks.'

'No problem.'

'Have you eaten?'

'No, I didn't get a chance. I don't always feel like it when I'm busy anyway.'

'You need to eat,' Nate said before stopping suddenly.

'What's up?'

'Come to mine. I've got more food in there than I need and it would make me feel better for you missing out on eating because you were covering that other waitress's tables.'

I laughed. 'Ooh, don't let her hear that you've forgotten her name. She always aims to be unforgettable when it comes to men like you.'

'Men like me?'

I waved a hand up and down briefly. Nate shook his head.

'Well, then I've failed in her eyes already so I guess those are the breaks. Will you come? Bryan would love to see you.'

I laughed. 'Ha! No using cute dogs as bribery.'

'Well, the whole body of a god thing is apparently lost on you so I've had to pull out bigger guns.'

I looked up, laughing, and felt my heart lighten as I saw Nate's eyes sparkle with the joke, and the sound of his laugh carry on the crisp air. It was a wonderful sound and I only hoped I would hear it more.

'You know my weakness.'

His smile widened and we put out heads down as a sharp wind blew in off the sea, stinging our faces and making our lips taste salty as we headed for the beach house.

15

The following morning, I'd just locked my front door and turned to the street as the postie strolled by with his letter trolley, handing me one with a smile as he passed.

'Thanks, Paddy.' I took the envelope and stuffed it in my basket to look at later. From the heft of it and the expensive feel to the paper, I assumed it was from my ex's solicitors. Who were also very expensive. I'd taken a chunk of money when I left. Half of everything was mine, after all, but I knew now I should have taken more. I'd been rather naïve about how long this amount would last me and also in thinking that my ex would play fair. He'd quickly disavowed me of that belief. Hence the need for the job at Ned's and being grateful for Holly's offer of the cleaning job. I wasn't sure what would happen once Nate went back to Australia, whether Holly would still want me to keep up the cleaning, but I would cross that bridge when I came to it. It might also depend on what was in that envelope. In theory, if I could get access to it, I had enough money not to work if I didn't want to. Or to take the time to find something I actually wanted to do. The investments my father had made for me before he died had been wise ones. Unfortunately, I hadn't been so wise in agreeing to put everything of mine into joint names. Looking back on it now, I could see how stupid that was. Unfortunately, my father had passed away several years earlier. Had he not, I knew things would have been a lot different. But I'd been a dutiful daughter to my mother and followed her advice in regards to both money and marriage. A huge error in hindsight. But then marriage as a whole had been a revelation for me, and not in a good way.

Still, what was done was done. I just had to move forward now. Leaving had filled me with a mixture of terror and a sense of release. I knew I'd been lucky to end up here in Wishington Bay, and to have met the people I had. Initially I'd thought a faceless city where no one really knew anyone would be better for me to blend away into, but fate had other ideas. As I'd said to Nate, I really had run out of petrol here. It was late and I'd been exhausted so it had seemed as good a time as any to take a break. Waking up in the bed and breakfast the next day, I'd had every intention of moving on and finding that city, but it had been such a lovely day, and the view from the window had been so enticing, I'd decided that a walk round the village might do me good after the hours of driving the previous day. It hadn't taken long to fall in love with the place. By lunchtime I was already looking for property. My husband hadn't realised I'd left for good by then and so the account was still accessible. I viewed the empty flat above Flora's shop, which had just come on the market that day, and took it immediately, paying the asking price in full so as not to get outbid, advising I wanted to move in as soon as possible. With no chain, and me able to use my name to ensure I could withdraw enough cash almost immediately to seal the deal, I was at least reassured I'd have a roof over my head. After that, I'd gone for lunch at Ned's where I overheard him mentioning to Eloise that he needed to advertise for another waitress. Everything had fallen into place almost as though it was meant to be. Ned had been great about the fact I had no experience and Eloise was so kind in showing me the ropes. Corinne had been aloof and full of herself even then but I'd just got on with my job and taken her in my stride as much as I could. Admittedly, her behaviour the other day was a step up but then it wasn't every day we had someone who looked as good as Nate decorating the window seat.

I headed down the slope that led to the house and felt the paperwork burning a hole in my bag. Reaching in, I retrieved the envelope and began opening it as I walked along.

Dear Mrs Huntingdon-Jones,

We are in receipt of your latest correspondence and have consulted with our client as to how he might wish to proceed.

In order to try to bring this matter to a swift and final conclusion, our client has decided to agree to the terms detailed in the previous correspondence, although he wishes it be known that this is only because he is 'rather tired of the situation' and would prefer it now closed as soon as possible.

I took a few deep breaths, the cool sharp air of the winter morning filling my lungs as I did my best to remain calm. I'd only ever asked for what was mine out of that marriage but my ex had made things as difficult as he could from the beginning, from emptying the joint bank account once he realised I wasn't coming back – an idea I wish I'd thought of first – to questioning every single point with regards to the divorce, probably knowing that each query would cost me in both money and time. Anything he could do to make life difficult, he'd done. And now suddenly he was ready to settle, and as soon as possible. Whatever the reason for this sudden about-face was nothing to do with him being fed up of dragging things on. I'd watched him do this in business and in his personal life for years. If Jeremy could drag something out and make things uncomfortable for someone, he would. No, whatever this was, it was in order to make things easier for him and him alone. Which probably meant he'd met someone. Well, good luck to her. She was going to need it.

I felt a weight lift off me as I stuffed the paperwork back into my bag. I'd been getting by with the waitressing and cleaning jobs, but I knew I hadn't realised how privileged I'd been, never having to even think about, let alone worry, about money before. I understood that now and, although it seemed like I was going to be in a far more comfortable position again now that Jeremy had deigned to agree to what were already pretty damn reasonable terms, I knew I'd never again take my situation for granted. I decided not to make any rash decisions about whether to give up the waitressing or not yet – I actually enjoyed meeting the customers and working with Ned, Carrie and Eloise. Corinne and her attitude, however, were a different matter and something I definitely wouldn't miss if I left. Anyway, until the ink was dry on those documents, I still didn't trust my ex-husband not to renege, so I wouldn't count any chickens just yet.

'You look like you've got a lot on your mind.' The quiet, deep voice drifted into my thoughts and I snapped my head up. My mind busy, I'd arrived at the house quicker than I expected, and seeing Nate leaning against an open doorjamb, Bryan resting against his chest, brought a smile.

'Nothing important,' I replied, tickling Bryan under the chin as he basked in all the attention.

'Come in. I've just unwrapped what looks like a very delicious apple cake and it'd be a shame to eat it alone.'

I stepped into the warmth of the house and pulled off my boot which Bryan, now back on the floor had a good old sniff round as I yanked the other one off, over balancing slightly and reaching out blindly for whatever was closest to steady myself. That something turned out to be Nate and the chest I landed against felt as solid as the wall I was aiming for.

'Woah, you all right?' His hands rested gently at my waist as I looked up.

'Umm... yes.' I dropped my hands from his chest so that I, temporarily, stood as straight as a toy soldier. 'Sorry.'

'No worries,' he said as he stepped back, my body suddenly cool from the loss of contact. 'Tea or coffee?'

'I'm supposed to be working,' I grinned, following him and the dog into the kitchen.

He looked round at me. 'Sorry. I'm sure you have plans after this. I wasn't thinking.'

'No,' I reached out and laid a hand on his arm. 'Actually, I don't. I... I guess I just feel a bit cheeky sitting here drinking tea and eating cake with you when I'm supposed to be working.'

'You're hardly a slacker, Sophia. This place always looks sparkling after you've been. It makes me feel bad to use anything after and mess it up.'

I laughed. 'Please, mess it up all you like. A home is supposed to be lived in, not look like a museum piece or a show home. It can always be tidied up again.' I had too much experience of being afraid to sit there or touch that which is why I'd been so thrilled at Nate's compliment the other day about my flat looking homely. 'Thanks,' I said, as Nate put a steaming mug of tea, the perfect colour, down on the breakfast bar in front of me along with a very generous slice of cake.

'It's a good job I'm doing the housework after this,' I said, peering at it. 'I'll need to burn some of those calories off.'

He gave me a look. 'There's nothing of you.'

Not entirely true, but kind. I'd always kept in shape and never really eaten what I wanted at home, mainly because that's what everyone else did. But the stress of an unhappy marriage and the act of finally walking away from it and, as it turned out, the rest of my life, had resulted in me losing more weight than I'd planned. I'd gradually put some of it back on, but it had been slow going. But that, like everything else, would settle in time. That was the motto I'd created for myself, and one I did my best to live by. I took a forkful of the cake as Nate picked his up with his fingers, nodding at me.

'I figured with that accent you'd want a fork.' The tease flashed in his eyes and played at the corners of his mouth and I tried not to think that, right now, he looked about as delicious as the cake in front of me.

We sat in companionable silence for a few minutes, eating our cake and watching the sea through the glass.

'Do you mind if I walk back up to the village with you when you're done? I need to drop something at the post office.'

I thought of the paperwork in my bag. 'Not at all,' I pulled my bag towards me. 'I've got something I could do with sending too, actually.' Reaching in, I withdrew the large envelope and rummaged through for a return envelope. Nothing.

'Bloody cheapskates,' I muttered.

'Everything all right?'

'I don't suppose you've got a spare envelope, have you? I need to return something and they haven't included one.'

'Sure.' He got up and went across to a bureau Holly had reno-vated in the palest shade of soft green and opened one of the drawers. 'This OK?' He called, holding up a white A4 envelope.

'Perfect.'

Nate crossed back to the kitchen stool and laid the envelope in front of me.

'Thanks.'

'Looks important.' He nodded at the paperwork. 'Sorry, I

didn't mean to seem nosy. I just... you look more serious than I've become used to seeing you now we've got over our bumpy beginning.'

'Oh, don't remind me!' I laughed, happy for the distraction.

'I'm really glad we worked it out.'

I looked up at him, smiling, pleased to see his own shy smile appear. 'Me too.' I glanced back at the paperwork. 'And I'm fine. Hopefully I'm getting to the end of all this malarkey now. It will be good to be able to move on properly.'

Nate frowned. 'What is it?'

I pulled a face. 'Divorce papers. My ex-husband hasn't exactly been the most helpful so it's rather dragged on. Of course, now he's suddenly agreed to things and seems to want it all tied up as soon as possible so I'm guessing something's changed in his life that he needs to be free of me for.'

'Funny how that happens.'

'Isn't it? Anyway, I'm just happy the end seems to be in sight now.'

'I'm hoping mine will be a bit less stressful than yours sounds to have been.'

'Oh God, Nate. I'm so sorry. That was thoughtless. I didn't mean to—'

He laid one large, lightly tanned hand over mine. 'It's all good. Really.'

I didn't feel convinced and he gave a gentle squeeze of my hand. 'Really. You don't need to walk on eggshells with me. In fact, it'd be a relief if you didn't. I feel like that's how people have been forced to be around me for way too long because of my relationship with Serena. I didn't see it before but it's amazing how things become more clear when you put some space between you and a particular situation. I know it hasn't been easy for my family and I feel bad about that.'

'You shouldn't. It's only putting extra pressure on yourself and they wouldn't want that, I'm sure. All they want, and all they'll ever have wanted, is for you to be happy.'

'Sounds so easy, doesn't it? Two little words. Be happy.'

'It does. And those who are make it look so simple. I know you haven't met Holly in person but you said you Skype Gabe?'

'Yep. Holly's been there sometimes and I know what you mean. Everything looks easy and relaxed with them. I'm not sure I ever truly had that with Serena. I was so busy being completely head over heels and wanting to do everything that she wanted, just to make her happy, I kind of missed that things were perhaps a little more one sided than they should have been.'

'I'm sure she loved you. She married you, after all,' I smiled. I wasn't entirely convinced that always went hand in hand, speaking from my own experience but then Nate thankfully hadn't had generations of ancestors and long standing traditions to try to appease with his wedding.

'Yep,' he nodded, his mind clearly somewhere else. 'I think she did. In her own way. At least for a while.' He gave a little headshake. 'You don't need to hear all this.'

'But I'd like to. If you want to tell me.'

He splayed out his hands on the cool granite worksurface. 'There's not much to tell really. Beautiful girl, completely smitten bloke. It all seemed fine to start with. I loved doing things for her, and got a kick out of it, making her happy. But then work sometimes meant I couldn't make a particular party or I'd want to visit my parents instead of some friends of hers that I barely knew and really had nothing in common with. I'd always been close with my parents. Gabe and I both were, or are. Even living over here he seemed to do a better job of keeping that bond than I did living just down the road.'

'Didn't your wife get on with your family?'

'I think they saw through things a hell of a lot quicker than I did, and that kind of got Serena's back up.'

'That she couldn't get away with the same stuff as she did with you?'

'Pretty much. Funnily enough they weren't influenced by the beautiful face and hot body.' He gave a small smile and I sucked in my stomach a little.

'Mum and Dad are pretty easy-going and so's Gabe, so I was surprised that things seemed strained when we all got together. Of course, I couldn't see what they saw and just ended up resenting that they couldn't accept my choice of partner.'

'Not always that simple, is it?'

'No,' he said. 'Gabe and I had a proper falling out one time he came home which of course, upset Mum and Dad.'

'Oh dear.'

Nate ran a hand across his chin, a day's dark growth shadowing the hard planes of his face. 'Yeah. They rubbed each other up the wrong way from the start, him and Serena.'

'Gabe's so easy-going, usually.'

'He is. I guess he's also got pretty good at reading people. Assessing them. I'm sure it helps in his job. And Serena apparently made a pass at him quite early into our relationship.'

My eyes widened. 'No!'

'Not that he told me. I only found that out more recently. And now I know he certainly wasn't the only one.'

'Nate, I'm so sorry. You're a lovely man. You deserve better than that.'

He turned, his blue eyes holding my gaze. 'I'm sure if I'd told you that the first time we met, you'd have said I deserved everything I got.'

'No, I wouldn't have. No one deserves to have their heart

broken. Even if they do come across as rather grumpy and appear to question my brilliant cleaning skills.'

He closed his eyes but a smile played at the corners of his mouth. Opening them again, he looked back at me. 'Was I that bad?'

'Yes. But luckily I've forgiven you.'

'Lucky.'

'Yes, you've grown on me.' I pushed the breakfast stool back and slid down. 'Like a fungus.'

He laughed, the sound filling the room with joy.

'I'm not sure whether to say thanks to that or not. I think I'm pleased about the first bit, but I might have to come back to you on the fungus part.'

I swiped the plate from in front of him and made a move towards the mug.

'I can do that.'

'I'm here to clean.'

'I can put stuff in the dishwasher.'

'You're supposed to be writing.'

'I will be, shortly.'

'Good. Right,' I said, grabbing the cleaning caddy. 'I'm going to start upstairs so you can get stuck in.'

Nate smiled, raised a hand and turned back to where his laptop sat on the table.

* * *

I fluffed the cushions one more time, stepped back to the door and snapped a picture on my phone.

'Why do you photograph things when you've cleaned?' The deep voice broke into my cleaning fairy reverie and I jumped.

'Jeez, where did you come from?'

'Downstairs,' he answered honestly.

'How can someone so big be so quiet?'

He shrugged broad shoulders. 'Serena's a really light sleeper. I guess I got used to creeping around when I had an early start.'

'Well, try to make some noise now, if you can. You're going to give me a heart attack popping up behind me like that.'

'I'll work on it.'

'Thanks.'

'So,' he nodded his head at my phone. 'What's with the photographs?'

I gave a shrug. 'I'm sure you'll think it's daft.'

'I doubt it.' His face and words were sincere.

I leant against the wall. 'When I moved here, I deleted all my social media accounts and stuff. I wanted a clean break away from my old life. But I missed following some of the old accounts I'd liked, and I had always enjoyed the record keeping aspect of it. So, I started up a new Instagram and just followed a few people. When I started the cleaning, I was kind of surprised how much I enjoyed the rhythm of it all, and the results.'

Nate frowned at me. 'You'd never cleaned before?'

'I can see you trying not to wrinkle your nose,' I grinned. 'I didn't live in a hovel. I just... was lucky enough to have a cleaner.'

'Your whole life?'

OK. I wasn't exactly prepared for these questions right now. But neither was I ready to let everything out just yet either. I knew I'd have to, one day. Just not now. Instead I gave a shrug and carried on.

'Anyway, I enjoyed trying out new tips and when I found a good one, I shared it in my stories, and it's picked up a bit of traction. The photos of a gorgeous room looking perfect make me happy and seem to be quite popular.' I suddenly looked up at

Nate. 'I did check with Holly and I never share the location. I don't even mention the county.'

'I didn't doubt any of that. Can I see it?' He pulled his phone out of his back pocket.

'What?'

'Your feed.'

I blushed. 'Oh, you don't want to see that. It's just a bit of fun.'

'Contrary to popular opinion, I'm not averse to fun.'

'I didn't mean it like that, and you know it.'

He gave me that smile again and I forgot everything for a moment. 'I know,' he said. 'So, come on, what's it called?'

'You have Instagram?'

'I had strict instructions to like all of Serena's posts so I kind of had to get it. But actually I've found a couple of accounts I enjoy so it's not been a total loss.'

I told him the account name and he found it under a search. 'These are cool. I like the mix you have.'

'Thanks. I know these brand people say everything should look similar and have a similar theme but I'm not doing it as a business. I like the eclectic look. I think it's more interesting. At least I find it interesting. Basically, if I see something I like, I take a picture, hence it being rather a hotch-potch of beaches and sunsets, flowers, yummy food – all sorts really – as well as the house type stuff.'

'Was this on your wreath making course the other day?' He was looking at the picture of the girls and me with Billy.

'Yes, that's it.'

'I ran into Ned as he was putting the little one in the car to come and get you all. Looks like you had a good time.'

'Yes, it was fun to do something different and spend time outside work with Carrie and Eloise.'

'No Corinne?'

'She turned her nose up at the invitation, although when she saw that picture, she seemed a bit put out.'

'Because of him?' Nate pointed at Billy.

'How did you guess?'

He remained silent for a moment, looking at the pictures.

'Mind if I follow you?'

'Keeping an eye on your brother's place?'

'No. That's not the reason.'

I looked up at him, wondering what the reason was. Suddenly, Bryan dancing about near the door caught my eye. 'I think someone needs a visit outside.'

'Oh, Christ. Sorry mate!' Nate scooted down the stairs, Bryan doing his best to trip him up in his own haste and shortly after I heard the door to the beachside open and close. Turning back to the room, I snapped another shot as a sunbeam lit the interior softly through the gauzy curtains, then tucked the phone back into my pocket and headed downstairs to clean there.

I dusted and cleaned to the gentle accompaniment of Nate's keyboard tapping rhythmically, and surprisingly speedily.

'Do you mind if I vacuum now?' I asked, reluctant to disturb his concentration.

'Not at all,' he said through a yawn as he stretched, leaning back and reaching his arms to the ceiling.

'Sounds like it's going well,' I said, glancing back as I checked the charge in the cordless appliance.

Nate grinned at me. 'Like I said, you seem to be my lucky charm. Do you think you could come here every day?'

'I don't think you make enough mess for me to come and clean every day.'

'I could try. But it wouldn't have to be for that.'

I looked up at him and he suddenly looked awkward. 'I think that might have come out wrong.'

Grinning, I tilted the handle back on the vacuum. 'You might want to be careful going around making offers like that. Corinne would certainly be interpreting them differently.'

Nate swallowed and gave an eyebrow raise. 'Are things OK between you two? I didn't mean to cause any problems or make things difficult for you at work.'

I gave a dismissive wave. 'It's fine. She's never taken to me anyway so it's no great loss. She's a bit more frosty than usual but the wonderful thing about youth is its confidence. In her eyes, there is no way you could possibly be more interested in anyone than her, so she's certainly not considering me any sort of threat.'

'Am I supposed to do something tomorrow night? I mean, what she said about going to see the lights together.'

I shrugged and tried to ignore the uncomfortable twist my stomach gave at the thought of Corinne draping herself all over Nate. 'That's up to you, I guess.'

'Sophia, I never asked her out.' His tone was earnest. 'At least, I don't think I did.'

I looked up. 'You don't need to explain yourself to me, Nate. What you do, and who you do it with, is entirely up to you. I'm just here to make sure the house is comfortable for you, not report back on your activities.'

'That's not what I meant. Gabe would probably be quite happy for me to see someone else.'

'Then what are you worried about?'

He gave me a patient look. 'What do you think?'

My eyes widened a little in surprise. 'Me? Why?'

He gave his shadowed chin a quick scratch. 'Because I... value your opinion.'

'Oh.' Disappointment sagged inside me like a deflating balloon. The more I'd got to know Nate, the more I liked him. It was ridiculous, I knew. I lived here. He lived on the other side of the world and both of us were mired in the process of getting divorced. But I couldn't help it. I liked him. And frankly, it had been such a long time since I'd felt that way, it was novel and exciting. And utterly pointless. Nate might not be interested in Corinne, not that she had any plans to give up on that particular conquest yet, but he clearly wasn't interested in me either.

I stole a glance as he took his seat back in front of the laptop. As if sensing me watching, his gaze flicked up, catching me in the act. If I looked away now, I may as well have just hung a sign round my neck that said, 'Why yes, I was staring at you.' Instead I smiled in what I hoped was a casual manner, before stepping on the vacuum switch, filling the room – and hopefully my mind – with a distracting roar.

By the time I'd finished downstairs, I had got my thoughts, and libido, back in check. Nate was gorgeous, yes, but keeping it just friends was perfect. That way we got to enjoy each other's company without all the hassle that taking it further could bring. By keeping it just friends we could chat and have a meal together without me worrying whether I'd shaved my legs that morning, or deal with the bother of Nate's large, strong hands exploring my body as that sensuous mouth pressed down on mine, his body close to me as he – oh, bugger. I definitely needed to work on this.

'You done?' he asked, closing the lid of his laptop.

'Uh-huh,' I said, yanking my runaway imagination back into line and giving it a good talking to as I busied myself tidying away the cleaning gear.

'Still up for that walk to the post office?'

'Yes.' I cleared my throat and took a couple of deep breaths before turning to face him. 'Absolutely. I just need to sign the papers and write that envelope.'

'I'll get you a pen.'

I sat back down at the breakfast bar and spread the papers out

in front of me, reading through again and checking what I
needed to do. Half of me was curious to know what Jeremy's
sudden rush was but the other half was more in the 'good
riddance, moving on' camp. That seemed the healthiest mindset,
and I took another mental step towards it as I signed the paperwork in a manner my mother had always told me had 'rather too
much flourish'.

'All done?' Nate asked as I pulled the sealing tape from the
envelope and ran my finger over the flap, ensuring it was all
secure.

'I think so.'

'How do you feel?' His expression was serious.

I thought about it for a moment. How did I feel? The divorce
had dragged on far longer than I had expected. Although I
knew Jeremy could be awkward when he wanted to be, the
levels he had sunk to had surprised and disappointed me. It
made me wonder whether he had ever felt anything for me at
all. If he had, would he have been quite so vicious in his
handling of the divorce, determined to make everything as difficult and expensive as possible for me, knowing he'd already
taken the bulk of our money? Could you really do that to
someone you'd loved, even if it had only been for a short time?
Although I suppose the news and magazines are full of people
who had once stood in front of their family and friends and
professed everlasting love only to subsequently do vile things to
each other, so perhaps I had got off lighter than some and
should be grateful.

'Sorry. I shouldn't have asked that. I guess there's a whole slew
of emotions.'

'No, it's fine. But you're right. When I sit back and think about
it all, a whole host of emotions tumble about – sadness, disappointment, surprise – but right now, looking at this envelope and

knowing that I'm so close to being able to finally close that chapter, the main feeling is relief.'

Nate nodded.

'Have you...' I wasn't entirely sure how to phrase the question.

He finished it for me. 'Started divorce proceedings?'

It was my turn to nod, as I dropped the envelope in my bag.

'Kind of. Although things don't seem to be progressing that quickly, but I guess she's busy with her new life.'

'How do you feel about that?' The words popped out before I could censor them. 'I mean, only if you want to talk about it.'

'No,' he stayed me momentarily with a hand on my arm. 'Actually, it feels a bit of a relief to discuss it with someone who understands.'

I gave him a smile. 'I'm always happy to listen, Nate. Any time.'

'Thanks, Sophia. I know I'm lucky to have Gabe and Mum and Dad, but I don't want to burden them with all this.'

'I'm pretty sure they wouldn't see it as a burden. From what I know of your parents, and certainly Gabe, whatever they could do to help, they would.' I felt a sad twist of envy as I voiced this.

'But sometimes it's easier to talk to someone who isn't involved... if that makes sense? A step removed from the family.'

'It does.'

'So,' he held out my coat for me and I slipped my arms into it. 'Thanks.'

'Basically, I'm waiting on her to agree to what I've proposed. When she gets round to it. I think she will. My lawyer wasn't that happy about things and says she's got a pretty good deal so hopefully she will see it that way too.'

'Sounds like you've made it very simple for her,' I said.

'Yep. I guess I was pretty easy to play. Pretty much whatever she wanted, I gave her. It made it easy.'

'Goodness, I wish I'd divorced you instead,' I said, then frowned. 'Sorry. You know what I mean.'

A resolved expression tinged with sadness hovered over his features. 'I do. I guess that all makes me sound a bit sappy.'

'Not at all,' I said, pulling my woolly hat on and checking my reflection in the hall mirror, before straightening the hat a little. 'So long as it doesn't leave you on the streets, and what she asked for isn't something that means a lot to you, then perhaps it was the best way forward for you.'

'Yeah, that's kind of what I thought, too.'

'Do you have your parcel for the post office?'

'Oh...' he dashed back, grabbing a small square box off the table. 'I do now. Thanks.' He moved the box from one hand to the other. 'It's just a little thing for one of our cousins. She used to be a ballerina. Well, I guess she still is, but she teaches at a school in Sydney now. I saw it in Flora's shop the other day and thought she'd like it.'

'The little china ballerinas?'

'Yes. Do you think she'll like it?'

'Well, obviously I've never met her, but I do think they're beautiful and I know Flora's had trouble keeping them in stock, they're so popular. I'm sure your cousin is going to love it.'

'Thanks. We're a similar age and always got on well.'

'It's lovely you're still close.'

'Yeah, she and her husband have been pretty supportive,' he said, busily employed in doing up Bryan's coat.

'When you let them?'

Nate gave a shrug as he reached around me and opened the front door, Bryan's lead looped over his wrist and the little dog dancing about by my feet in excitement at the prospect of a walk.

I smiled. 'That's what I thought.'

'So, did you have someone you could talk to about it all? I mean, it sounds like you've had a tougher time of it than me.'

I fidgeted with my hat and hoiked my bag up on to my shoulder. 'Not especially, no.'

Nate gave me a look. 'And there you are telling me off for not opening up.' I looked up and saw the gentle teasing in his eyes.

'Flora knows I'm getting a divorce. I mean, everyone at the restaurant does, too. But you're right, I haven't really taken much of my own advice about opening up when it comes to that. It wasn't something I was used to doing and I guess most of the time I've wanted to keep it separate from my new life here, as much as that's possible. I'm happy here and I wasn't happy before.'

'You didn't want to risk tainting this happiness.'

'Exactly.'

'I get that.'

We walked on in silence for a moment, Bryan's toenails tapping out a happy rhythm as we walked.

'But if you ever want to talk, I'd listen. I promise not to taint anything.'

I looked up at Nate as I walked, seeing the smile in his eyes, the sincerity in his voice. 'I'll remember that. Thank you,' I said, softly.

And then I fell on my face.

16

'Oh my God! Are you all right?' Nate's concerned voice reached me through a fog of mortification that I now felt from my toes to the tips of my ears.

'Absolutely fine,' I said, being terribly British about it all and pushing myself up from the floor. I'd been in such a hurry to meet the pavement, I'd failed to find the time to put my hands out and had instead opted to break my fall with my chin with back up from my nose.

'Here, let me help.' Nate's arms were round me before I could answer as he helped me stand, guiding me away from the patch of pavement the weak rays of winter sun had failed to reach, leaving last night's ice remaining in place. 'Oh crikey, Soph.'

I finally met his eyes. His brow was covered by his beanie but I guessed he was frowning as his entire gaze focused upon me. In any other circumstance, I might well have relished this attention but right now, embarrassed and sore, I could think of a hundred places I'd rather be now than under Nate McKinley's scrutiny.

'I'm fine,' I said, reaching up to brush the grit off my face. Ouch.

'We need to get you cleaned up.'

'Really, Nate, it's noth—' I glanced at my cream mitten which was now artfully decorated with a bright red streak. I stared at it for a moment longer then looked up at Nate.

'Oh. Oh dear.' And then it all went black.

* * *

'I think she's coming round.' Muffled voices swam in my head and I tentatively opened one eye. Above me Nate and Flora were both hovering, concern written across both faces. I closed my eye then opened both together.

'Hey.' Nate's voice was soft, and a gentle smile broke through the worry and despite knowing at some point I was going to have to deal with a flood of embarrassment worthy of Niagara Falls in full flow, I smiled back.

'Hello.'

'How are you feeling?'

'OK.' I made to push myself up and Nate was there immediately, helping me to a sitting position, stuffing another pillow behind me as I sat on my sofa, my legs out, covered by the soft blanket that normally lay across the back of it.

'Shall I get you a drink, love?' Flora asked.

I nodded. 'Thank you, Flora. I'm fine. I'll do it myself in a minute. Just need to gather my thoughts a sec. Who's minding the shop?'

'George. I rang him the moment Nate rushed into the shop with you in his arms.' Behind Nate, she gave me a wide-eyed look and wiggled her eyebrows a couple of times. 'I'll go and make us all a nice cuppa.' With that, she disappeared through to my tiny kitchen and I heard her getting mugs out of the cupboard and the kettle beginning to boil.

'I fainted, didn't I?'

Nate smiled. 'Quite spectacularly.'

'Oh, God.' I dropped my head into my hands. 'I'm so sorry. As soon as I saw the blood I knew it was going to happen. I'm so embarrassed.'

Nate's hands closed softly round my wrists and tugged gently. Reluctantly I looked up. Letting out a sigh, I met his gaze. 'Why couldn't I have done it without an audience?'

Nate's brow creased. 'I'm very glad you didn't or you would have hit the pavement pretty hard. Again.'

'I'm rather covering myself in glory today, aren't I?'

Nate smiled and gave my hands a squeeze before standing and relieving Flora of the drinks she'd just bustled in from the kitchen with.

'Actually, I'm going to take mine down to the shop and just check on George, if that's all right? I think Nate's got everything in hand here.' She gave me another cheeky wink. 'I'll pop the mug back later. Take it easy, sweetheart.' Flora bent and gave me a quick kiss on the top of my head, squeezed Nate's forearm and headed back downstairs.

Nate passed me my drink and took a seat on the coffee table opposite me.

'Is my face a mess?'

'Nope,' he said taking a sip of tea. 'Flora found me your first aid supplies and helped me clean you up while you were out. Bit of gravel rash and a small cut on your chin which was what leaked all over your glove.' He nodded towards the kitchen. 'She's got them soaking in a bowl of something or other in the kitchen to get the blood out.' At the mention of the word, I felt the room swim a little.

'Sorry. I won't say it again.'

'It's fine. Really.'

'You look kind of green.'

'It'll go off. And thanks for cleaning me up. And for catching me and bringing me home.' I raised my eyes to the ceiling and gave a small head shake.

'What's up?'

I let out a sigh. 'It's just embarrassing. Smacking my face on the pavement was bad enough and then I had to give a finale performance of fainting like some eighteenth-century heroine.'

'If it helps, it wasn't like that at all. More like someone dropping a sack of spuds.'

I wasn't sure if that helped or not but it brought a smile to my throbbing face so there was that.

'That's better.' Nate returned the smile.

'So not a fan of the B word then?' he asked, taking my mug from me as I reached forward, to place it beside his own on the side table. I glanced round. There were even coasters underneath them. Whatever his ex thought, I knew a lot of women would definitely file Nate under the 'keeper' category. There was a good chance I might even be one of those women but my head was too sore to think about anything like that right now so I focused back on what he was saying instead. Which was definitely harder than it looked.

'No, it's something that's happened ever since I was a child. Absolutely mortifying, really.'

'Nah, you're all right.'

'How would you like it if it happened to you?'

He moved his head from one side to the other and shrugged. 'Probably not so much. I'm pretty sure you wouldn't have been able to catch me and I know you wouldn't have been able to carry me so I'd probably still be splayed on the pavement like that proverbial sack of spuds.'

'You're hilarious.'

He grinned and I immediately forgave him. Damn.

I drew my knees up towards me. 'Here. Sit on here. It's more comfy.' Nate obeyed, moving from the oak coffee table to the softness of the sofa, settling back, and turning to look at me.

'So, any particular reason?'

'Huh?'

'This reaction.'

'Polo.'

His brows raised momentarily. 'Not the answer I was expecting but with that voice, I guess I shouldn't be surprised.'

I poked his thigh with my toes and he grinned. I felt a bolt of warmth fizz and pop in my stomach before shooting out in a variety of directions, none of them helpful.

'I was watching, not playing.'

'Because that makes all the difference.' His laugh was soft and welcome.

I stuck my tongue out and he laughed again.

'Sorry. So, tell me what happened.'

I gave a shrug. 'Some friends of my parents were playing a match and we'd gone to watch. In the second chukka, one of the players became unseated.'

'Is that a posh way of saying he fell off?'

'Yes. I suppose so.'

'And?'

'He landed rather badly. Right in front of us and there was this awful noise. Next thing I know, I'm looking on horrified as he's lying on the ground in agony and his shin bone is sticking clean through his jodhpurs about a foot in front of me.'

'Oh. Wow. Ouch.'

'Quite. I stared in horror for a couple of seconds and then passed out apparently, much to my mother's disgust.'

'Really?'

'I was showing emotion. That's always been rather a no-no in her book. Thankfully my father was still alive then and he was always far more understanding. He scooped me up and took me back to the car. But I'm afraid I've had rather a drastic reaction to blood since that day.'

'Understandably.'

I gave a shrug. 'I probably ought to see someone about it.'

'Who?'

I pulled a face. 'I don't know. Maybe a hypnotherapist or something. They help people stop smoking and conquer a fear of flying. Maybe they could help with this sort of thing too.'

'Might be worth a try.'

'I need to wait until everything is settled with the divorce first. Just so I know for sure where I stand financially.'

'Oh, about that. I'm afraid your letter didn't go in the post. I was more concerned about getting you home and cleaned up.'

I glanced at the clock. The post office would be shut by now. 'It's OK. He can wait an extra day. God knows he's dragged it out as much as he can when it suited him.' I thought for a moment. 'Did you go and get your present posted though?'

'No,' he looked at me. 'I was worried. I didn't want to leave you.'

I swallowed, suddenly full of emotions I wasn't quite ready for. It had felt a very long time since anyone – especially a man – had said anything as caring to me. The fact that it had come from Nate made it all the more special. Not to mention complicated.

He's only here temporarily, Sophia. Don't get attached.

My head knew this was the case. Unfortunately, my heart seemed too busy skipping ahead to listen to anything I tried to tell it. I gave myself a mental shake and sat up a little more.

'Why don't you leave your parcel here, and I can take it to the post office first thing tomorrow before my shift at Ned's?'

'You don't have to do that.'

'You scraped me up off the pavement, brought me home, and patched me up. I think it's the least I can do in return.'

'You don't need to do anything in return. Anyone would have done the same.'

I pondered whether my ex-husband would have done the same and came to the conclusion he just would have blustered a bit, got angry and probably stepped right over me on the way to his next meeting. Or next affair.

'No,' I said simply. 'They wouldn't. So thank you. And I've got to go to the post office anyway so it's not like I'm going out of my way.'

Nate read my determination to do something to repay him and held up his hands. 'OK. If you're sure you don't mind. I'll leave you some cash,' he said, making to stand and, I assumed, retrieve his wallet from his coat. I stretched my legs out and did a very poor job of pinning him to the sofa. He looked down at my feet, then at me, then back at my feet.

'It's symbolic.'

He grinned. 'Good, because the fact I could sling you over my shoulder earlier means I'm pretty sure I can move a pair of dainty feet.'

I pulled my feet up towards me. 'You slung me over your shoulder?' I cried, my voice pitching in what probably wasn't the most attractive way, but I had other things on my mind. Like the fact my backside had been on show to the entire village as Nate had strolled back to my flat with me tossed over his shoulder like a caveman.

Nate shrugged. 'What's wrong with that?'

I threw the blanket back and stood up, felt the blood rush to my head and sat down again.

'You might want to take it easy for a bit.' I looked up and met his concerned gaze. Even that face wasn't quite enough to still the churning in my stomach. I'd been brought up not to make a scene, to blend in, once my mother had informed me that neither my looks nor figure, the only things that mattered in her opinion, were good enough to enable me to stand out. Although stepping out into the world on my own and moving here had helped me build some of the confidence I'd been lacking, making a scene and drawing attention to myself was still anathema to me. It was bad enough to have fainted in front of Nate – in front of anyone. But the thought that I'd been brought home caveman-style somehow was even more embarrassing than I had already pictured things to be.

'What are you worried about?' His voice was calm and reasonable which only made it worse.

'You slung me over your shoulder and then paraded me through the village, bottom first. That's what I'm worried about.' I stood up again.

Nate began to smile.

'I'm glad you find it funny!' I snapped.

'Come here,' Nate reached up and gently took my hand. I pulled away but he caught it again and gave the tiniest tug. I followed his hint and sat down again. He didn't let go of my hand and I made no attempt to remove mine. Somehow it felt right to let it remain there.

'I'm sorry. I was just teasing you.'

I looked up, meeting his eyes. He smiled as he reached his other hand to push the hair back from my eyes. 'In the interest of full disclosure, I carried you in my arms, and had tipped you in a little so your face was close to my chest, rather than on display for everyone to see. Not many people know who I am so if they'd seen me, they wouldn't automatically assume it was you I was carrying so I think we're still under the radar so far as most of the village is concerned.'

'Thank you,' I returned his smile, his thoughtfulness swimming round in my head. And my heart. 'I know it sounds silly to get worked up about it, but...' I drifted off. I didn't really have an excuse.

Nate gave a small shrug, apparently not requiring one. We sat in silence for a moment and I tried not to think how comfortable it all felt.

'Oh!' Nate shifted suddenly, releasing my hand. I tried not to notice the loss of his heat and focused on his face. Probably not the best option as it was way too handsome for my own good, but I had to pick something. 'There was a pile of stuff delivered for you today apparently. Flora had taken it in, but I brought it up when you were off in the land of nod.' He disappeared into my tiny hallway for a moment before reappearing with a selection of boxes which he placed on the coffee table in front of me.

'Gosh! Thanks.' I peered at the senders' labels quickly before getting up and drawing the curtains against the darkness. The clock on the mantel showed it was gone five. 'Do you need to get back?' I ran the sentence back in my head. 'Not that I'm trying to get rid of you,' I added hastily.

'No,' he checked his watch. 'I probably should get out of your way. We left Bry downstairs to keep Flora's husband company in the shop so I'd better check and see how much mayhem he's caused.'

'If you both wanted to stay, I could do some dinner.'

Nate hesitated and I suddenly felt awkward. Like a gawky teenager back at the school disco, clumsily asking one of the boys from the visiting school out. 'I mean, only if you want to. As a bit of a thank you, you know, for helping me up once then not letting me smash my face for a second time and bringing me home, not like a sack of spuds but—'

'That'd be great. So long as you're sure we're not putting you to any trouble,' Nate, thankfully, interrupted me. 'But only if you let me help with dinner.'

'There's not a lot to do. I made a huge lasagne yesterday, so it's just a reheat deal really. Nothing fancy.'

'Sounds great.' He grinned at me and I made a concerted effort to keep my legs in a non-jelly like form. When Nate smiled, it transformed his face. The blue eyes sparkled as the skin around them crinkled, even white teeth showed in a wide smile that immediately reminded me he was Gabe's brother. 'What?' His voice startled me from my daydream.

'I... well... I was just thinking how much you look like Gabe when you smile,' I replied, which was fairly close to the truth.

'Well, I guess there's worse blokes to look like, going by how popular he used to be whenever we went out to bars together.'

'That's true. Neither of you exactly fell out of the ugly tree, did you?'

Nate laughed, soft and low, but the sound wrapped itself around me. 'I think that's a compliment.'

'It is. Be grateful,' I grinned, glancing up momentarily as I ran a scissor blade along the top seal of the first box.

'Oh, I am.' There was something in his tone that made me look back up but he'd turned away, heading towards the front door. 'I'm just going to nip down and get Bryan. Anything else you need?'

'No, I don't think so, thanks. Take a key. It's just hanging on the hook there.'

'OK, back in a sec.' And then he was gone, the flat suddenly feeling emptier without his sizeable bulk helping to fill it. Knowing Flora, Nate might be down there for a little while so I set about unpacking my delivery and flattened the boxes, before putting them in the recycling tub. Spreading the goodies out on my coffee table, I began looking through. A short while later, I heard the sound of a key in the lock, immediately followed by doggy paws pit-pattering on my hall floor. Moments later, a small mostly-Dachshund rocket raced into the living room and launched himself from the floor into my lap.

'Manners, mate. Manners,' Nate laughed, shaking his head.

'Oh, you're all right, aren't you?' I said to Bryan, fussing over him as he snuggled so far into me I thought he might pop out the other side.

'Remind me to come back as a cute dog.'

'Oh, pfft. I'm sure you get more than enough fussing.' I waved a hand in his general direction and grinned. For a moment there was a pained look on his face, but it was smothered so quickly I questioned as to whether I'd imagined it. But as it replayed in my mind, I knew I hadn't.

'You're looking worryingly pensive.' He cocked an eyebrow.

I pushed myself up from the sofa and crossed the room to join him. 'Why worryingly?'

He looked down at me and I tried to ignore the way my breath wanted to shorten as I took in a faint scent of the citrus and woody notes of Nate's aftershave, the warmth of his body as he moved closer momentarily in order to avoid Bryan who was now dancing round our feet.

'Mate,' Nate laughed, bending briefly to scoop up the hound. 'We've had a talk about this before and agreed that you were going to keep out from directly under my feet because if I step on you, I'm going to have to change my name and emigrate to Antarctica. Remember that conversation?'

Bryan cocked his head as though trying to recall it. I grinned at the exchange and felt myself take a step closer to something I wasn't sure was such a good idea but, without asking permission, my heart had given my head a good shove and ploughed ahead anyway.

17

The next hour was spent talking easily about everything and nothing and all that lay in between. Nate was far more relaxed than he had been when I'd first met him. Back then his whole body had seemed to thrum with tension but, in these last few weeks, Wishington Bay had begun to work the same magic it had done on me when I'd arrived, slowly untying those knots, loosening the nerves that had been strung as tight as piano wire until finally I'd begun to feel like me again. Or, more accurately, it had allowed me to discover who that person really was, now she was finally free to live her own life and make her own decisions. Sneaking a glance at Nate, I could see that same process unfurling. It might not be finished yet, but it was certainly in progress.

'It's rude to stare.' His words caught me off guard as he looked up and met my eyes.

Oops!

'I wasn't staring.'

Liar.

Nate didn't say anything but everything about his face told me he didn't agree. Which was fair enough, as I was indeed lying through my teeth.

'OK. Fine, so I was staring. But not in the way you think.'

'And what way is that?' The tiniest flicker of enquiring eyebrow accompanied the question.

Oh crap. I was digging myself a bigger hole with every word that tumbled out of my mouth.

'I was just...' I gave what I hoped was a casual clear of my throat and began again. 'I was just thinking how much more relaxed you seemed now. I mean, from when you first came here. And that I'm happy about it. For you, I mean. Obviously.'

Inner me was slapping a hand to her forehead and trying to make herself as unobtrusive as possible in a corner. Outer me had to sit here and brazen it out.

'Obviously.'

Was that the flicker of a smile?

I shrugged. Again, as casually as possible but it felt like I had a coat hanger in my jumper so I wasn't entirely sure I'd pulled that one off.

Nate remained where he was for a moment, those inconveniently gorgeous blue eyes still studying me, as though he was still trying to decide quite what to make of my last declaration.

'I am,' he said, eventually. 'More relaxed, I mean.'

I let out a breath I didn't realise I'd been holding.

'That's good. Really good.'

He scooped Bryan up from where he was trying to climb up Nate's leg and plopped him on his lap where he then walked around a few times, determined to find just the right position. As he placed his paws in a rather delicate area, Nate shifted and frowned down at the little dog.

'It's a good job you're not bigger. Come on, mate.'

Bryan looked up at him, apparently considering his words, before he made one more turn and settled himself down on Nate's lap, curling himself round like a furry Cumberland sausage.

'Thank you,' Nate said.

Bryan let out a long sigh in reply. Two minutes later he was snoring gently.

'I'm not sure I can remember the last time I felt this relaxed, to be honest. Not that I noticed I was particularly stressed. I guess you get so used to a state of being that it ends up becoming the norm. It's only when something happens, something like this, that it suddenly throws everything into relief.' He drew a hand across the five o'clock shadow of his jawline. 'I suppose that can be both a blessing and a curse.'

I shuffled round to face him, tucking my knees up to my chin. 'In what way?'

He gave me a brief glance before dropping his gaze to the dog, his hand rhythmically stroking the dark, shiny fur.

'It's kind of made me face up to just how unhappy I was. I can't think Serena was happy either.' He gave a little outward huff, not quite a laugh. 'Well, obviously she wasn't, otherwise she wouldn't have left, but... I don't know. I'm not explaining this very well.' He gave me that shy, insecure glance again.

'It's OK.'

'I'm not really used to this.'

'What?'

'Spilling all my deepest, darkest secrets.'

I shrugged. 'They're not all that deep, or dark.'

'Again... intriguing,' he said, a glimmer of that beautiful smile playing round the corners of his mouth.

'Not really,' I shrugged, and waited for my nose to grow.

Inside, I felt that familiar knot that only ever appeared when I thought about my old life, and the fact that I'd hidden that life from everyone in my new one. I knew at some point I was going to have to tell them about it. But every time I thought about doing it, I chickened out. I'd had too much experience of people changing their attitude towards me – not necessarily for the better – in the past and so I always talked myself out of it. Next time, I'd tell myself. Next time the opportunity arose I'd tell them. And yet here I was, eighteen months later still with no one any the wiser. And, if it hadn't been for the fact I wasn't a natural born liar and therefore the secret sat heavy on my conscience, I'd have happily left it like that for ever. As far as I was concerned, I wasn't that person any more, so why should it matter? But I knew that, for friendships to be real, the truth mattered.

'That's what I like about you, Sophia. You're honest.'

'Huh?' I jerked my head up from my momentary drift in concentration.

'You. You were honest – brutally so, in fact.' He gave me a look and my mouth curved automatically, with no intentional input from my brain. 'When we first met. It was...'

I raised an eyebrow, half dreading whatever was coming next.

'Refreshing,' he finished.

I gave an unladylike snort. 'I bet that wasn't what you thought at the time.'

His lack of immediate reply gave me his answer.

'That's what I thought.'

'To be fair, it was all a bit of an adjustment. I was still jet lagged, and completely unconvinced that coming over here was the good idea my brother, not to mention my parents, insisted it would be.'

'And then I was rather blunt with you.'

'With good reason. I think I'd probably spent far too much time on my own in the preceding months, outside of work. My job deals in facts and figures and quantifiable statistics. I never sugar coat anything at work. It is what it is and we're trying to keep people safe. When Serena left, it was a shock. I mean, I knew things weren't right. Anyone could see that, but I couldn't see a way to make it right. Everything I tried seemed to make it worse.' He glanced across at me. 'Oh man, don't give me that face.'

'What face?' I asked, frowning.

'That, aww, poor sad bloke. What a drip.'

'I am not!'

'Yeah. You are.'

'This is just my listening face!'

His expression suggested that he didn't entirely believe me, but I gave him my best snooty look and he gave me a resigned one in return. Good to know some of my previous skills could still come in handy.

'Carry on,' I prompted him.

'There's not much else to say. One day I came home and she'd gone.'

'That was it?' I frowned. 'You didn't talk about it?'

Nate smiled but there wasn't any humour in it. 'Serena isn't really a big one for discussing things. Basically, it's her way or nothing.'

'That can't have been an easy foundation to build any relationship on, let alone a marriage.'

He sat back, relaxing into the sofa, Bryan still snoring on his lap. 'I didn't see it as a problem for a long time. I didn't really see it at all, I don't think. Others did, which caused friction, but you can't tell a person in love stuff like that, can you? At least you couldn't tell me. I didn't want to hear it. As far as I was concerned,

Serena was as close to perfect as I thought a woman could be, and frankly I was just amazed that she was interested in me.'

'Seriously?'

'What?'

'Oh, come on. We've had this conversation already – you're kind of hot.'

He looked away and I smiled. 'I'm not sure about that. Gabe's always been the one the women fell over themselves about.'

'Or maybe you only saw those ones.'

He pulled a face. 'Anyway. I was frantic when she didn't come home. Stupidly, it never even occurred to me that she might have actually left me. I guess that sounds kind of arrogant, but it wasn't like that. Like I said, I'm not great at explaining stuff sometimes unless it's to do with my work. I'm shit hot at that.' He grinned, lightening the moment.

'I'm sure,' I grinned back. 'But I know what you mean. You get into a routine. It's not happiness but it's life. This is how it is. How it's going to be and after a while you just accept that. Until you, or someone else, does something to change it.'

'That's it, that's exactly how it was. I earn pretty good money and Serena definitely liked that aspect of our lives. When the TV and film stuff came in, that was a bit of kudos too as far as she was concerned. I consulted on a couple of big name disaster movies and we got to go to the premieres. Serena was in her element then. She's made to be seen – it's like she comes alive in situations like that. Frankly, although the work itself was interesting, I'd have happily skipped the premiere stuff.'

'I'm guessing that wasn't an option.'

'I'm pretty sure she would have left me a lot sooner if I'd have done that.' He gave that a moment's thought. 'Maybe that would have been better.'

'You can't rake over what you should have done or not done

now. The past is the past and we can't change it, no matter how much we might want to.' God knew there was plenty I'd change if I could.

'That's true. What's done is done. When I realised she was gone, it was the strangest feeling. Half of me wanted to beg her to come back and the other half, I don't know… Does it sound bad if I say it felt like some sort of relief? Mixed in with the pain and upset and all that other stuff blokes aren't supposed to admit to.'

'If men admitted to more of that stuff, I'm sure there would be a lot less of them pretending everything was fine until it's too late.'

Nate nodded. 'You've probably got a point there.'

'I definitely have a point there.'

He looked across and laughed. 'See? This is what I mean. You know who you are. You're honest about it. You don't need constant validation. Not that I mind. It was pretty hard not to compliment Serena, to be honest. But you know what I mean.'

I couldn't remember the last time I'd received a compliment from my ex so to be honest, as much as Nate was right, as much as I now lived to please myself, and made my own decisions, be they right or wrong, there weren't many people who didn't enjoy a genuine compliment from someone from time to time.

'I do,' I said, simply.

He looked down at the dog in his lap, and gently laid the pad of his thumb on the top of Bryan's head, and began a series of slow, gentle strokes.

'If everything that has happened has taught me anything, it's that honesty is the most important thing. If we'd have been honest with each other about how unhappy we both were, we might have been able to fix things. Or at least realised that we couldn't and avoided a hell of a lot of extra drama.' He looked up from the dog, straight into my eyes. 'Honesty is key, really, isn't it?'

I nodded, the action feeling stiff and unnatural as I agreed with him, feeling like guilt was written all over my face as Nate sat there, telling me he valued my honesty when all the time I knew I was living a lie.

18

Eloise smiled and gave a little wave to a customer over by the door. As she turned to look at me, the mischievous expression on her face told me there was only one person it could be.

'Stop it,' I said, trying not to smile, which would only encourage her.

'What?' she shrugged.

'You know what.'

Eloise maintained her innocence. 'Probably ought to go and serve him though. Wouldn't want him marking us down on Trip-Advisor for lack of attention, would we?'

I tucked my pad back into my apron as I walked towards where Nate was waiting. Suddenly, Corinne rushed past me, heading towards the door and coming to a halt in front of Nate, her wide, youthful smile beaming out at full wattage. I stopped, still a few steps short of where Corinne now had her hand on Nate's arm, laughing with him as though they were old friends. He was looking down at her, concentrating on her words, and possibly her newly plumped, pillowy lips, enhanced today with a bright, scarlet red. As she turned to lead him to a table, conveniently in her section of the restaurant she caught my eye, and gave a smaller smile, this one brimming with smug satisfaction.

I turned back to where Eloise was now at the till station.

'Corinne's a conceited madam if ever there was one,' Eloise said, throwing a quick glance over her shoulder. 'She's always been thoroughly spoiled by her parents. She's a nice looking girl but her attitude, and ego, both need some serious adjustment.'

I shrugged. 'It doesn't really matter who serves him. And if she's fawning all over him we can probably be sure of that good rating on TripAdvisor after all.' I gave her a nudge with my hip.

Eloise was less inclined to be persuaded. 'From him, maybe, but you know we're going to be left to pick up the slack on all her other tables now the Australian god has arrived.'

I looked over in as casual a manner as possible. Corinne was leaning forward, hanging on every word that Nate said. And from the looks of it, he was actually giving her quite a few to hang on to. He was clearly feeling more comfortable in himself and his surroundings these days. His body language was far more relaxed than it had been on previous visits to the restaurant and a lot more relaxed than when he'd first arrived in the village. Corinne said something, resting her hand on Nate's arm as he laughed in response.

Turning away, I squished down the strange feeling in my stomach and resolutely denied that it might actually be jealousy. Which was ridiculous. Of course it wasn't jealousy. Nate and I were friends. Nothing more. He'd already told me, perhaps unnecessarily bluntly, that he had no interest in beginning anything during his stay here and I'd been more than happy to agree. Of course, that was when I'd thought he was a total arse and wouldn't have spent a moment longer with him than I absolutely had to. Without any direct consultation with my brain, other parts of me had apparently now decided that spending more time with Nate McKinley might actually not be the worst thing in the world. In fact, it might be really rather nice. All of which was stupid because I most definitely wasn't the type to have a fling. I'm not sure I entirely knew how to have a fling. What constituted a fling anyway? Was there a set length of time where a fling ticked over into 'short term relationship' territory? And if so, what was it? Did it vary from continent to continent?

'Well, you're deep in thought.' Ned's voice startled me.

'Oh! Sorry. Miles away.'

Ned nodded. 'Everything all right?'

'Absolutely.'

'What's all that about?' he asked, subtly inclining his head to where Corinne was now delivering Nate's drink to him. A task that should take all of two minutes but which she was managing to stretch far longer.

'What do you mean?' I asked. I certainly wasn't a fan of Corinne's true colours but I wasn't a snitch either. Ned, however, wasn't buying it and gave me a look that said as much.

'It's Gabe's brother. You said to make sure he's looked after well when he comes in.' I gave him a casual smile, but Ned's expression remained blank.

'Corinne seems to be taking that instruction to include a hell of a lot more than what's on the menu. Is something going on between them?'

'Not that I know of.' I glanced round and couldn't help notice the difference in Nate's body language between the last time he was here and now and had to refrain from adding 'yet' to my reply. 'He's a big boy, Ned. And it's not like he's fighting her off,' I said, feeling the twist in my stomach again and stamping on it with the determination of a five-year-old faced with a plateful of sprouts.

'That's not the point. I promised Gabe I'd look out for his

brother. He's been through the wringer already. Corinne setting him in her sights is the last thing he needs.'

Across the room, Nate laughed and Corinne gave him a flirty look before heading over to where another customer was trying to get her attention.

'Or perhaps it's exactly what he needs,' I said to Ned, giving a shrug and resting my hand on his shoulder for a moment. 'You're doing all you can but he's a grown man. If he can be so easily seduced by youth and beauty, then who are we to stand in his way.'

Ned tilted his head a little, smiling. 'If I didn't know any better, I'd say that comment had a distinct whiff of envy about it.'

I made a shocked 'O' with my mouth and placed a hand on my chest. Ned's grin widened and he gave my hand a friendly squeeze. The pager hooked on my apron vibrated.

'Order up.'

'Thanks, Sophia. I'm going to have a word with Corinne anyway. I've already noticed her missing several of her tables while she's busy making cow eyes at Nate and it's not the first time. I'm happy to have him here as much as he wants and they can do what they want out of here but she needs to rein it in a bit while she's on shift.'

I didn't know what to say to that, so instead I pointed at my pager. 'Better go.'

'Yep. Thanks.'

I headed off to the kitchen and picked up my order. Making my way over to the table, arms full of plates, I saw Ned and Corinne huddled in a space just behind the booking lectern where we stored customers' coats, out of sight. Ned's face was uncharacteristically serious while Corinne's had the livid but sulky expression she'd likely been cultivating since her teenage years. Whatever Ned was saying, it definitely wasn't going down well. I'd never seen Ned have to reprimand any of his staff in the time I worked there. Corinne had mistakenly interpreted this as thinking he would be a pushover but Ned, like most people, had limits. The restaurant was his and Carrie's life. They'd built it from nothing, cultivating its stellar reputation and, with a young family to support now, keeping that reputation was more important than ever. The rest of us knew this, but Corinne apparently needed her memory refreshing.

The phone by the lectern began to ring, and I headed over to answer it. As I approached, Corinne's gaze moved from where it had been petulantly staring over Ned's shoulder and met mine. Her eyes burned with rage and she narrowed them slightly as she stared. I looked away and answered the phone. Clearly she felt that her dressing down from Ned had come at my behest and, having that added to my crime of Nate walking me home the other day, had only increased her dislike of me. I wasn't a great one for conflict, having done my best to avoid it for most of my life, as and when possible, even if that meant making myself unhappy. I didn't particularly relish an even more difficult relationship with Corinne as I loved working at Ned's, but I also wasn't about to be intimidated by a twenty-something with a crush. Life was too short. Glancing over at where Nate was now sat alone, looking out to sea, I realised that perhaps Corinne hadn't been the only one with a bit of a crush. But I'd got over far bigger things than this in the past eighteen months, and this too would pass. Besides, if he preferred taut young bodies with pert boobs, full lips and thick extension-enhanced hair, that was up to him. It was hardly a revelation. My own ex-husband had certainly veered in the same direction on more than one occasion. And that was just the times I knew about. Sometimes there was just no accounting for taste.

* * *

The crowd was thinning a little as Eloise met me at the lectern.

'Isn't it time for your break?' she asked, glancing at the clock above the door. 'Ooh, and perfect timing.'

I frowned and followed her eyeline. Billy Myers was at the door. And before either of us could move, so was Corinne.

'Bloody hell, it's like she's got some inbuilt tracking device for good looking men,' Eloise said. 'And men too old for her at that.'

I gave a shrug. 'Age is just a number and all that.'

Eloise didn't look like she agreed particularly, but her focus was on Billy and Corinne.

'Hi! Welcome to Ned's. I'm Corinne.'

'Hi. I was actually looking for Sophia.' Over Corinne's head, he smiled. I raised a hand and gave a small, acknowledging wave.

'Oh. Right. Well,' she posed a little and looked up at him through her lashes. 'We're not really supposed to have visitors when we're working.'

Eloise made to step forward but I stopped her. Billy's entire being was relaxed, and confident. Just as it had been at the hotel. My friend looked round at me and I gave a small head shake.

'That's OK,' he said, 'I already cleared it with Carrie.'

'I see.' Corinne replied, tilting her chin up. 'Well, I guess a posh accent gets you special privileges.' She gave Billy a smile but being apparently immune to her charms, he'd now dropped in her estimation and there was no warmth in it. She stepped out of the way and threw me a cold glance. 'I'll leave you to it.' With that she stalked back on her Bambi legs, inevitably towards Nate.

'Got a real fan there,' Billy grinned. He was dressed in dark jeans, chunky boots, and a cosy looking royal blue padded jacket. His hair was a little shorter than before and the tips of his ears were pink with the chill, as was his nose, contrasting with the green eyes that were currently sparkling with mischief.

'Oh yes. She and I are like this,' I nodded, crossing my fingers

He laughed. 'Hi,' he said after a pause.

'Hello.'

'Nice to see you again, love,' Eloise said, giving him a quick hug. 'Soph was just about to take her break anyway so you've timed it well. See you again soon, I hope.'

'I hope so too,' he replied, smiling at Eloise before sliding his gaze across to mine. My friend patted my arm quickly and then headed off towards one of her tables.

'How are you?'

I nodded. 'Fine, thank you. You?'

'Yep. Pretty good. I've just finished for the day. Half day. Thought I'd try and get some Christmas shopping done and it seemed like it might be an opportunity to see you. I missed you when I dropped the wreaths off the other day.'

'Yes. I'm sorry about that. I have another job and was at that.'

He studied me for a moment.

'Do you want—'

'Billy! How lovely to see you again so soon.' Carrie's warm smile greeted us both as she gave him a one armed hug, the other being occupied in holding her son on her hip.

'Hi, Carrie, and you. And who's this fine fellow?'

'This is Will.'

Billy grinned. 'Now that's a fine name if ever I heard one. Hi Will.'

The little boy studied Billy for a moment, giggled then snuggled his face into his mother's shoulder.

'I've already been warned that I might be getting Sophia into trouble by visiting but I understand she's just about to take a break anyway.'

Carrie raised a brow. 'I can imagine who warned you off but that's OK. You missed her the other day and, whatever she likes to think, that particular waitress does not own the restaurant.' Carrie glanced across the floor and then down at the ledger. 'Actually, we're pretty quiet today. Sophia only has a couple of hours left of her shift anyway and I think we've got this covered so why don't you two go off somewhere.'

'Oh! Carrie, I couldn't. Really. I mean, no offence Billy, it's just that—'

'I insist. And, of course, you'll get the full pay for the shift. Goodness knows you earn it. She's one of our best, you know,' Carrie said.

I felt a flush in my cheeks, both at the compliment and at the fact that the concern I had about short wages had apparently been so obvious.

'I'd love that... but only if Sophia's up to it. I have rather turned up out of the blue.'

I looked back across the restaurant. Carrie was right, it was quieter now. Even with Corinne spending most of her time at Nate's table, the rest was easily doable by the staff without me.

'It's just that...'

Carrie had disappeared for a moment and had now returned with my coat and bag. A not very subtle hint.

'Go,' she grinned and I took the items off her, before leaning over to give her a kiss on the cheek and Will a light one on the top of his fair head.

I rested my bag on the counter and went to put my coat on. Billy took it from my hands, his brushing my own lightly as he did so and held it out for me as I slipped my arms in and belted it tightly.

'Thank you.'

'Pleasure,' he said, looking down at me before turning to my friend. 'Thanks, Carrie.' Across the room, Eloise waved, a broad grin on her face. We headed out, and I caught my breath at the crisp cold air after being cocooned in the warm fug of the restaurant. It was a beautiful winter's day with a deep blue sky. The wind was light and the sea shimmered in the cold sun.

'Where would you like to go?'

'I don't mind. You said you wanted to do some Christmas shopping. Is there anything in the village that might suit?'

'Only one way to find out. And even if not, I'm sure there's somewhere I can buy you a coffee.'

I nodded. 'There is.'

We turned and began to walk along the path that would take us from the edge of the sea towards the centre of the village. As I adjusted my bag on my shoulder, I glanced through the large plate glass window of "Ned's", my gaze catching Corinne's who was, unsurprisingly, once again loitering around Nate. By the look on her face, me bunking off early had just earned me yet more popularity points in her eyes. I looked away, my gaze unintentionally meeting Nate's. His eyes flicked briefly to Billy, then back to me before he raised a hand in a brief wave. I returned it before looking back ahead of me and asking Billy what sort of things he had in mind for possible gifts.

'I don't really know yet. I'm hoping for inspiration.'

'Then you've come to the right place!' I laughed.

'I think I already knew that,' he replied, giving me a direct look, which I met briefly.

'Can I ask something?' he spoke again after a moment.

'Of course,' I said, trying to inject a lightness into my voice which I didn't feel. Those simple four words always sent a shiver of unease throughout my body, prickling my skin. I knew why. And I knew how to fix that constant worry. If you don't have anything to hide, there's nothing to be uneasy about. But I did.

'The guy in the window seat back there.'

'Uh-huh?'

'Is there something... I mean, do you two... have some history?'

I looked up, genuinely surprised. 'No, not at all. Why?'

'I don't know. Just the look he gave me.'

'Oh,' I gave a quick dismissive wave of my hand as I shoved it into my glove. 'Don't take that personally. He just has one of those serious faces.'

'He was smiling at that other waitress enough while I was waiting for you.'

'Well, yes, she seems to have that effect on a lot of men.'

'I don't think she's my biggest fan.'

I looked up at him. 'Somehow I think you'll manage.'

He grinned back. 'I'm not sure a year's wages would cover the price of the watch I saw that bloke was wearing when he waved at you so, yeah, I think my ego will recover on that front alone.'

'Well, that's a relief.' I flashed him a look and he laughed.

'This is such a pretty village,' Billy said as we approached the main street. 'I can't believe I've never really been here. I think I've driven through a few times.'

'It's lovely, isn't it?'

'They go to town on the decorations, don't they?'

'Yes. Everyone really gets into the spirit,' I smiled, as I looked through the butcher shop window, itself decorated with tinsel and fairy lights, and waved at Pete.

'The restaurant looks great. Especially those wreaths dotted everywhere.'

I laughed. 'We made them ourselves, don't you know?'

'Is that so? You must have had a brilliant teacher.'

'Oh, he was all right,' I shrugged as Billy let out a good natured laugh.

'Tough crowd.'

'Come on, I'll buy you coffee to make up for it.'

He caught the hand I'd freed from my pocket to wave at Pete, and we stopped at the side of the pavement. 'I already called dibs on that one.' His voice was softer now and the green eyes focused on me as his fingers lightly held mine.

'Fair enough,' I agreed. 'There's a lovely tea shop just up here. How about we start there and maybe make a plan of attack for your present shopping.'

'I have a confession to make.'

'Oh dear. That sounds worrying.'

'No, I just thought, in the interests of being completely open, I'd better confess that my main reason for coming here was to see you.'

'So you're not Christmas shopping?'

'I am... if I saw something. But I really just wanted to see you again.'

I wasn't exactly sure what to say. It had been a long time since someone had said anything like that to me.

'You seem surprised,' Billy said, his expression half smile, half puzzlement. 'I didn't think I was particularly subtle at the workshop.' He shrugged. 'I've been told subtlety isn't exactly my strong suit.'

'No, it's not that. I mean, yes, I suppose I am a little but not...'

He waited. And I waited too, trying to get my brain to finish the thought but it refused to. Probably because it had no idea where it had been going with that sentence in the first place.

Billy gave a roll of his shoulders. 'OK. Let's start with this. Did your heart sink when I walked in the door?'

'What?' I looked up, horrified that might be what he thought. 'Of course not.'

'Good. Then that's a good starting point. Now, where's this tea shop?'

I pointed up the road and he held out a hand, inviting me to start walking again, the relaxed expression back on his face as we headed towards Miranda's warm, cosy tea shop, talking about our weeks and stopping occasionally to look in the decorated windows of some of the tea shop's closest neighbours.

* * *

'So?' Eloise pounced when we had a momentary lull the following lunchtime. 'You were very vague on your message when I asked how it went.'

'It was... nice.'

Eloise's face fell. 'Nice?'

'Yes,' I shrugged. And it had been. 'Lovely.' I tried to exude a bit more enthusiasm but her expression remained.

'Oh dear.'

'Why oh dear?'

'Are you seeing him again?'

'I... don't know.'

She pointed a shocking pink nail at me. 'That is exactly why "oh dear". What's wrong with him?'

'Nothing.' I shook my head and avoided her eye. 'Nothing at all. He's lovely. You know that.'

'I do. Which is why I don't understand why you're not seeing him again. He's obviously pretty keen on you.'

If I was honest, I didn't understand it too well myself. Everything Eloise had said was true. Billy was lovely. And we'd had a great time. He was relaxed and comfortable with who he was, not to mention funny and cheeky and bright.

'I do like him.'

'But?'

'But what?'

'I don't know, but there's definitely a "but" because otherwise you'd already have another date set up.'

'It wasn't really a date.'

She gave a small shrug as though that was irrelevant anyway, and she was probably right.

'I think he'd be good for you, love. God knows you could do with some fun.'

'I have fun!'

'Not nearly enough.'

'I just—'

'Hey,' Nate caught my arm and I jumped as I felt electricity fizz through me as I turned. Ned was escorting him to the front of the restaurant, chatting easily while at the same time ensuring Corinne attended to the tables she'd yet again been neglecting since the man had walked in the door today.

'Hi,' I said.

'Sorry, I didn't mean to interrupt.'

Eloise gave me a momentary enquiring look before turning to Nate. 'That's all right, love. How's you? Feeling a bit more at home here now?'

'I'm good, thanks. And yes, I think so. How are you?'

'Fine, thanks, Although I'd better go and get this,' she said, silencing her pager. 'Lovely to see you as always, Nate.' She patted his arm and headed back towards the kitchen to collect her order. Ned shook Nate's hand, reminded him to come in as often as possible and headed off in the same direction.

'How are you?' Nate asked when we were alone.

'Fine, thanks. Did you enjoy your meal?'

'It was fantastic, as always.'

'I'm glad you enjoyed it.' *You certainly seemed to be enjoying the service*, a small, petulant voice in my head added. I gave him a quick smile and turned away, doing my best to ignore my inner monologue. I'd done my best to ignore Corinne's over the top flirting today but her tinkling laugh occasionally caught my attention, which, from the look on her face whenever I turned, had been part of the plan. The third time I kept my head lowered and just looked up surreptitiously, then gave myself a good mental kick for being baited at all.

'So... Corinne said it's the Christmas light switch on in the village tonight.'

I bet she did, the little voice whined again. I remembered back to what Corinne had said the last time Nate had been in, about him meeting her the following week. When he'd awkwardly said that he'd been waiting for me outside the restaurant later that day, rather than her, I'd stupidly assumed that had perhaps meant something. His protestations that she was a bit full on had felt genuine at the time but today he'd seemed far more open to them. And even after Ned had spoken to her yet again about neglecting other customers and reining in the flirtatious behaviour, I noticed she was still strutting around like the cat that had got the cream. I flicked my glance up to Nate, and got the distinct feeling I was looking at that proverbial cream right now.

'Yes, it is,' I said, unnecessarily tidying the booking ledger in front of me.

'Are you going?' Nate prompted.

'Oh, I expect so,' I replied in what was hopefully a casual and carefree manner.

'It's just that I saw you with that guy the other day,' he cleared his throat. 'So I just thought maybe—'

'Ooh, are we talking about Sophia's gardener?' Corinne swanned up, butting into the conversation.

'He's your gardener? I thought you only had the flat?'

'He's not *my* gardener. He's *a* gardener. It's his job.'

'I suppose there's something to be said for the outdoorsy type, but I prefer a man whose mind is his main tool.' Her eyes drifted up to meet Nate's but he kept his gaze up and was looking at me.

'Well, we might see you there then.' Corinne was clearly bored with the conversation, despite never having actually been invited to join it. Her voice dripped with self-satisfaction as she laid a hand on Nate's arm. 'Mightn't we, Nate? I'm showing him some of the sights by night beforehand so I'm not sure what time we'll get there.'

'What time does the switch on happen?' he asked but I wasn't really listening. My mind was turning back to when I'd offered to show him some of the sights and get him out of the house. All I'd got was a sharp rebuttal but now, despite all his protestations about Corinne being too young and too obvious for him, here he was, lapping up all the attention she and her perky chest could throw at him. From everything I'd heard about his wife, Nate was certainly partial to a pretty face, and Corinne was undeniably beautiful. Not to mention a good fifteen or so years younger than me. Gravity had begun to take a rather unfair hold on certain parts of my anatomy while she was still in that wonderfully youthful stage where everything defies such laws and you blindly believe this will always be the case. Of course, one day you look in the mirror and to your horror discover that things most definitely aren't where they started out.

I'd once done my best to counteract this with personal trainers, regular tennis matches and sessions at the gym, but you can only do so much. Nowadays, rushing round at the restaurant, cleaning, and walks in the fresh air with the sea crashing on to the beach beside me probably burned more calories anyway.

Many of my – well, I'd called them friends but time had disavowed me of that belief – acquaintances had long since turned to the plastic surgeon's knife for a helping hand, but that was one step too far for me. I'd booked several appointments but ended up cancelling every time. Something about it hadn't seemed right. I didn't care if others did it, especially if they gained confidence from it. But lurking in my mind was the knowledge that this wasn't really something I wanted. I was doing it because everyone else was. Because my husband had suggested it might be a good idea to 'perk things up a little'. Because my mother, who could barely smile these days, even if she had wanted to, told me it was my duty as a woman to look the best I could. I could practically hear suffragettes spinning in their graves when this gem of wisdom was imparted to me.

Watching from the corner of my eye, I saw Nate tilt his head down as Corinne made a comment in a low voice, and I knew what I needed to do. I needed to step back here before my imagination got carried away even further in thinking that my friendship with Nate had ever had the slightest potential to become anything else. It was stupid to have even entertained the idea. I'd been asked out and spent time with a man who, as Eloise had said, would probably be far better for me than Nate McKinley ever would. And actually lived in the country. Billy Myers was everything I should have wanted. But it was Nate McKinley who made my blood fizz with electricity when he touched me, not Billy. And that wasn't fair to such a decent man so when he'd asked me out again at the end of our afternoon of coffee and trailing the shops, I'd had to say no. I didn't want Nate to have that effect on me – and I would get over it. But I couldn't pretend that Billy did have that effect when he didn't. I'd already had a lifetime of pretending and I wasn't about to start again.

I didn't disbelieve that Nate hadn't been looking for anything to happen during his time here. His whole being had resonated as a man who'd shut himself away from any possibility of being hurt again, and I understood that. But as he'd opened up, relaxed into his stay in Wishington Bay with Bryan and begun to enjoy the process of writing his book, something had obviously changed. He'd become more relaxed with me, which I was happy about. He'd also apparently decided that being a monk, forever worshipping his ex, wasn't the life for him after all. Corinne wasn't looking for anything serious, as far as I knew. And Nate can't have been either really... could he?

'It must be so wonderful to be able to sit on the beach on Christmas Day,' Corinne sighed. 'Just stretching out under the sun in a bikini.' She did a languid cat stretch for the full effect. 'Don't you think, Sophia?'

'Umm... yes. I suppose so.' I glanced across the room and noticed one of Corinne's customers trying to catch her eye. Unfortunately, their waitress's own gaze was firmly fixed on Nate.

'Table five is calling you.'

Corinne let out a sigh and gave Nate a dramatic eye roll. 'Working is such a bore.' She moved round me, pressing herself close to Nate in the process. 'See you tonight,' she said breathily and sauntered over, swaying her hips more than usual, confident that Nate was watching. Under my lashes, I stole a glance. He wasn't. I tried not to smile and tried not to feel bad about the fact I wanted to.

'So, will I see you later?' Nate asked.

I shrugged, flicking the pages of the ledger back and forth importantly, as though searching for something although I wasn't taking in anything written there, my mind instead whirring away in a different direction entirely. For all I knew, Kermit the frog could have booked a table for two this evening and I wouldn't have noticed.

'Maybe,' I answered, aware that I was being vague and

annoyed with myself for letting Corinne's date with him bother me quite so much.

'Is something wrong?'

I looked up and saw the genuine concern in Nate's eyes which only served to make everything just a little bit worse.

'No,' I shoved a smile on to my face. 'Not at all.'

'It'd be nice to see you this evening if you're able to make it.'

Across the room I could see one of my tables ready for attention. 'I'll probably be around somewhere but honestly, I'm not sure you're going to have much time to notice anything but Corinne. She's a full attention type of girl. I'd better go, sorry.' I made to move but Nate caught the fingers of my hand lightly with his own, halting me, and I looked up, trying to ignore all the sensations his touch set off.

'I'm not seeing Corinne. I mean, it's not a date.'

'Nate, you don't have to explain anything to me. It's up to you what you do. You're single and she's single.' I gave a shrug and pulled my hand from his.

'But it's not a date,' he repeated, apparently determined to get this across to me, but I needed to get on and put it out of my mind. What Nate McKinley got up to during his time here was nothing to do with me. Now I just had to get my heart to listen to my head. I gave Nate a quick smile.

'I'm pretty sure Corinne thinks it is. Maybe you should just go with it. Sorry, I need to get back to work. Enjoy the lights if I don't see you.' And with that I stuck a smile on my face and headed over to where my customers had now decided which of the several delicious puddings Ned offered had taken their fancy.

19

'You know she'll eat him alive,' Eloise said in a confidential whisper as we finished our shift.

I made a brief attempt at pretending not to understand what she was referring to, which my friend saw off with one look, so I gave up.

'He's a big chap. I'm sure he can look after himself.'

'You heard what Gabe said about him. It sounds like he ran himself ragged trying to provide for and please his ex, and she still went off. And now he's agreeing to take Corinne on a date, who between you and me, sounds very much of the same ilk as his last one?'

'Apparently it's not a date.'

Eloise gave me a look and I shrugged.

'That's what he told me.'

She made a 'pffft' noise. 'I heard he was supposed to be quite the brain box.'

'He is.'

'Not in this area, it would seem.'

I shrugged. 'Corinne's pretty and vivacious. Maybe he has a type.'

'A type that is no good for him by the sounds of it.'

I belted my coat and pulled my hat down over my ears. 'I guess we'll see. Maybe it's just what he needs. Who knows?'

Eloise tilted her head at me momentarily. 'Are you trying to convince me, or yourself?'

'Why would I care?'

She reached over and gave me a hug. 'Quite. Why would you care? If he can't see what he's missing, then he's nowhere near as clever as he's been portrayed.'

'Honestly, I'm not interested in Nate McKinley, Eloise. He's only here for a short while and I've had more than enough of relationships to last me a lifetime. Yes, he's pretty to look at but, as is blatantly obvious, underneath most men are all the same. Swayed by youth and beauty and, frankly, Corinne's welcome to him.'

Eloise looked at me for a while. 'That's a very wounded heart you're carrying round in there, my darling. Be sure not to wrap it away so securely that no one can ever touch it again.'

I shook my head. 'That's actually been working pretty well for me, to be honest, and I'm definitely not about to change it for him.'

Eloise looked at me for a long moment before giving a slight nod, realising that the discussion was closed.

'Will you be at the lights tonight?'

'I expect so,' I said, more positive this time. 'It's lovely to see all the shops and streets lit up. I'm not sure what time yet, though.'

'Fair enough,' Eloise replied, clearly not wanting to push any further than she already had. 'Just give me a ring if you're around and we can get together for a hot chocolate or maybe something stronger.'

I gave her a grin and a hug and headed out into the chill air, waving at Bob as I did so before tucking my chin down and battling against a fierce headwind that was doing its best to keep me from the cosiness, and security, of my flat. Winding my way through the cobbled streets and relishing the shelter provided by some of the buildings, I finally arrived at Flora's shop. Like many of the others in the village, it would be opening late tonight and just as I approached, George was climbing back down off a stepladder beside the blue and white striped awning.

'Hi, George. Everything all right?'

'Hello, love. Yes, thanks. I was just giving the lights a quick test and one of the blasted things blew. Still, luckily I'd bought a few spare so we should be all systems go tonight. You're coming, aren't you?' he asked.

'Yes, I expect so.' As much as I loved the village, and having thoroughly enjoyed the lighting ceremony last year, my enthusiasm for tonight had been waning the more I battled against the bitter north-easterly on the way home and even all the beautifully festive shop windows couldn't boost my excitement. If I was honest with myself, I knew that the possibility of seeing Corinne's smug expression as she paraded her newest conquest around really wasn't adding to the desire to be outside when I could quite easily be cuddled up with a blanket and a good book, or a binge-worthy series on Netflix. But on the other hand, this community had helped me heal and I knew it was things like tonight that made it special.

'That's good. Oh, I think Flora wants to see you, if you've got a minute.'

Right now, I just wanted to get in and put my feet up for a bit but instead I gave George a pat on the arm and turned to head into the gift shop. As the bell tinkled announcing my entry, Flora glanced up, bright eyes smiling in her attractive face. She'd once shown me pictures of herself in what she called her 'heady days of youth' and it was no wonder George had fallen for her. She'd been an absolute knockout and she still retained a more mature, elegant sense of that today. I only hoped I could look as good as she did when I got to her age.

'Oh, Soph, there you are. How's the face?' she asked, taking my chin gently in her hand and tilting it a little to inspect it.

'It's fine,' I said, shrugging it off. 'Looked worse than it was.'

'Nate was ever so concerned.'

'Probably worried he'd have to clean his own house for the rest of his break.'

Flora raised an eyebrow and I flapped a hand. 'Sorry, I'm just a bit tired and grumpy. Long shift.'

'Oh. Then I'm afraid you probably aren't going to be thrilled at why I've called you in either.' Something in her tone sent a creeping chill of discomfort through my veins.

'Why? What's happened?'

Flora held my gaze for a moment then pulled a magazine from beneath the desk. 'My granddaughter dropped in earlier and she knows I love all these magazines so she left me a bunch. This one just came out a couple of days ago. It's got a gossip section and I couldn't believe it when I saw it.'

'Saw what?'

She turned the magazine round for me to see. There on the second page of a double page spread was a picture of my Instagram account, with a couple of smaller snapshots of posts I'd done. Above it was the headline:

The new Mrs Hinch? But why the mystery?

My stomach churned as I flicked my gaze up to meet Flora's. She knew about my account and had been eager to spread the word about it in order to help me to gain followers. I'd had to explain that wasn't something I wanted to do. That this was something I did purely for my own entertainment and had no interest in becoming any sort of influencer. Whatever happened organically was fine, so long as I was in control. The name I'd given to the companies who'd sent me stuff to try was fake, and as Flora often took parcels in for me, I'd had to come up with an explanation for this. I'd merely told her that I'd had a messy split with my ex and that it had caused a big family rift and, as I had no interest in them discovering where I was, or what I was doing, it was easier to keep the account just for myself and not risk anyone linking it to me. It was a truth of sorts. By the look on Flora's face, I guessed she had worked out there was probably more to it than the glancing overview I'd given her, but thankfully she didn't probe.

'Are you all right, love?'

I nodded, my eyes still on the gossip piece. 'How did these people even find my account?'

'I suppose the same way any of these accounts get noticed. One person tells another and at some point, it might reach someone with influence. Or at least with access to the media. The fact you purposely avoid your voice or face being in any of your posts... well, I guess people think there might be more to that than there is. And people love a mystery, not to mention a bit of gossip.'

I felt sick. I'd never thought anyone would notice my account. It was fun and for once I'd been posting things I wanted to, rather than curating the look of a lifestyle expected of me as I'd had to in my previous life. I enjoyed it but I'd never dreamed it would ever be at risk of attracting any attention like this.

'Do you think I should just delete the account?' I asked Flora as I worried a thumbnail with my teeth.

She glanced back down at the magazine. 'I don't really know, love. I know you wanted to keep things a little mysterious for personal reasons. Deleting it might do the trick. Of course, depending on how invested the person that wrote this is in finding out why you stay anonymous, it might be just adding more kindling to the fire.' She closed the magazine. 'It's hard to tell these days. Everyone always seems to want to know everyone else's business.'

'I just... like my privacy.' It was true but even to my own ears it sounded weak. Flora was right. It might all blow over. But if someone got a sniff of who I actually was, things could get a bit sticky. Thankfully, I'd sent off the divorce papers now and hopefully that would finally be over before Jeremy could change his mind on anything else, especially if he got extra ammunition. I could just see him raging over the headlines now. His propensity for a tipple had resulted in a gradually deepening pink tinge to his skin over the last several years, something he tried to cover up with tans from trips abroad and sessions at the salon. However, it was unlikely a tan would be able to hide the beetroot purple apoplectic rage he'd explode into if this came to light. In his eyes it would be an absolute disgrace for me to have debased myself by cleaning. To him, I'd be no more than a servant, which to my eternal embarrassment was what he had always called the household staff. I swear sometimes it had been like living in the eighteenth century. Perhaps it was his aversion to women working at all that had caused him to 'rescue' so many young ladies from their jobs as waitresses and bartenders. The altruism he showed in these cases, judging by the trinkets, clothes and occasionally cars, they were given, was incredibly generous...

'Has anyone contacted you about this?' Flora asked.

I gave a shrug. 'I've had a few DMs asking me for info, but I ignore them. I wasn't interested in giving any more information out so I just thought they'd go away. Why are they even interested?'

'Why's anyone interested in anything? That other girl has done pretty well doing a similar sort of thing and I guess they thought you'd be keen for the same. Most people seem to be eager to grab onto any hint of fame these days, so the fact you blanked them has probably made their antennae perk up.'

I let out a sigh. 'That was the opposite of what I meant it to do.'

Flora gave me a squeeze. 'Don't worry too much about it, love. I'm sure it'll blow over. There's a tonne of other things for their magpie brains to latch on to.'

'Yes, you're right. But do you think I should respond?'

'And say what?'

I shrugged. 'I don't know. Thanks for the interest but I'm not looking for any publicity.' I turned to her. 'Would that work?'

'It might do. Or, depending on what side of the bed they got out, it might just encourage them.'

I dropped my head back and rolled it from side to side, trying to release the day's knots.

'Come on. Let's forget about it for now. Are you coming out to see the lights switch on tonight? Perhaps bringing that rather gorgeous man of yours? Or is there a choice now?'

News travelled fast in a small village like Wishington Bay.

I gave a very unladylike snort. My mother would be so proud. 'Nope. No choices at all. And if you're referring to Nate McKinley, he's most definitely not mine.'

'That's not what I'd have said the way he was looking at you the other day. I've never seen someone so concerned.'

'Well, see how he's looking at Corinne this evening when she parades him about the village and get back to me on that.' I hoiked my bag up on to my shoulder.

'Corinne?'

'Yes. She's been all over him in the restaurant whenever he comes in and tonight he has a date.'

'Surely not. I thought he had more sense than to be taken in by a flibbertigibbet like that.'

'Apparently not.' I gave her a shrug. 'He did say it wasn't a date but that's definitely how Corinne's looking at it.'

'Well, maybe she's got a shock coming.'

'Who knows. He didn't seem to mind the attention from what I saw today.'

Flora tilted her head. 'Is that a little of the green-eyed monster peeking out there?'

I pushed my shoulders back. 'Absolutely not. Nate McKinley can see and do whatever he likes. Not my business. I'm just here to make sure the house is cared for.'

'Right.' Flora looked at me, her slightly raised brows telling me she didn't believe a word of it. To be honest, I was having my own struggles, but I figured the more I told myself that, the more I would believe it.

'So, you're coming?'

'Yes, I'm coming.' Why should I stay in just because Nate was spending the evening with Corinne? The best way to show them both that it didn't bother me was to go about my business as usual. I'd loved the ceremony and the festive evening last year and there was no reason I should miss it this year. Especially no tall, dark and handsome Australian reason.

'Good. I'll see you in a while, then?'

'Definitely. I'll just head up and have a shower and then come down and grab something for dinner. Maybe some fish and chips from Jake's?'

Flora's eyes lit up. 'Ooh, now you're talking.' Jake the Hake's fish and chips were legendary in the village.

'I'll get you and George some too. We can have a picnic in the shop.' As I spoke, I felt excitement for the event begin to seep into me, replacing the worry of the magazine comment piece, and the... whatever it was I felt about Nate and Corinne. I wasn't quite yet ready to admit to Flora's diagnosis of jealousy, even if I had the sneaking suspicion that she might be right.

'Right, see you in a bit. And thanks,' I said, giving Flora a quick hug before scooting out of the shop.

* * *

A short while later I was back outside my flat, having washed and changed and bundled myself up against the cold. The night was bitterly cold. Pinned to the dark sky, a full moon peeked out every now and then through swift moving clouds that were heavy with the threat of snow. Waving through the window to Flora and George I made an eating motion with my hands and pointed up the road. Flora gave me a thumbs-up and then turned to George, I imagined to fill him in on tonight's menu.

The queue for Jake's was out of the door, as usual, snaking back past his window and almost past the shop next door. I joined the end and stamped my feet a little to get some circulation back into my toes. Slowly the line advanced and I passed the time chatting to residents of the village as they meandered by, all wrapped up against the chill. Eventually I placed my order, enjoying the warmth of being inside the chip shop, its windows steamed up as the heat from the fryers hit the cold glass. As I waited, I flicked through a local free paper absentmindedly, my stomach rumbling loudly as delicious smells wafted round. I dropped the paper and folded my arms across my tummy until my order was called.

Clutching the warm, precious parcel to me, I hurried back to

Flora's and unwrapped it, handing out a parcel each to her and George, along with a wooden fork. We sat in companionable silence, eating our chips, warm fluffy potato with just the right amount of crisp, fish coated in the lightest of batters that just melted in your mouth. Customers and browsers wandered in and out and we took it in turns to serve them. Manoeuvring a slightly over-large piece of fish into my mouth, I looked up to see Nate and Corinne stood just inside the doorway to the shop watching me. Corinne gave a tiny raise of one artfully styled brow. I ignored it. Fair enough, I'd underestimated that particular forkful but I'd had a lifetime of eating right, doing right, looking right and I wasn't about to be intimidated by what Corinne thought of my manners.

20

I gave a wave of my little finger from the hand that held the fork. Nate smiled.

'Hey,' he said, before glancing round the shop, almost as if he was looking for something.

'Hello,' I said, remembering the chat I'd had with myself to be casual and forget the silly hint of a notion I'd had about getting cosier with this man. Annoyingly, he looked just as attractive as usual this evening, which wasn't helped by the fact that Corinne was, as I'd suspected, looking terribly pleased with herself as she tucked her arm possessively through Nate's. I had to admit, though, Nate wasn't looking as thrilled as I'd expected he might. His hands were shoved deep in the pockets of his cashmere coat and as Corinne tilted her head to rest against his arm, I could see his body tense. I looked away. I probably hadn't made the best job of convincing him that what he and Corinne did was his own business, but I wasn't about to let him see it bothered me now. I set my face to disinterested and looked past them into the street where the cobbled roads were filling with villagers and visitors, ready for the big switch on.

'Having a nice evening, Nate?' Flora asked, as she took the empty fish and chip wrappings from George and me.

'Yes, thanks,' he smiled at her, disengaging himself from Corinne to accept Flora's hug. Was it me, or did he look just a little relieved? Shaking George's hand, he then looked over at me. 'How were the chips?'

'Good, thanks. They're from Jake the Hake just up the road.' I inclined my head in the direction as I, unnecessarily, tidied up the gift wrap supplies on the desk. 'You should try them some time.'

'I will, thanks.'

'Ooh, we could get some tonight, Natey.' Corinne slipped her phone from the back pocket of her sprayed-on jeans and checked the time.

Natey?

Nate didn't answer and was instead showing great interest in a small decoratively painted elephant made from ceramic. Behind him, Corinne pouted. Flora shot me a look, quickly mouthing the word 'Natey'. I gave a tiny shrug in reply and continued with my task, preparing some ribbons by curling them with one blade of the scissors.

'It's an incense holder,' Flora said, wandering over to him as Corinne let out a sigh before picking up and putting down a few of the gift shop offerings, a thoroughly bored look on her face.

'It's pretty.' He paused for a moment, turning the item over in his large hands. He'd been less tanned than I expected when I first met him. I'd automatically expected him to be similar to Gabe, if not more so, with reliable weather in which to access the gorgeous beaches he had at his disposal but he wasn't. His light olive colouring had certainly had a little colour but less than I'd have supposed. Of course, it had made sense when I thought about it. I'd got the feeling that, much of the time, Nate saw little but his work computer. Well, that and the inside of a gym, I'd guess from the sneaky looks I'd stolen at his body. Whether these activities were solely as a mechanism to help him not think about his imploded marriage, or whether he was naturally a bit of a workaholic, I wasn't sure. Either way, at least here, having to look after Bryan was getting him out of the house and some fresh air. Talking of which...

'Where's Bryan?' I asked, frowning.

'I don't really like dogs,' Corinne answered before Nate got a chance.

'So?' I replied.

She let out an impatient sigh, clearly annoyed at having to spell out to me what she felt should be obvious. 'So, I don't want dog hair all over me. I don't get why people go so mad over them to be honest. They're such a tie and just ruin your clothes.'

I felt my blood rising and Nate stepped in front of me, the little elephant in his hand.

'So you just left him on his own for the evening? Why didn't you call me? I would have come and got him if it was too much trouble to take him on your date!'

Nate's features hardened but I didn't care. Poor Bryan! Having to miss out on a walk and all the fun sniffs and sounds this evening would have offered, not to mention all the socialising, just because Corinne demanded it.

'Flora, I'm going to go and get Bryan. I'll be back in—'

'He's not at home.'

'What?'

Nate fixed me with a look that was as chilly as the temperature outside. 'I didn't leave him at home. I wouldn't do that.'

'So where is he?'

'With Ned and Carrie.' He tipped his wrist up, glancing at the face of another extremely pricey watch. Corinne caught the movement and I saw her eyes widen slightly as she took in the brand. Nate was toast.

'See?' Corinne said, coming back to stand by him. 'No need for all the drama. Honestly, Sophia, it's just a dog.'

It? *It?*

I opened my mouth to reply but Nate beat me to it, turning to face Corinne. 'Bryan is a he, not an it, Corinne.'

She gave him a pouty smile.

'All right. There's no need to be so tetchy,' she said, leaning into him. He leant back and she mis-stepped, a look of surprise on her face.

'I'm not tetchy, Corinne. I just don't appreciate you speaking about him that way.'

Corinne looked away and rolled her eyes. 'Honestly, Nate. I think you're taking it all a bit seriously.'

Nate looked at the back of her head for a moment, before giving a small shake of his own. He switched his gaze to me. I met it coolly.

'Carrie was missing him and called me earlier to ask if they could have him this evening. Their little one is full of a cold so Ned was going to give Bry a quick walk so he can say hello to everyone and then have a cosy evening in. I'm going to collect him after the lights thing.'

'I thought we were going to dinner?' Corinne protested in a tone that had a distinct edge of whine to it.

A flicker crossed Nate's face.

'Do you think Holly would like this?' he asked, placing the little elephant down on the desk in front of me. 'You know her better than me.'

I hesitated for a moment, catching the annoyance on Corinne's face as Nate ignored her question.

'I... um... yes. I think she would. I know she's bought incense sticks from here before, hasn't she, Flora?'

My friend picked up the thread. 'She has,' she said, coming to stand next to me as we both became aware of the daggers I was now receiving from Corinne. 'I think she'd love it, Nate. That's very thoughtful of you.' She smiled, giving the hand he'd rested on the counter, taut with tension, a tender pat.

Nate looked up, smiling for the first time since he'd entered the shop.

'I'll take it then, please.'

'Nate, can we go now? I want to get a good spot to see Zane Hudson turn the lights on.'

He frowned and a small sigh escaped. 'Who's Zane Hudson?'

'Oh my God, really?'

He looked round at her exasperated tone and shrugged.

'He's a massive soap star and had a best-selling album earlier this year and did a world tour, including Australia. You must have heard of him.'

'Nope,' Nate said quietly, handing over a note to pay for the gift.

'We're really going to have to bring you up to speed, sweetie,' she purred, back at his side now.

'Actually, I'm quite happy with my current speed,' he replied, concentrating on receiving the change I handed him. Corinne's perfectly painted mouth dropped open a little.

Beside me, Flora suddenly found something interesting to faff with just below the desk. I slid my eyes to her and tried not to catch her giggles.

'Are we done here? We're never going to be able to get a good place otherwise. I'm dying to see him!'

'Well then, perhaps you should go. I'm not quite ready.' Nate's voice was even and he kept his eyes lowered, focusing instead on my hands as they wrapped the little elephant in a pretty package ready to give to Holly.

'So, we're not going to dinner? You said you'd take me to dinner!' The whining tone was now in full flow.

Nate lifted his head and turned. 'No, Corinne. I didn't. You said did I want to come along this evening so you could show me round a little more, and that you were meeting friends. Somehow that seems to have become a dinner date for just the two of us, which I told you at the time, as tactfully as I could, wasn't something I was interested in.'

Corinne by now had an expression as black as the sky outside. 'Well, how would you even know if you don't try?' she snapped. 'You're never going to meet anyone if you just hole yourself up every day with that dog. Especially not someone like me!'

A muscle flickered in Nate's jaw.

'As I said before, I'm not interested in meeting anyone.'

Corinne made a show of adjusting her scarf. 'I see. Well, I'll leave you to it then.' Her eyes switched for a moment between Nate and me. By this point, George had wandered off to the pub and Flora was busy still finding things to sort under the desk, her eyes widening with intrigue at the exchange going on above her. I returned Corinne's look, keeping my expression disinterested before moving away from the desk to tidy one of the nearby shelves. 'You don't know what you're missing.'

I sneaked a glance at Nate as he gave a small, conciliatory nod. 'I'm sure that's the case, Corinne.'

She seemed to perk up at the thought that Nate realised he might be a fool, passing up the opportunity of dating her. Tilting her chin up, she turned on her four-inch spiked heel and strutted out of the shop. Nate let out a long, audible sigh as Flora bustled over to him.

'You all right, love?'

'Yeah, sure. I feel like kind of a sh—' He stopped himself and Flora grinned.

'No need to mind your language on my account. I've heard it all before, and probably used a good deal of it too. These angelic looks hide a multitude of sins.' She gave him a devilish wink, bringing a smile at last to his tense features. 'And you shouldn't. If she tried to make it all into something it wasn't, then that's her look out.'

'Maybe.'

'No maybe about it, is there, Soph?' Flora looked over to me.

'No,' I said, struggling to put a lot of effort into my reply.

Nate shoved his hands in his pockets. 'Somehow I don't think Sophia believes that.'

I remained silent. Flora flapped her hand.

'Of course she does. We all know what a flirt Corinne is and having you on her arm to parade round the village would be right up her street. You're not the first she's set her sights on and won't be the last.'

'I did try to make it clear to her I wasn't looking for anything... romantic.' He gave a shrug with one broad shoulder as if he wasn't sure that was the right description. I wasn't sure that was the right description for what Corinne was usually after either, but I remained silent. 'I thought she understood that.'

Flora patted his arm. 'You can't blame a girl for trying. Gorgeous chap like you swanning in and causing ripples in the village.'

'Hardly,' he smiled, giving a small head shake.

I echoed the gesture to myself, but for a different reason.

'What was that for?' The question was quiet and calm but I could feel the undercurrent of tension, and I was pretty sure Nate could too.

I turned to face him. 'What?'

'That headshake. Clearly you have something to say so perhaps it would be best if you just said it.' He held his body tense, its language defensive.

I gave a shrug, denying all knowledge of what he was talking about. He shifted his weight and held my gaze, not buying it in the slightest, his eyes remaining fixed on me.

'OK, if you really want to know, I can see how Corinne got the wrong idea.'

'Oh, you can?' Again, the voice was calm, but I could see the fire building in his eyes.

'Yes.'

'And just how do you figure that?'

I gave a small head tilt, accompanying it with another shrug. 'Just in the restaurant the last few times. You haven't exactly seemed averse to her attentions.'

'Yes, she's always been very friendly in there. I don't really know what else I'm supposed to do as no one else seems to want to wait on me. Would you have me ignore her all the time when she's serving me?'

'Not at all, but you can't flirt and laugh and then be surprised when she expects more.'

'I was not flirting!'

'Really,' I said, flatly, disbelief lacing my tone.

'Yes, really,' he fired back. 'She suggested something at the beginning of the meal that time and I told her, as gently as I could, I really wasn't interested. She laughed it off and said I'd got the wrong end of the stick and that she'd just been inviting me out to this thing tonight as one of a group. I have to say I was relieved. After that she was just really casual and friendly so I let it go and thought maybe getting out like that would be a good thing. Especially as you'd been such an advocate of it.'

He had me there. Bugger. Hoist with my own petard!

'Anyway, as it turned out, that was obviously not what she had in mind at all but I didn't know how to extricate myself without upsetting her.'

'Maybe you should have just gone along with it,' I shrugged. 'You might have enjoyed it after all.'

'I wouldn't. And I wasn't. Been there, done that.'

'Done what?' Flora asked, intrigued.

We both turned, having momentarily forgotten Flora was there.

'Oh...' Nate adjusted the beanie on his head. 'Just...' he looked round, but the shop was empty of customers.

'Sorry, I'm a bit nosy at times,' Flora smiled, giving his arm a squeeze. 'George is always telling me off about it.' She grinned sheepishly.

'No, it's fine.' Nate smiled down at her. 'Actually you remind me of my mum a bit. She'd like you.'

Seeing a chink, Flora pursued her question. 'So, what did you mean? Been there done that?'

He smiled a little wider and looked over at me. 'She's persistent, isn't she?'

I couldn't help but return it. 'That she is.'

'I just meant the whole spoilt princess thing. That probably sounds bad and I'm sure Corinne is a lovely girl.'

Flora gave a small cough.

'But I don't think I could go through all that again. Initially I enjoyed trying to make my wife happy but in the end, when nothing was good enough, it just got exhausting.'

Flora studied him for a moment, then reached up and gave him a big hug which he returned. Pulling back, she rested a hand on his cheek.

'There's someone out there who's right for you, love. Someone who knows love is a two-way street.'

Nate pulled a face. 'Maybe, maybe not. Right now I'm just enjoying taking things as they come, and spending some quality time with Bryan.' He rubbed a hand across his forehead. 'I should never have said yes to coming out with Corinne.'

'Oh, you weren't to know what she was up to. And in the meantime,' Flora glanced up at the clock on the wall, 'It's nearly time for the big switch on. Let's lock up, go unearth George from the pub and then find a good spot to watch from. What do you say?'

He nodded. 'Sounds good to me.'

Flora waved me over. 'Come on, Soph.' I picked up my coat from the hook and shoved my arms in as Flora dashed to the back room to get her own.

'Are you still annoyed with me?'

I looked up at his question. 'I'm not annoyed.'

'See, your mouth is saying that, but your face is saying something else entirely.' There was a hint of smile at the corner of his lips which, irritatingly, made it quite hard to be annoyed with him. He had explained and really it was none of my business anyway. I should just be pleased he'd been able to laugh and relax, even if it was with Corinne, especially as, remembering the strain his face had shown when I'd first met him, it hadn't seemed like he'd done much of either for a long time.

'I'm not. Really,' I said, feeling myself relax.

He studied me for a moment before accepting. 'Good. I don't want to fall out with you, Sophia.' His voice was soft and low, both of us aware of Flora bustling about in the next room.

'No, me neither.'

His smile widened a little and I felt myself respond in kind.

'Just so you know, it's not that no one else wants to wait on you at the restaurant – it's more that none of us get the chance these days.'

'Ah. I see. Well, somehow I can't see her being in a rush to serve me again after tonight.'

I shrugged. 'Who knows with Corinne.'

'So...' he looked round again before his gaze dropped and met my eyes. 'I maybe thought you might be here with someone tonight.'

I frowned up at him.

'The guy from the photo. I saw you with him the other day and thought that, maybe...'

'No,' I replied simply, as Nate's question tailed off into silence.

'Busy?'

I shook my head. 'No. My choice.'

'Oh.'

I felt the corners of my mouth turning up. 'Whatever it is, just say it, or ask it as you look about as comfortable as someone with a hedgehog rambling about in his trouser leg.'

'Ouch.'

'Quite. So what is it?'

'Your gardener,' he held up a hand. 'Sorry. The gardener. I just... I guess I thought you and he were... an item. Maybe.'

'We just went for coffee, Nate. People here do love a gossip. You shouldn't listen to it.'

'I haven't listened to anything. I'm just going by the way he was looking at you at the restaurant.'

'Oh, I don't think he—'

'He definitely was.' Nate's voice was soft but didn't invite argument.

I looked up.

'Billy's lovely but... he's not for me.'

Nate let out a breath and for a moment it looked as though he was about to say something but just then Flora came back through, now bundled up. Efficiently, she hurried us out of the shop, and towards the pub to find George. As we walked, Flora tucked her arm round Nate's. He tilted his other elbow, the hand stuffed in the pocket, so that I could do the same. I hesitated a moment before catching Flora's eye. She gave the tiniest head shake and then nodded at Nate's arm. I tucked my arm through and we went off in search of George and the big switch on.

21

'So, this Victorian fayre thing? Worth a visit?' Nate said, looking up from the laptop screen and stretching.

'Definitely. If you can spare the time,' I said, nodding at the keyboard as I wrestled the vacuum back into place in the cupboard under the stairs.

'All work and no play makes Nate a dull boy,' he said, as he came to stand beside me and leant in to the cupboard, rearranging the space a little in order to make it easier for me to replace the appliance. 'At least so I was told.'

I looked up. 'That's not exactly what I said.' I thought back to when I'd first met him. I remembered suggesting that he get out and see some of the area but that was it. Wasn't it?

He shook his head, closing the door on the cupboard. 'No, you didn't. Not in so many words.'

I felt the hint of a blush.

'Oh, I didn't mean... I was... it obviously came out a bit wrong. It was just that I didn't think...' I stopped as I looked up again to see a wide smile on Nate's face. Frankly, that smile was enough to make anyone stumble in their tracks, but right now, still close to him, able to smell the soap of his early morning shower, and feel the warmth of his inconveniently sexy body next to mine, my sensible, ordered thoughts weren't flowing quite as easily as they ordinarily did.

'What are you grinning for?' Not that I was complaining, which was probably evident by the smile on my own face.

'Well, for one thing, I've found it's actually a lot more fun than being a miserable sod all day.'

'I'm not going to argue with that.'

'So you agree I was?'

'That's not what I said, and you know it,' I replied, poking him in the chest.

'Not in so many words.'

'Not in any words,' I laughed, giving him another prod.

He tilted his head down. 'You have excessively bony fingers.'

I pulled my hand back. 'I do not have bony fingers.' I held my hand up. 'I have regal, elegant hands.'

'Regal?'

I shrugged. 'Maybe.' Actually, that was closer to the mark than he knew, but now wasn't quite the time to divulge that information.

'And I didn't say they weren't elegant. But they're still bony.'

'Perhaps you just need a bit more meat on you.'

He raised an eyebrow. 'Was that the thinking behind you stocking the fridge and cupboards with irresistible food? My brother thinks I needed feeding up or something?' He looked down and poked his tummy.

'Oh, pfftt, there's nothing there.'

'There would be if it hadn't been for this little mutt.' Nate inclined his head to where Bryan was lying with his feet in the air, the paws moving rapidly as he chased something or someone in his dreams.

'Hardly.'

'And back to the original question, I didn't mean you were calling me dull. Even when your temper is up, I don't think you'd have been that mean.'

I leant against the wall as Nate held the kettle up in silent invitation and I smiled in acceptance.

'Certainly not intentionally.'

He flicked the kettle to boil and turned back to me. 'The comment was one often repeated by my wife.'

'Then she's wrong.'

'Not necessarily. I did work a lot.'

'That doesn't automatically mean you're dull. People spend a lot of time at work for all sorts of reasons, not least to earn money to do things that are fun.'

'That's true.'

'Can I say something?'

Nate poured water into the teapot and set it in front of us on the coffee table to brew as we took a seat each on the sofa. 'Am I going to like it?'

'I don't know.'

He took a deep breath, turning a little more towards me. 'Come on then, let me have it.'

I smiled. 'It's not that bad, don't worry.'

'A statement which makes me even more concerned.'

I bumped my shoulder against his and grinned before looking back up at him, my smile fading a little as other feelings took its place.

'So, what is it?' he asked, pouring the tea.

'I was just thinking that maybe it's time to start letting go of all the more uncomplimentary things you may have been told over the years.' Nate shifted position a little, keeping his eyes averted.

'I know it's not that easy,' I said, resting a hand briefly on his arm. 'It's always easier for us to believe the bad stuff for some reason. But there comes a point where we just have to stand up for ourselves and be our own cheerleader.'

Nate placed a perfect cup of tea in front of me. 'If I didn't know better, I'd say that this advice was coming from personal experience.'

I lifted the drink and he met my eyes over his own mug. 'It might be.'

He fixed me with a look.

'OK,' I said taking a sip before returning the china mug back to its coaster. 'It's definitely coming from experience. And that's why I know how important it is for you to let go of all the bad stuff. All it does is eat away at you, making you more and more unhappy and insecure, and for what?' I turned to face Nate more. He'd replaced his tea on the table, beside mine, and now it felt like his whole being was focused on me. It was a little hard to concentrate with that amount of hotness centred on me, but I made the effort.

'It's just one person's opinion of you, Nate. I know you loved her very much, but you can't let words like that shape you for the rest of your life. At some point, you need to take back control and decide who you are, and who you want to be and start taking steps to make that happen.'

For a moment, Nate said nothing. I sat watching him for a moment, wondering if I had overstepped the mark.

'It's not that easy though, is it?' His gaze flicked up and met mine, a half smile on his lips but sadness in his eyes. 'I mean, it sounds so easy. Be positive. Move on. Simple words. And you sit there thinking, how hard can it be?' He shifted position and glanced out at the sea, the foam being whipped by the beginnings of a storm weather forecasters had announced coming in from the Atlantic. 'Turns out those little words are some of the hardest to live by. At least, it seems that way to me for the moment.'

'Sometimes it's the smallest words that can have the biggest impact.'

Nate gave me an even look.

'Oh God,' I laughed, breaking the tension. 'I sound like some cheesy self-help book.' I was glad to see that this time his smile reached his eyes. 'And I'm not knocking self-help books. God knows I've gone some way to keeping that particular part of the publishing industry in business over the past couple of years!'

'Is that right?'

'Well, I certainly seem to have acquired quite the collection.'

'Did any of them help?'

'I think some of them did, actually. Some of them weren't for me but different things work for different people. And I think a good proportion of it was that I felt like I was taking back control. That I was making an effort to make the changes I wanted in my life, even if I wasn't entirely sure what it was I actually wanted. The most important thing is that I realised what I didn't want.'

'And what was that?'

'A life where I felt irrelevant.'

'You could never be irrelevant, Sophia.'

'Oh, you'd be surprised.'

'I would,' he returned, 'You've got an energy about you. A drive. There's no way you could ever just be... anything less than you are now.'

'I was. Believe me. And I'm determined never to be that way again.'

Having finished his tea, Nate relaxed back into the soft cushions of the sofa. 'So, what's the story with you then? Everyone seems to already have a good idea as to what's happened with me, something I need to have a word with my brother about, but you've lived here for some time now and no one seems to know that much about your history.'

I felt a discomfort creep through my bones.

Yes, and that's exactly how I'd like it to stay.

'Have you been spying on me?' I asked, forcing a lightness into my tone that I wasn't entirely sure sounded natural.

'Not at all. People just seem to talk here. A lot.'

'That is true, but they don't mean anything by it. And don't be cross with Gabe. It's pretty hard to keep a secret in this place.'

'You seem to have managed pretty well.'

I laughed off the comment. 'It's no secret I walked out on an unhappy marriage and ran away to the seaside.'

'That can't be all there is to it?'

'Can't it? Isn't that enough?' I asked quietly. 'People the world over do the same thing every day in one way or another. People who once believed in those vows they made, who couldn't imagine a life without that person they were joining themselves to. And then somewhere, somehow, for one reason or another, or maybe for no particular reason at all, suddenly it's not working any more. This thing they'd believed in, that they'd both wanted, now wasn't something they wanted at all.'

'Or maybe only one of you still wants it.'

I sat back, both of us facing out towards the large glass doors, watching the clouds darken, turning the sea a heavy leaden grey. Seagulls swooped low and erratically as the wind caught them and blew them off course, their screeches competing with the strengthening storm.

'And do you?'

He rolled his head on the back of the sofa lazily, and I turned at the movement.

'What?'

'Still want your marriage.'

'I thought I did. For a long time after Serena left, I thought I did. Despite all the rows and tantrums and stress, I thought that if I just did this or that, it would be different if she'd just give us another try.'

'And now?'

'No. Not any more.' He let out a sigh. 'When I first came here, I dreaded having to walk the dog.'

I frowned, hurt on behalf of my four-legged friend.

Nate smiled. 'Don't look at me like that.'

'I can't help it,' I replied, honestly.

'Let me explain before you judge me.'

'Fair enough. I'm listening.'

'It wasn't the dog walking as such I was dreading, it was the time. Time I'd have to turn things over in my mind. Time alone with my thoughts.'

His comment now made more sense and I understood exactly what he meant.

'When I came here I did a lot of walking. On the beach, out in the countryside, round the village. But I never went anywhere without my headphones and an audio book, or a podcast or the radio. Something, anything to keep the thoughts out of my head.'

Nate sat up a little. 'That's it. That's it exactly. I did the same thing.'

'So, what happened?' I asked quietly.

'I guess I realised that keeping things parked out of sight only works for so long. And it was kind of hard to keep track of my book or whatever when Bry was always charging up, ready to play. It felt unfair to him to only give him half my attention.'

I smiled and looked over at him. 'You're a big softy really, aren't you?'

He gave a quirk of his eyebrows. 'For my sins.'

'There are far worse things to be.'

'I guess that's true.

'So, how's it going then? Letting all these thoughts in?'

'Not as scary as I'd first thought. Some days are worse than others but I suppose that's all part of the process.'

'I think so.'

'I wasn't convinced of Gabe's idea of coming here. I felt that I could write anywhere. That soulless hotel room in Sydney you mentioned when we first met, for one. But my baby brother has more insight than I gave him credit for. For him it was always about more than me just having a quiet place to write. It was a place for me to start healing. To start, for lack of a better turn of phrase, and at the risk of sounding a bit hippy dippy, finding myself again. Like you said, discovering who I am and who I want to be and getting on the road to making that happen.'

'And how do you think that's going?' I asked.

Nate shifted on the sofa, turning to face me a little more. 'Better than expected. Admittedly there was a small hiccup with nearly getting caught up with Corinne, which I definitely hadn't planned on.'

'But you felt you did the right thing?'

'Definitely. I wasn't looking for anyone when I came here, just like I told you, albeit rather clumsily now I think back on it.'

I shrugged it off. 'Sometimes things happen when we are least expecting them. That doesn't mean we should automatically write them off, just because they weren't on our plan.'

'No, that's true,' he said, before letting out an 'oof' noise as Bryan, who had now woken up from his nap, wandered over and decided to join us. His aim as he leapt up on to the sofa was either slightly off, or spot on, depending on what view you took. Nate's own view was now through watering eyes.

'Bryan, sweetie,' I said, lifting him off Nate's lap and settling him on my own for a few moments as Nate shuffled and recovered. 'You're totally adorable but you have to look where you're going occasionally. We promised Gabe that we'd hand Nate back in one piece. You might be small but you know how fragile these male humans can be.' Bryan tilted his head to one side and emitted a small squeak as he yawned.

'I know, and yes, we still love you.' At this, Bryan let out a contented sigh, walked round on my lap a couple of times and curled himself into me. 'Don't get too comfy down there. I've got to go in a minute.'

'Do you have to leave?'

'I've got a few things to pick up in the village and I've already disturbed your work for long enough.'

'You're not disturbing me. I like the company.'

I couldn't help but grin. 'Bet you didn't think you'd be saying that a few weeks ago.'

'Aah, come on. Give a bloke a break. I wasn't that bad. Was I?'

I pulled a face and he grinned. To be fair, I didn't think I'd be sat on this sofa musing on just how knee-meltingly good a smile Nate McKinley had a few weeks ago either. At that point in time, I wasn't even convinced he could smile, so I guess in that respect we were pretty even.

'Luckily, you improve with time. If you know what I mean.'

'Are we back to the fact I've grown on you like a fungus?' he laughed.

'Just focus on the "grown on me" bit of that if the fungus part bothers you so much,' I replied, happy to hear his laugh and feeling utterly relaxed myself.

'I will.' Nate lifted the dog off me so that I could get up. Bryan looked askance at him for a moment before burrowing under one of Holly's beautiful cushions and making himself a little den instead.

'So, this fayre?'

'Uh-huh?' I said, grabbing my coat from the hallway hook and swiping a couple of times to find the second sleeve.

'Are you going? I mean, could I... we... kind of go together. Here.' He moved behind me, found the sleeve hole and aimed it at my arm.

'Thanks. Oh, sorry. I can't,' I said, turning back to face him as I belted the coat.

'Oh. Right. No, that's fine.' He fiddled with the cuffs of his jumper for a moment. It was kind of adorable. 'I didn't mean to make you uncomfortable and after I just made the whole big speech thing about not getting together with Corinne. I mean, I know what it sounds like and I totally understand that—'

As cute as Nate was right now, stumbling a little over his words and explanation – a fact I was doing my best to ignore – I had to put him out of his misery.

'It's all right. I didn't think you were asking me out so you can relax. I'd have been happy to show you round the fayre ordinarily but it's just that I've kind of got roped into taking part in it this year. It's Flora and George's wedding anniversary so he's whisking her off somewhere for the night. The fayre is always a good night for sales, especially if the weather behaves, which it's supposed to. Flora's been so good to me so I said I'd mind the shop for her for in the evening.' I took the hat he was holding out for me and pulled it down low over my ears. 'You're welcome to come and help too, of course.'

'In the shop?'

'Yes. I can show you the ropes and I'd be grateful for the company. But only if you want to, of course.'

'I'm not sure I'd be much of an asset. It's a long time since I had to deal with the public face to face. Normally it's just me and suits talking about very dry statistics.'

I stole a glance at him. He was definitely more of an asset than he thought. Suddenly he dropped his gaze and locked straight on to mine. A smile broke on his face. 'You know what? Why not? It might even be fun.'

'It will be fun!' I laughed, taking the bag he'd now handed me. 'You sure Flora will be OK with it?'

Flora was already a huge fan of Nate McKinley and constantly encouraging me to become a bigger one myself. Something that would be very easy to do, had circumstances been different. But in the meantime, his company as a friend would be good and it would be another step in getting him out and mixing and building his confidence back up. It was a win-win situation.

'She'll be fine but you're welcome to come back with me so we can run it by her together.'

'That's a great idea. Can you hang on a mo?'

'No problem. Shall I get Bryan ready?'

'Would you mind?' he asked, leaning back over the stair banister.

I shook my head, smiling, leaving him to finish taking the stairs two at a time until I heard him in the bedroom, opening a wardrobe door and grabbing whatever it was he needed from there before rushing back down the stairs again. I had by this time coaxed Bryan out from his sofa den by merely lifting his lead from the hook. Before I could even turn round, I felt two small paws resting on my calf. Lead clipped on, Nate quickly unhooked the cosy coat he'd bought the little dog from where it was hanging and in moments, had snuggled his four-legged pal into it. Bryan was now looking from one of us to the other, and then at the front door, clearly wondering what we were all waiting for. Nate stuffed his feet quickly into the boots he'd kept near the radiator, zipping up the thick jacket he'd slipped into at the same time.

'I know the dog's in a hurry but there's no rush,' I laughed as he tried to pull his hat on at the same time, dropping it in the process.

'I don't want to hold you up.'

'I'm not in a rush,' I repeated, slower this time as I picked up the hat from the floor. 'It's fine. Now stand still,' I said, before reaching up to place the knitted beanie on Nate's head, taking a moment to adjust it, although in all honesty, it already looked perfect. He was one of those people who just automatically looked good in anything. Bit sickening really. But it was clear he didn't realise this, which made the trait even more attractive.

'Thanks,' he said, quietly, once I'd finished.

'You're welcome.'

'Ready?' I asked, opening the front door and catching my breath as an icy breeze pierced the bubble of warmth we'd been ensconced in.

'Let's hope this has passed before the fayre opens!' Nate said, raising his voice to carry over the wind that was now howling round us.

'It's supposed to,' I said, glancing up at him, and staggering slightly as a rush of wind pounded into me.

'Here,' he said, holding out his arm. 'Let's tackle it together. Bryan can pull us along,' he laughed, looking down at the little dog, who was trotting into the wind, his ears almost at right angles to his head as he occasionally snapped at it, catching an interesting smell or two. Tucking my arm through Nate's, I smiled as he pulled it closer to his body, bringing me along with it.

'Ready?' he asked, as we faced the wind again. Nate's nose was turning pink from the cold, but his face was more relaxed than I'd seen it since he'd come here. A gust blew around us and caught him, snatching any other words he might have been about to say away. He shook his head and tried again, laughing. 'Come to England, they said. It'll be great, they said!'

I squeezed his arm. 'It is great, and you know it. It's just a bit...' I powered against the wind. 'Breezy!'

Nate laughed again, pulling his arm tight in order to make us a smaller target for the wind, and we pushed on together up towards the village.

22

In accordance with the wishes of an entire village, the day of the fayre saw no trace of the previous storm, save a few small, misplaced branches snapped off in the wind and carried away. The sky was a cool, bright blue, dotted here and there with the wispiest drapes of white cloud. Outside on the little streets, the village was buzzing with activity as signs were erected, the main road closed to traffic and rows of temporary stalls began to take shape on the main thoroughfare.

I waved through the window at Flora as I made to pass by on the way to get some groceries and restock my currently sad-looking fridge. She made a beckoning motion and I poked my head through the door.

'I won't keep you,' she said, bustling over to me for a brief hug. 'You sure you're all right to cover tonight still?'

'Of course.'

'And Nate's still coming?'

'As far as I know,' I said, shrugging casually.

'He seemed a bit hesitant once he knew he'd have to dress up.'

'But he didn't say no.' I got the feeling that Nate had done very little out of his comfort zone for quite some time so this actually could be good for him. An opportunity to build some of the confidence that had been chipped away at. I knew something about that. But I also knew it was possible to rebuild it. And sometimes you found reserves you never even thought you had.

'I have a feeling he's going to look rather wonderful as a Victorian gentleman,' Flora gave me a nudge and I shook my head, smiling.

'I'm sure he will.'

'Well?' she asked.

'Well, what?'

'You. Him.' She made a gesture as if to say the rest was obvious.

I gave her a smile and a roll of my eyes. 'Hardly.'

'What? Why not?'

'I can think of about ten thousand reasons to start with,' I replied.

'Oh, what's distance when it comes to love?'

I gave her a look.

'Fine, fine. But it seems like a bit of waste. Both of you single and you seem to get on well.'

'We do. Which is nice, but Nate's not looking for anything, and I'm not about to get involved with someone who may or may not still be in love with his ex-wife.'

'Do you think he is?'

'I think it's a possibility, whatever he says. Plus, I'm not really the type for flings, which is all it could ever be. He's leaving again in a few weeks' time.'

'And here you are wasting all this time you could be sharing a bed!'

I laughed, half in amusement, half in exasperation. 'I have to go now. I'll see you later.' Waving, I stepped out into the cold

December morning, closing the door behind me hurriedly in order to keep as much warmth as possible in the cosy shop. The chill air cooled my skin and I relished the feeling as Flora's comment about Nate's bed had sent a rush of unexpected warmth through my body that wasn't exactly helpful, bearing in mind I had to spend the entire evening with him later. And yes, once Nate had got over the surprise that his volunteering to help in the shop this evening would involve him dressing up, there had been some fleeting thoughts of how sexy Richard Armitage had looked dressed as a Victorian gent in *North and South*. But that was TV and no one last year had had the ability to induce the kind of reaction Mr Armitage elicited in his Victorian costume so, as lovely as Nate was, there were definitely no plans for swooning in my foreseeable future.

* * *

Ten minutes before I was due to re-open the shop for the evening's fayre, the door rattled as someone tried to enter. I looked up to call that we weren't open and saw Nate raise a hand in greeting through the glass of the door. Hurrying over, I pulled the bolt and stood back to let him in.

'Hi,' he said.

Suddenly there seemed a lot less air in the room, which was only due in part to the tightness of my corset. I stole another look at Nate. And I'd thought Richard Armitage looked hot... All I could think of right now was where I might be able to obtain some smelling salts.

'You OK?' he asked.

'Hmm? Yes. Definitely. Just a bit nervous, you know. I've never run the shop on my own before and I'm just a bit, well, you know. Want to get it right and everything. You look nice.' The words rushed out in a torrent and I sucked in a breath at the end. Well, as much breath as this damn corset would let me. I knew I shouldn't have let Flora help me with it.

'You've already got a gorgeous figure, but we may as well go for broke, eh?' she'd giggled as she had given the laces on it another good yank. 'If not tonight, then when?'

That was a fair question as now, between only having half my lung capacity and Nate looking hotter than any man had a right to in a stiff Victorian collar, I wasn't entirely sure if I was going to make it through the evening.

'Thanks,' he said, giving the lapels on his coat a bit of a nervous tug and consequently making it lopsided.

I faced him, gently batting his hands out of the way before straightening the coat back up. 'There.'

'I'm not really used to anything like this.' His hands began to travel nervously back up and I caught them.

'Stop fiddling. You look great.'

'Sure?' he asked.

Looking up I saw the genuine disbelief on his face.

'I'm positive. In fact, I might just have you stand at the door and wait for the female stampede.'

'Oh, ha ha.' He gave me a half smile, the merest hint of blush tinting his cheek.

I turned away and began to walk back to the cash desk. Probably safer that way. 'The funniest thing is you think I'm joking.' I glanced back over my shoulder. Yep, he looked just as good from a distance. Damn. Still, it was only for a few hours. I could do that, and like I'd told Flora, I wasn't in the market for a quick fling.

'What can I do?' Nate asked, following me across the shop.

I looked up at him. 'Relax, for starters. This is supposed to be fun.'

'It's a little out of my comfort zone.'

'Maybe that's a good thing.'

He gave a little head wobble. 'Maybe yes, maybe no.'

Ugh. The layer of vulnerability added to the already undisputable package of gorgeousness wasn't exactly helpful.

'Let's go for yes,' I grinned up at him and he returned it more fully. Oh crikey. Where the hell were those smelling salts?

* * *

An hour and a half later, and the shop was humming with activity. It was always busy but I hadn't missed the stolen glances sent Nate's way, some far more obvious than others. He, in contrast, missed them all entirely but did seem to be enjoying himself and after a little while had got into the swing of it. His shoulders were no longer rammed up by his ears and he was chatting and laughing with the customers far more easily. The large glasses of mulled cider the grocer had popped over with earlier may have helped a little with this, but most of it was Nate just being who he was. Perhaps because he was finally being allowed to be himself, or at least rediscover that man?

'Hello, Nate.' I glanced over from where I was rearranging some goods to fill the spaces where we'd sold out and saw Nate look up from where he was leaning on the counter and come face to chest with Corinne's cleavage. Rather than the more demure look many of us villagers had gone for, Corinne had chosen to head down the busty serving wench road. And frankly, she looked like a knockout.

'Oh... umm, hi Corinne.' Nate stood straight.

'I just wanted to pop in and say that I hope we can still be friends.' She moved to the side of the counter and wrapped her hands round his arm, pressing herself against him and gazing up.

His eyes flicked down then back up again. Even the most determined of men would be hard pushed to avoid what Corinne was clearly on a mission to flaunt.

'Sure. Of course. No hard feelings.' He smiled briefly and looked over towards me, an unmistakeable plea in his eyes. I took the hint.

'You having a nice evening?' I asked, heading back towards the counter, doing my best to keep my tone light and conversational, despite the lack of friendliness in Corinne's own eyes.

'Yes, thanks. I'm just waiting for my date.'

'Oh, right.' Corinne never was one to hang around but I got the feeling, from the quick look she threw at Nate, that this comment was more for his benefit than mine. 'Have you been round the fayre already or just heading out now?' I was aware of the inanity of my words but I seemed the only one there attempting to make any sort of effort. Nate's shoulders were back welded to his ears, and Corinne was busy lazing over the counter, flipping through the magazine Flora had left stashed under there.

'Yeah,' she replied, not looking at me and clearly not listening to me. I met Nate's eyes. He issued a small shrug and I gave up.

'God, that looks just like Holly's place. Don't you think?' Corinne turned the magazine to face Nate and I felt my face colour, suddenly realising what Corinne was looking at.

Nate looked down at the picture under the gossipy headline about the mystery of the popular house-proud account. 'I guess. Lots of places look the same though now, I think.' He flicked a glance at me and met my eyes. He knew. 'They're all styled just to get Likes and stuff.' He shrugged as Corinne looked up at him. 'Or that's what my ex-wife was always saying.' I could have kissed him. And not just for the obvious reasons.

'I guess,' she replied. 'Although do you reckon this could be Holly? I mean, I only saw the place when I came round to see you so I haven't exactly got intimate knowledge of it.' She lowered her voice on the word and gazed up through a teasing look. 'But it really does look like it. I know Holly has a lot of individual pieces since she started that sideline of revamping furniture and that cabinet just seems so familiar.'

'I think she's got an account so maybe she posted something and someone's copied the idea. I guess that happens?' Nate's tone was nonchalant.

'Yeah, I s'pose. Shame. It'd be cool to get in with a proper influencer. She might be able to help me boost my own account. I'd love to do something like that. But with clothes and make-up, obviously. They get all this stuff given to them for free! And sent all over the world, staying in top hotels. I'd be so good at that.'

'I'm sure you would.' He smiled at her, and she returned it, pacified, it would seem. Or else just basking in that smile, which I totally understood too.

'Ready, babes?' The Peaky Blinder lookalike who'd just entered the shop took in Corinne still standing close to Nate, and we both saw the assessment in his eyes. 'Didn't you have something in that jeweller's you wanted to show me?' The platinum pinky ring, set with an exquisitely cut ruby, together with the very un-period Rolex hinted that Corinne's date had more money than his market trader accent initially suggested.

Corinne's eyes lit up. 'Oh hi! Yeah, let's go. I'm dying to show you. I mean, it's way too expensive but I'm hoping to save up for it.' His arms wrapped around her as she reached him. He threw a glance back at Nate. Nate smiled, no hint of jealousy on his face. The other man studied him for a moment, and it was hard to work out whether he seemed pleased about that or not.

'Bye, Nate.'

He raised his hand briefly as they left the shop.

'Bye, Sophia,' I mumbled in a high-pitched voice, glancing over at him. He grinned.

'Just be thankful she's gone.' He pointed to the magazine. 'This is your account, isn't it?'

I let out the breath I hadn't realised I'd been holding. 'Yes. Thanks for covering for me. Corinne's the last person I want finding out that's mine. I'm still thinking it might be better to take it down completely.'

'Do you want to?'

'Not especially. I enjoy doing it. I've just no interest in making it a big thing. I know to people like Corinne not wanting to be "discovered" might seem impossible to understand but it's never been about that for me. It's merely a bit of fun.'

'So keep it then. This will all blow over. You know how long an attention span people have these days.'

I let out a sigh. Well, as much as I could in this damn corset. 'Yes, I suppose you're right. I don't really want to be dictated to as to what I can and can't do. But I don't want the attention either.'

'Would it really be so bad if you did get some?'

I thought of my mother finding out I knew one end of a toilet brush from the other. I'm not sure she'd ever recover. And of course, then she'd know where I was, which was far worse.

'Yes. It really would.'

Nate shifted his weight and looked at me. 'You're not on the run, are you?'

I let out a breath that was part laugh. 'No. I promise.'

'Shame. I could have done with a bit of living dangerously.'

'I'm sorry to disappoint you.'

Nate reached out, hooking one of the curls that had escaped the myriad hair grips I had plunged into my updo earlier and tucked it behind my ear.

'Now that is something you definitely don't do.'

I looked up, meeting his eyes, the warmth of where his hand had rested against my face still lingering.

'I do, however, get the feeling there's a whole lot more to know about you than you've told me.'

'Oh, I'm not sure you're missing out on anything.'

He took a step towards me. 'You know, actually I think I really might be.'

'Nate...'

He moved again, one hand lifting to rest at my waist as he stepped closer.

'Sophia, I—'

The bell on the back of the door jangled loudly and we both jumped, moving apart quickly, me stumbling as I caught the heel of my boot in the hem of my long skirt. Nate's arm was back around me, steadying me quickly as I simultaneously tried to act normal for the small group of customers now entering the shop.

The next couple of hours passed in a haze of activity as the fayre got into full swing and Flora's shop did brisk business. There was little time to think over the moment that Nate and I had had. I mean, I think it was a moment. It felt like one, but then it had been a heck of a long time since I'd had anything like that, so maybe I'd been mistaken.

At half past nine, I waved the last customers out of the shop, turned the sign to closed and locked the door. Underneath I tacked the sign that Flora had made, announcing the shop would be opening a little later, at ten, tomorrow morning, which gave her and George time to get back from their night away. Leaning against the door for a moment, I let out a sigh. Nate came over from where he'd been tidying the counter of the remains of the gift wrapping supplies, ensuring we left it perfect for when Flora returned. His eyes fixed onto mine and I knew that, however out of practice I was, I hadn't imagined anything.

'You look exhausted.' His words were soft, brow creasing in concern.

'I'm fine,' I said, knowing my face and body probably told another tale. 'But I am glad you were here. I had no idea we'd be quite so busy. Thank you for helping. I don't know what I'd have done without you.'

Nate reached around me, pulling the blind down to cover the glass of the door. 'I'm glad I was here.' His body stayed close. 'Truth is, I don't know what I'd have done without you the entire time I've been here. I thought I knew what I did and didn't want from this break but then I met you and it kind of threw a spanner into the entire works.'

23

I couldn't remember the last time I'd felt like this. I knew it was complicated for all the reasons I'd listed to Flora but right now, stood here with Nate, it didn't seem complicated at all. I didn't reply but closed the final distance between us and leant my head on his chest. Nate's arms wrapped around me and for the first time in a very long time, I felt wanted and safe. Valued for who I was – not for who people thought I was, or what they thought knowing me might be able to do for them. Of course, I would tell Nate the truth, but somehow, I didn't think it would matter to him. I just had to find the right moment. But right now, all I wanted was to feel his arms around me.

I felt him shift and I lifted my head.

'I think we need to get you off your feet.'

'It's fine.'

'OK. Then I'm knackered and need to sit down. I was just trying to couch it in a way that made me look less of a wimp.'

I laughed, stepping back, sorry to feel his arms drop away but thrilled as he caught my hand before I could leave his touch entirely. 'You're not a wimp. Shop work isn't as easy as it looks, is it?'

'Definitely not,' he said, letting go of my hand as I checked that all was as it should be for Flora's return, scribbling a note of the takings and tucking it under the charity box for her to see in the morning. We stepped out into the night air, and I shivered. The Victoriana dress I was wearing may have had plenty of layers, but none of them were doing much to keep me warm against the cold night.

'Here,' Nate made to slip the longline coat off and hand it to me but I stopped him.

'It's all right. It's not like we're going far and you're more likely to freeze than me. I'm accustomed to the temperatures.'

'That's true but generally you have more layers on.'

'You'd be surprised at how many there are going on under here!'

He grinned. 'I always was keen on history. I'm happy for you to enlighten me on that aspect of it.'

I gave him a playful prod in the chest. 'Don't think that smile is going to get you anywhere.' Although in truth, right now, it'd have taken him pretty much anywhere he wanted to go.

'I wasn't. You just make me smile.'

'And those smooth lines aren't going to work on me either.'

He laughed, pulling me close to him.

'I'm not sure I've ever used a line in my life.'

'Now that I don't believe.'

Actually, I did. He really didn't seem the type and frankly, the way he looked, I'd guess that lines weren't terribly necessary.

'It's true,' he said, curving a finger under my chin. 'Besides, I'd never want to use a line on you, even if I could. I've had more than enough of trying to say the right thing. I love that you just say what you think and let me be the same. I think the first thing I noticed about you, once I'd recovered from the fact there was an extremely hot woman in my bathroom aiming a toilet brush at me, was how honest you are.'

'I'm surprised that appealed.'

'Admittedly, it was a little more honesty than I'd been expecting, but on the other hand I realised that for the first time in years, I knew exactly where I stood with someone. Even if it that somewhere felt like it was in the middle of a massive cow pat right at that moment. But still.' He looked down, meeting my eyes. 'I think I'm in big trouble here.'

I knew exactly what he meant.

'And how do you feel about that?'

'Pretty damn good, actually.' His mouth grazed my temple as he spoke and I shivered again as the words whispered softly into my ear, but this time it was nothing to do with the cold.

'You're cold. We should—'

I didn't know what he was going to say and didn't care. All I wanted was Nate and, pressing myself closer, I tilted my face so that my lips caught his. Instantly, his arms tightened around me as his lips pressed down on mine, opening gently, inquisitively, as we staggered slightly against the window of the shop. His body shifted as he hands moved up, cradling my face as the kiss deepened. I forgot where I was, that I was kissing a man I didn't actually know all that well in the street for everyone to see. I forgot that I'd been brought up to look upon such behaviour as common and that my mother, had she seen it, would have been the one in need of the smelling salts. None of that occurred to me. None of that mattered. All I thought of, all I could feel, was Nate.

'So I guess you were looking for something after all?' The voice cut into the moment and sliced it apart.

Nate lifted his head, resting it momentarily against mine as a small sigh escaped. Both of us recognised the voice, and neither of us had missed the tone that accompanied the words. He turned towards Corinne. She was standing a few feet from us, swaying slightly. The man who'd followed her into the shop earlier was on the pavement a little way back talking into his phone intently, his attention on something other than Corinne, which probably explained some of her annoyance. The rest of it was firmly centred on us.

Nate met her eyes but didn't reply. His arms remained around me, and his look was even, his body language confident. He had no reason to explain himself to her, and clearly no intention of doing so. I fell a little bit more under his spell.

Corinne shifted her weight, glancing back at her date with irritation. 'Are you going to be on that phone all night?'

He waved a hand and turned away, continuing the conversation. Corinne narrowed her eyes momentarily before looking back at me.

'I guess he's got a thing for older women. Some men get off on all those wrinkles and saggy bits.' I felt Nate tense against me. She gave her already hoisted breasts another hoik so that they were in danger of escaping the bar wench's outfit altogether.

'I guess so,' I said casually, giving a one shouldered, unconcerned shrug. 'Lucky me.' Nate's embrace tightened.

Corinne's mouth dropped open a little and I met her fiery gaze with my own cool one. Turns out certain experiences at a private girls' school could prove useful later in life after all. I'd suffered my share of bitchiness and had found, after some trial and error, that not rising to the bait was one of the most effective ways of dealing with the comments.

'Sorry, Babes.' The man approached her, slipping his arm round her waist, his eyes resting on her boosted cleavage.

'Finally!' she snapped.

'I know. Come on, let's get back and try that jewellery on

you...' His lecherous gaze indicated that might be the only thing she would be wearing. Corinne softened a little in the light of the obvious adoration.

'Fine. But no more phone calls or I'm going home. Alone.'

He made a show of putting his phone in his pocket and pulled Corinne closer to him. 'Promise.'

She tossed her hair, her eyes on Nate rather than the man beside her.

'Have a nice evening,' she said, the tone implying all hopes were for exactly the opposite.

Nate nodded at them both before returning his attention to me. 'Come on, you're freezing,' he said, wrapping his long line jacket round me despite the fact he was still in it. I snuggled in against him, the feeling of care and attention unusual. It was a simple gesture but it meant such a lot and I couldn't remember the last time I'd felt that way. Like I was something special. Something, or rather someone, who was worth taking the time to care for.

From the corner of my eye, I saw Corinne give a parting glare as we turned towards my door and I fished in a pocket for my key.

'I'm sorry about that,' Nate said as we closed the door on the cold outside. 'I should have been more wary.'

'Oh, don't worry about it. She's never liked me anyway. Scared off a previous waitress apparently too. You showing up with all your hotness just made it worse,' I winked at him. 'But I can handle Corinne,' I said, giving a little shiver as the warmth of my cosy flat began to permeate into my bones.

'I have no doubt of that,' Nate replied, pulling me back against him gently. His warmth, plus the faint lingering smell of his aftershave all wrapped up in the scent that was Nate caused another shiver, but this one was for an entirely different reason.

'You're still cold.'

'No.' I looked up at him and saw the concern in the bright blue eyes. 'Really, I'm not.'

He gave me a disbelieving look that was half smile, half frown and entirely sexy.

'I'm not.' I bumped against him gently.

'Well, I think I still need to try and keep you warm.' The frown disappeared and the smile widened. 'Just in case.'

'Always better to be safe than sorry.'

'That's what they say.'

I couldn't get any closer to him now and still it wasn't enough. Despite the layers of Victorian style clothing, there was no denying Nate was of a similar opinion. At least, parts of him were, and when I looked up into his face, the darkening heat of his eyes confirmed his mind was on the same track.

'I have no idea what I'm doing but, with you, somehow it feels right.'

'I know what you mean,' I said, taking a step back and reaching up to remove the hat from his head, tossing it onto the chair. 'I've no idea either but, at this point, I don't really care because I don't think anything has ever felt so right.' I pushed the coat from his broad shoulders as I said this, and he wriggled, helping it slide down his arms. It landed in a puddle behind him and I was already working at the buttons on his waistcoat. My fingers, in their haste, struggled with the small fastenings and Nate's large, warm hands took over, ensuring a quicker progress. I didn't take any chances with the shirt buttons and instead pulled the fabric. Buttons pinged in various directions.

'I'll sew them back on tomorrow,' I breathed as Nate smiled down at me, his hands around my waist, the long fingers working at the button of my skirt. Of course, I'd first have to learn how to sew a button on but the chest beneath the fabric was worth whatever effort it took. Smooth, tanned and broad, I slid the palms of my hands across it, feeling its strength beneath my touch as I linked my fingers behind his neck and his mouth met mine at the same time the heavy skirt fell to the floor. Without parting our lips, Nate pushed my fitted jacket I'd now unhooked back over my shoulders and began to work on the lacing of the corset beneath.

'What the hell?' he growled, pulling away, his voice thick with a desperation that made my knees feel weaker than they already were. His hands gently but firmly turned me round so that he could see the problem. Within a couple of moments, he'd loosened the ties and I was able to wriggle out. Not the most elegant of moves, but at this point both of us were beyond caring, as the remainder of our clothes tumbled to the floor, and we tumbled to the sofa.

At some point, we'd made our way to the bedroom, and when I woke late the next day, it was to the unfamiliar feeling of a man's arms around me, his hard body pressed against mine under the warmth of the duvet. I turned my head as far as I could but couldn't see his face. For some reason, I wanted to. Needed to. This was all a new experience. For one thing, I'd never slept with a man on a first date – and I wasn't even sure that Nate helping me out in the shop qualified as a date at all. But I'd known plenty of people who had. And I'd listened to them lament the throes of passion that had led them into it. But I wasn't lamenting anything. My body ached in a way it never had before and a happiness, a peace, flowed through me in an entirely new manner. All I could hope was that Nate felt the same way.

'Good morning.' The words were deep and raspy with an early morning huskiness that did nothing to quell the flames already flickering in my stomach.

I shuffled round so that I could face him.

'Good morning.'

His hand lazily stroked up my thigh and the smile on his face matched the sentiment.

'You OK?'

'Um-hmm,' I nodded, pushing my fingers gently back through his hair.

Suddenly he moved, scooping me underneath him as he propped himself up on an elbow, and now rested above me. There was no need for any more words as he lowered himself enough to begin tracing the line of my shoulder with soft, butterfly light kisses. I felt my body respond as his did to mine. A small, sensuous moan reached my ears and I realised it had come from me. Something else new then. Nate pulled back and gave me that lazy smile again before reaching back for the duvet and pulling it up over both of us as his free hand moved lower.

* * *

'So, I'll see you later?' Nate asked as he leant against the door jamb, looking far too attractive for a man I was having to force out of my flat when what I really wanted to do was drag him back in.

'Definitely,' I replied, standing on tiptoes to plant a kiss on his smiling mouth.

'Good,' he checked his watch. 'I'd better go and pick up Bryan from Ned and Carrie, take him for a walk and then get back to the book. I'll come and meet you after your shift though.'

'You don't need to do that.'

His arm pulled me close. 'I know. But I want to. I really, really want to.' The last words were muffled as his head dipped and his lips skimmed the curve of my neck.

'You'd better go or I'll have no job to be met from.'

Nate made a noise that mixed complaint with regret, but he took the hint.

'I'll see you later,' he said, stealing one last kiss before turning and jogging down the stairs and out the front door onto the street, pulling the door closed behind him.

* * *

The look on Eloise's face told me she'd already heard the news about Nate and me.

'About bloody time too,' was her greeting as she gave me a hug and helped me tie my apron before turning me back to face her. 'So?'

'So, what?' I asked.

She gave me a look and I grinned. I couldn't help it.

'That,' she said, pointing at my face, 'just answered my question.'

'I don't know what you mean,' I said, aware that there was a still a big smile plastered over my face and had been for the majority of the weekend.

Eloise looked at me, laughed and moved to the door to greet our first customers.

* * *

'You know he's married.' Corinne had been late starting her shift. The look on Ned's face suggested she was trying his good nature but, for now, she was here and apparently eager to burst any bubble I may have been occupying.

'I'm sorry?' I said, turning briefly.

'Nate. You know he's married, right? I saw some pictures of his wife online. She's absolutely stunning.' Her glance flitted over me and the rest of her opinion, although unvoiced, was clear. I knew I shouldn't reply. Should let her words just wash over me, but the dig that I was seeing a married man had lodged in like a barb. I'd been on the receiving end of that situation on plenty of occasions so the accusation that I was now doing the same thing rankled.

'He's separated, Corinne. And getting a divorce. His ex-wife is already with someone else.' I turned to face her. 'And funny that whole situation didn't seem to bother you when you were desperate for his attention.'

'I didn't know he was married.'

I shook my head. 'Corinne. The whole village knew Nate's situation before the poor man even got here and you were no exception. Table three is calling you.' I nodded in the direction of her customers, turned on my heel and walked back to serve one of my own, trying not to let her comments permeate. I'd managed it before and I would do so again. Nate was single. We'd sat at his breakfast bar discussing our respective divorce proceedings so I knew it was certainly happening, not to mention the small matter of his ex already living with another man. Corinne was just trying to put the knife in because, for once, she hadn't got what she wanted.

I did my best to put it out of my mind, and continued with my shift. The place was busy and Carrie and Ned had now put the Christmas tree up, adding to the festive atmosphere and lending the restaurant a cosy feel. During a brief lull, I snapped a couple of pictures and uploaded one to my Instagram account. I avoided detailing the location and only part of the tree could be seen, but Carrie had done such a wonderful job decorating it, it seemed a shame not to share it in some way. Slipping the phone back in my pocket, I moved back and tidied the booking area before heading over to one of my tables to see if they could be tempted by some of Ned's famous puddings.

* * *

The wind coming in off the sea whipped my hair across my face, and the invisible droplets of lifted surf stung my skin as I waited for Nate outside the restaurant. Eloise and Bob had offered to wait with me but I'd sent them home to the warm. I knew Nate wouldn't be long and had probably just got caught up with his book.

Twenty minutes later I was beginning to feel less sure as tiny flakes of snow began to flutter down, catching on the bottle green of my wool coat. They lasted a moment, bright and white against the background before soaking in and disappearing. Pulling my phone from my bag, I checked the screen. No missed calls or unread messages. As I'd begun to lose feeling in my feet, I rang Nate. If he'd just got caught up and was now walking along the beach, I didn't want to start heading to Holly's place through the village and risk us missing each other. The number connected and rang. It carried on ringing until finally it rolled over to voice-mail. I hung up without leaving a message. The surf was roaring and if he was walking that way, it wouldn't surprise me if he hadn't heard the phone ring. I decided to head down towards his place and chose the beach walk. Bryan would have a good chance for a run around if Nate came that way, so it made sense he would choose that route.

Bracing myself against the wind and the now heavier falling snow, I walked fast towards the Art Deco place at the end of the beach, both enjoying and also being battered by the wild weather. If he'd forgotten about meeting me altogether, Nate better at least have the kettle on.

I rang the bell. Nothing. I rang again and this time, after a few moments, saw movement. The door opened and Nate stood there staring at me. The action was mutual. This was a completely different man from the one who'd left my flat earlier that day, and I hadn't seen him look this stressed since our first inauspicious meeting over the toilet brush.

'Hi,' I said when it became clear he wasn't going to speak first.

He ran a hand back through the dark, rumpled hair. 'Oh... er, hi.' Behind him, Bryan scooted round the corner, sliding like a car on ice, before regaining control and powering towards me. I bent and picked him up, letting his warmth thaw me a little as I remained on the doorstep, still not having been invited in. It was just as well one of the residents was giving out some warmth as there was definitely none coming from the little dog's temporary master.

'I thought you were going to meet me after work?' I said, my tone free of recrimination but even I could hear the sense of insecurity in it. Had I got this wrong? Was this not how it worked? I'd taken his words at face value, but was that what people said, whether they meant it or not, in order to save any awkwardness after a one night stand?

'Oh... right. Yeah. I... sorry. I forgot.'

I was still standing on the doorstep and feeling more and more awkward by the moment. Placing Bryan back down inside the house, I looked up at Nate. Something was off. A few hours ago he hadn't been able to keep his hands off me. It had been him that had suggested meeting up again, and the tone he'd used suggested he definitely didn't mean for a game of scrabble. Behind him I heard the unmistakeable sound of high heels clip clopping on the floorboards. Moments later, the owner of them came to stand beside Nate and looked at me, a mixture of curiosity and something else I couldn't quite place on her face. Her arm moved casually and rested on Nate's waistband. Her perfect face matched the toned body poured into a tight, Hermès-style bandage dress. It was a fake, I could tell – but a good one.

Somewhere in the back of my mind, I was glad that at least some of the skills from my previous life hadn't been entirely lost. The front of my mind, however, was more focused on what she was doing there. The pieces were slowly falling into place. And now, as the long, fingers with their elegant French manicure curved round Nate's waist, it was obvious what that expression I hadn't initially been able to name was.

'I'm Serena McKinley.'

It was possession.

24

I felt sick. And stupid. Hadn't I learned anything from the many years I'd been married to a cheat and liar? Apparently not. Despite all that experience, here I was again, being made a fool of by a man. And the worst of it was, I'd believed him. I'd believed the broken-hearted, used and abused person he'd pretended to be. Swallowed it whole like a creamy oyster. But now that oyster appeared to have been off and was making me feel like I wanted to throw up, preferably all over Nate McKinley's very expensive shoes.

'Hi.' I forced out in as casual manner as I could muster. I used to be good at the faking-it, playing-it-cool thing, but it felt awkward now and I was pretty sure she wasn't buying it. As she sidled closer to Nate, I knew for sure. She definitely wasn't buying it.

'This is Sophia,' Nate said, his voice sounding off and strained. 'She's...'

'The cleaner,' I finished for him. Not because I wanted to put him out of any misery. He could swim naked in shark infested waters for all I cared. My only aim now was to extricate myself from the situation as soon as possible.

'Oh, right.' Serena smiled, but it didn't reach her eyes. The beautiful make-up, which looked like it must have taken an age to apply, enhanced light brown eyes that almost shimmered with cold.

'I was just checking if Nate needed any supplies or anything. Holly and Gabe asked me to make sure the fridge was stocked at all times.' I gave what I hoped was a friendly, but detached smile. She wasn't really paying that much attention to me as I spoke, though, so I needn't have bothered.

'Oh, great. I'm vegan, so now I'm here we'll probably have to throw out anything that isn't suitable.'

I swallowed, picturing Nate's eyes practically rolling back in his head with pleasure the last time he'd had a steak at the restaurant and thinking of the couple of meals I knew were already in the fridge that I'd spent time, and Holly's money on, that were now apparently to be tossed away.

'Well, if they're going to go to waste, I can just take them back.'

'That's fine. I'll give you a list of dinners I want and you can swap them when you deliver those.'

I'm sorry. Did I miss the bit where I turned into Deliveroo?

'It's not really that sort of arrangement, Serena. Sophia's just dropped some food off from time to time. Most of the time I cook myself, now.'

'Oh. Well, we can eat out then I guess. Assuming there are some decent places round here. It didn't look that promising.'

I tried not to bristle at her dismissal of a village I loved and that she can have only seen for about ten minutes.

'Well, I'd better be going.'

Nate looked pained but I did my best to ignore it. Clearly his marriage wasn't as over as he'd told everyone, and I'd got caught in the middle of it. Typical. The first time in nearly two years I meet someone I actually like and, moreover, let something happen with him, it turns round and slaps me in the face.

Serena looked up from inspecting her nails and tilted her head.

'Do I know you?'

How on earth could this woman possibly know me? She lived thousands of miles away. I'd travelled to Australia in the past a couple of times on holiday but I highly doubted any passing contact, however remote the possibility, would have left any remembrance. Had I looked as good as Nate, the possibility might have been higher.

'No.'

'You look kind of familiar.' She was peering at me now and I shifted my weight under the scrutiny.

'I probably just have one of those faces.' I was pretty sure I didn't but I wasn't sure what else to say. 'OK then. I hope you have a nice trip. I'll be back to clean later in the week but you can just let me know when you're going to be out so I don't disturb—'

'Oh my God!' Her exclamation made both Nate and I jump. Serena's eyes were wide. 'It's you. You're Lady Sophia Hunting-don-Jones!'

'I think you've got me mixed up with someone else,' I said, desperately trying to keep any quiver out of my voice.

'No, I haven't.' She leant forward and I took a step back. 'It's definitely you. I read all the society stuff and it's been quite the mystery where you'd gone apparently when you walked out on your husband, although I don't blame you. Everyone knew he was cheating on you,' she added in a gossipy tone. 'Oh my God! What are you doing here? And why the hell are you calling your-self a cleaner?'

'She is the cleaner,' Nate stated, confusion crumpling his brow.

'I really have to go now.' I turned away, my stomach churning. I'd kept away from the media, the gossip, the people who'd hurt me, for over eighteen months without a problem, and now someone who lived thousands of miles away, who, as far as I knew, wasn't even supposed to be here, had the power to pull down the world I'd created. A world I was happy in – gorgeous Australian mishaps aside.

'Is it true?' Nate's hand on my arm stopped me.

'You should go back in, it's cold.' He was dressed in a t-shirt and jeans, without his customary thick jumper and, judging by the tiny dress his wife was wearing, Holly and Gabe's heating bill had suddenly taken a hike.

'Is it true?' he asked again.

I glanced over his shoulder. Serena was watching us. Suspicion clouded her eyes. 'Did you lie about who you were?' he pushed on.

'No,' I snapped. 'And I have no need to explain myself to you anyway.'

'What's going on here?' Serena narrowed her eyes. 'Nate? Are you sleeping with her?'

'Don't start on me, Serena. I'm really not in the mood.'

'You cheated on me!' she screeched. There was something in her tone that suggested the thought he would even consider doing this was more astonishing than the actual situation.

'I didn't cheat on you, Serena,' Nate snapped, whirling round on her. 'We were separated and getting a divorce. Remember that whole thing about you leaving me to go and live with your tennis coach?' A muscle flickered in his jaw as he ground the words out.

'Looks like you didn't waste much time being alone, though?' she snapped back.

He shook his head. 'I don't need to explain myself to you. I don't even know why you're here!' The snow of earlier had begun to fall more heavily now and was dampening his hair and soaking through his t-shirt, but he didn't seem to notice.

'I thought you'd be pleased to see me! I thought we could try to rebuild our marriage but I didn't realise you were already sleeping with your cleaner!' She practically spat the word out as she glared at me.

'Do you know what, Serena? It's actually been pretty relaxing to be away from you and all your drama. I didn't realise quite how bloody exhausting being married to you was until I got the chance to put some space between us.'

'From the sounds of it, space has been the last thing you've had.'

Nate let his head fall back for a moment, turning his face to the sky, the snowflakes landing softly before melting. From the waves of tension still radiating out from his body, they might be cooling his skin but they were doing nothing to cool the anger wound tight within him.

'Nate...' Her voice had softened now as she reached out. 'Come back inside. Let's talk about things. I made a mistake. Maybe we both did.'

Nate looked back down, his gaze fixing on me. 'Maybe we did.' The warmth his eyes had once held was gone and now they were as cold as the ice crystals that had settled on his long lashes. With that, he let Serena encourage him back inside and with one last cold look, she closed the door.

For a moment I just wanted to sit. To slump down on the cold, wet path. I already felt numb inside, so what would it matter if the rest of me froze too? Instead I forced myself to turn round and walk back towards the village and the comfort of my cosy flat. There I could lock the door and shut out Serena's glare, and

Nate's cold accusatory look. I never lied to him. Admittedly, I hadn't told him who I was, but I'd been planning to for the last couple of weeks. It wasn't really the sort of thing you just blurted out and I knew part of it was me not wanting to bring it up because that was the old me, and Nate and I were part of the 'new' me. Not that there was any Nate and I. Not now. I knew now I'd been stupid to think there ever would be. Women like Serena always got their way, however smart the man was. When it came to beauty and wiles like that, they didn't stand a chance. Nate McKinley might have thought his marriage was over and might have even been reconciled to it – but it appeared Serena had other ideas and I already knew, just as I was sure Nate did, that what Serena wanted, Serena got. And right now, it appeared she wanted her husband back.

I powered on back through the village, the snow soaking through my shoes, my hair now plastered to my head. As I passed Flora's shop, she waved at me through the window. I gave a brief wave in return but right now I just wanted to get inside and shut myself away from everyone. This morning the world had seemed bright and full of promise but now that had all seeped away. Why on earth had I let myself fall for Nate? Because I knew now that was exactly what I'd done, no matter how many times I tried to deny it to myself on my walk home. I'd had no intention of developing any sort of feelings for Nate, let alone love, and our first meeting had reassured me that wasn't something I had any need to worry about. But, as barriers were lowered on both sides, something had changed. Somewhere along the way my heart had decided to take matters into its own hands and, without any rational consultation with my brain, had decided to leap in with both feet. And while, initially, that hadn't actually looked like the disaster it could have been, the firm ground I'd landed on turned out to be quicksand, and I was now scrabbling to pull myself out before my heart became irrevocably damaged. Although, from the tight, painful feeling in my chest, it had already suffered far more injury than I'd anticipated.

Inside the shop, Flora was moving towards the door, flapping at me to wait. Pulling the door open, she beckoned me in.

'I can't today, Flora. I really need to get home.'

She studied me for a moment. 'You know already.'

I shook my head, pushing a stray, damp lock of hair back behind my ear. 'About Nate? Yes. I had the pleasure of meeting his ex-wife. Or apparently not so ex-wife. So yes, I know. Hence I just want to get inside, not to mention I'm soaked.'

She pulled me in. 'I can see that. Come in here a moment.' I didn't have the energy to protest any further. 'Nate's ex is here?'

'Yes.'

'But I thought...' she trailed off. I knew what she'd thought. She'd seen him leave my flat earlier this morning for a start.

'Yes, I thought so too,' I shrugged.

She gave a brief shake of her head. 'We'll come back to him in a minute.'

'There's nothing to come back to, Flora. Honestly. I'd rather just forget about it all.'

Flora gave me a look. 'Somehow I don't think that's going to be as easy as it sounds.'

I shrugged. 'It was just a couple of days. How hard can it be?' I tried to smile but the action felt alien and from the look on my friend's face, it didn't look much better from the outside. 'Anyway, what did you mean, what should I know?'

The sympathetic look on Flora's face caused my insides to twist into even more knots, which, considering how my day was already going, took some doing, but my stomach still managed it. She took my hand and led me over to the counter. From underneath she took a tablet and woke it up. The page displayed a website of a popular gossip magazine and right in the middle of it, splashed in big letters were the words 'Mystery Influencer Unveiled!'

Underneath was a picture of my Instagram feed, including the one I'd taken earlier today of Carrie's Christmas tree. And next to that was a shot of me in my apron, at work, clearly with no idea I was being photographed. With all the shit that was hitting the fan today, it would definitely have been a good idea to have been prepared with some make-up but, by the time Nate had left, I'd barely had time to shower and get dressed in order not to be late. Had I known someone was planning to sneak pictures which would then be spread over the internet, not to mention meet Nate's super hot ex, I might have made a different choice...

Sophia Jones, an unassuming waitress and cleaner from the small village of Wishington Bay on the south-west coast of England has been today, thanks to a secret source, unveiled as the mystery influencer behind the cleaning blog that's becoming a firm favourite among followers. Ms Jones has refused to reply to any of our attempts to contact her in order to explain why she wanted her blog persona to remain a secret but, having seen other similar blogs succeed and bring success to their owners, we can't imagine she'll be anything but grateful! Watch this space for more news.

Grateful? *Grateful*?! There were a lot of things I was feeling right now and not one of them was grateful. I was also pretty sure who their anonymous source was, but that was the least of my worries right now.

'Are you OK, lovely?'

I looked up from the screen and met Flora's eyes. 'I'm fine.' I was every emotion other than fine, but it seemed like the right thing to say. A very British thing to say and, had my mother ever been proud of me, she might have been so now for not collapsing into a puddle behind the shop counter.

'You don't look fine.'

I could believe that.

'Can I ask something?' she asked, her voice soft.

I nodded.

'Why have you been trying to keep it all a secret? Everyone seems so concerned about Likes and popularity these days. Why not you?'

I opened my mouth to reply but was stopped by the door flying open and Corinne bursting into the shop.

25

'Oh my God! You're a Lady?' She let out a laugh that was nothing but cold amusement. 'No wonder you didn't want anyone to know about your stupid Insta account! Did Nate know he had aristocracy cleaning his toilet?' Her laugh was high-pitched and annoying as a word that began with a capital F. 'I guess we should have all been bowing in front of you at the restaurant.'

'As a female, you should curtsey. Not that you'd know anything about manners,' Flora lashed out at Corinne, who for a moment looked stunned at this kindly, elegant lady putting her in her place. 'And I assume it was you who contacted this magazine?'

Corinne gave a smug smile. 'It was. And why shouldn't I? Got paid a nice bonus for it too. Some of us weren't born with a silver spoon in our mouths and have to earn our own money.'

'Oh, don't talk such rubbish. Your parents have spoiled you rotten from the day you arrived on this earth so don't act all hard done by,' Flora snapped back. I was still numb and although words screamed and raced in my head, nothing seemed inclined to make its way out.

Corinne flashed her a dirty look which Flora gave right back.

'I guess your little fling with Nate is well and truly over now. Even if his wife wasn't back, he had that big thing about being honest, and I guess finding out you've been lying to him, actually to the whole village, hasn't gone down well.'

I met the cold glare.

'Yeah, Serena and I have become really good Facebook friends after I found her page,' Corinne continued. 'We've got so much in common.'

That I didn't doubt.

'And then, of course, when I told her Nate was obviously miserable without her, she told me the thing with the tennis guy wasn't working out anyway so I suggested she come over and surprise him. I'm sure he's thrilled!'

He didn't look thrilled but then he'd looked pretty thunderous at me too, so I wasn't really in much of a position to talk.

'She messaged me after you'd been to the house. He's livid with you, by the way. But, of course, we both thought it was hilarious that you're supposed to be this super rich aristo type and there you are with a bog brush in your hand half the time. Oh my God! I mean, I can't even!'

'I think it's time you left,' Flora said.

'I'm not done yet.'

'Oh, you're done. You're more than done,' Flora returned in a voice that didn't offer space for argument. 'And I want you off my premises right now. Also, you're barred.' She hustled Corinne out of the door and shut it firmly behind her before looking back at me.

'You OK?'

I nodded automatically. 'I need to go home now.'

'Of course, love.' She rested her hand on the catch. 'Is it true?' Her voice was soft.

Again, I nodded. There was no point denying anything now. 'Yes. I'm sorry I didn't tell you before and I'm sure you have questions, which I promise I'll answer, but right now I—'

'You don't need to explain anything to me, love,' Flora said as she pulled me into a gentle hug. 'You're a wonderful person and that's the friend I love. It doesn't matter to me what your name, or your title is. I'm sure you have your reasons to have kept it to yourself, but they're your reasons and you should only explain them if you want to. Remember that.'

'Thanks,' I said, feeling the tears swim in my eyes but, with years of training behind me, I refused to let them fall in public.

She patted my hand, opened the door, and I quickly made my way to my front door, unlocked it, and bolted it behind me before dropping my bag and pelting up the stairs, barely making it to the bathroom before I threw up.

I woke to the unfamiliar sound of voices outside my flat. It usually took a while for the village to rise from slumber in the winter, and the peacefulness was something I loved about the place, having spent a great deal of time over the years in London. Shoving the covers back, I shuffled my feet into cosy slippers and moved across to the window. Peering cautiously through a gap in the curtains, I looked down to the street. Quickly I took a step back as my legs suddenly weakened. Putting my hand out blindly behind me, I felt for the end of the bed before sinking down on to it. The voices continued outside, but they were being drowned out by the clanging that now reverberated in my brain. This couldn't be happening. Not now. I'd worked so hard on building a new life. A life away from everything that had made me unhappy before and now all that had come rushing back, careering into the present and shattering the calm, happy existence I so loved.

'Lady Sophia! Lady Sophia!' The shouts permeated my thoughts and I could hear the front door being thumped and banged. I put my hands up to my ears, trying to shut it out. Perhaps, if I closed my eyes and pretended it wasn't happening, I could transport myself back into the better world I'd found. It didn't work. Of course, it didn't. I wasn't bloody Dorothy trying to get home from Oz, and no matter what I'd tried to pretend, I was Lady Sophia Huntingdon-Jones and it appeared that no one was going to let me forget that.

I headed into the bathroom and proceeded with my usual routine, some part of my brain craving normality, before I made my way into the kitchen. My stomach churned at the thought of food, so I fished out a ginger and lemon teabag and dropped it in a cup while I flicked the kettle on to boil with the other hand. Having got my drink, I took it through to the living room and sat on the sofa. Part of my mind was spinning wildly, but another part of me felt numb and like I was moving through thick, cold custard. Raised voices caught my attention, bringing me out of my fog. I stepped to the window, careful to keep myself back enough to still be out of sight to the telephoto lenses attached to the gutter press circling below. Flora was out there, waving her arms and yelling at the group of them now gathered outside the frontage of her shop.

A fresh wave of sickness and guilt rolled over me. The mob were completely blocking the door of her shop, enough to put off all but the most determined visitors, while window shoppers didn't have a hope of getting through. This was why I should have stayed in a city. I'd been foolish to think that I could just leave that life behind forever. There was always going to be someone who'd find a way to suck me back in. I'd been so careful. Even my ex-husband didn't know where I lived – my solicitors had been given strict instructions that neither he, nor anyone else, was to be told. Obviously I'd had to do all the legal stuff in my original name and, as much as I'd been trying to distance myself from it, in that instance, it had proved useful. The name of Huntingdon-Jones was old, and well known – a fact I knew to my cost – it had been one of the most attractive things about me, as far as my ex-husband had been concerned. I'd insisted on keeping it, the one thing I refused to concede. My father was no longer around but I was determined to hold on to his name. I'd tacked Jeremy's surname on the end of mine when we married but inevitably it sometimes got omitted in the interest of space in the press. My name carried weight, so what I requested, including utmost privacy and my mail to be addressed using my adjusted name, was immediately adhered to. No, this leak had come from the village. Serena had recognised me – how, I still hadn't worked out – but that was a worry for a different day, and her new best friend, Corinne, had done the rest. And, by the looks of it, Flora and her business were paying the price. I knew I should ring her. Try to apologise. Offer to somehow compensate her for any business she lost because of this, but right now there was one thing I knew I needed to do, and I couldn't put it off any more. Picking up my phone, I switched it on and waited for it do its thing. Once it had, I knew the situation was even worse than I'd imagined. Notifications poured in, beeps and pings, one after the other, lighting up my phone as bright as the Christmas lights I'd forgotten to turn off last night before falling into bed, upset and mentally exhausted, dreading the following day. But that day was now here, and as I looked down at the screen, I wasn't entirely sure how to proceed with it.

I dropped the phone as it rang, the sound startling me out of my bad dream-like state. The number wasn't one I recognised, and I immediately swiped 'decline'. No sooner had I done that, it rang again, this time with a different but again unrecognised number. Decline. Ring. Decline. Ring. Decline, decline, decline. According to my log, there were already more voicemails than my inbox could hold and a plethora of texts. Clearly Corinne had not only been free with my real name and address, but also my telephone number. I switched the phone to silent, deleted the voicemails wholesale, and did the same with the texts. Then I took a deep inhale and opened the internet.

Lady of the Loo!

Lady HJ Reduced to Cleaning Toilets!

Aristo's Fall From Grace

From Being Waited On Hand and Foot to Becoming the Waitress!

Lady Sophia – Cleaning Loos and Finding Comfort in the Arms of a Married Man.

On and on they went, all in the same vein. 'Inside sources' and someone 'close to Lady Sophia' gave all manner of information, the majority of it incorrect. I'd long since learned that such sources were often just the muck-rakers themselves, making up gossip to help sell their rags and boost their website hits. Not that it made it any easier. People believed it, and that was all they cared about. Facts were way down the list of things that such people held any concern for.

The whoop-whoop of a siren outside caught my attention. I dropped the phone and returned to my stealthy spot by the window. A police car had now pulled up outside and two officers got out, placing their hats on their head as they did so. The gaggle of press glanced towards them then back towards the windows of my flat as Flora bustled her way through to get to the policemen. I stood in the shadows and watched as she spoke to them, her arms flailing about as she did so. A tear crept down one cheek. Flora had been so kind to me, and this was how I repaid her. Even if I hadn't intended it, I'd always known it was a possibility and now she was paying the price. One of the policemen stayed with Flora as the older one moved towards the assortment of press. I couldn't hear exactly what he said but guessed he was asking them to move on. A car was now sitting in the narrow road, trying to get past the group that took up half of it as well as the pavement. It gave a beep and received a couple of rude hand gestures in reply. I recognised the car as belonging to a lovely couple who lived on the edge of the village as you walked up to it from Holly and Gabe's place. They owned the beautiful garden Nate and I had walked past and we'd had many a pleasant chat when I'd seen them working away in it. They didn't deserve that kind of treatment any more than Flora did. The policeman was doing his best, but the paparazzi weren't in any mood to listen to reason. I wasn't sure people like that ever were. They had their eye on the prize. And that prize was me.

Fine. If that's what they wanted, that's what they'd get. This village had been kind to me. I knew now my life here was over but the time I'd spent in this little community had helped me heal in more ways than I ever realised I needed. They didn't deserve this, and it was going to stop. I was going to make it stop.

26

Heading back into the bathroom, I yanked the shower pull switch on with a little more force than was probably necessary and stripped off my nightclothes as the water warmed. Fresh and clean, I quickly dried my hair and left it loose. Next, I pulled on jeans and a cosy Liberty sweatshirt before sitting down at the tiny dressing table. Since I'd moved here, I no longer wore the 'full face' I'd done day in, day out in my previous life. It never did to be caught without your make-up, and the thought of sitting around in jogging bottoms would have had my mother clutching her heart. My ex-husband definitely wouldn't have approved either – assuming he even noticed my presence, which in itself was pretty hit and miss. As strange as it seemed, curling up in front of the television or with a book in cosy lounge pants had been yet another revelation in my new life. But right now, I had to deal with fallout from my old life and, for that, I needed a bit of armour. I unzipped my make-up bag and went to work.

I sat back and studied myself for a moment. Better. I still looked like me, rather than who I'd had to be back then, but the magic of make-up had hidden the dark circles I'd woken up with after my fitful night, as well as disguising the slightly green pallor my skin still held thanks to this latest turn of events. Slipping my feet into my favourite pair of ankle boots, I grabbed my phone, shoved it in my back pocket and slid my arms into my long tan cashmere coat. I turned to the full-length mirror that hung on the wall in my tiny hallway. If I was going to face the wolves, I was going to do it looking pretty damn fabulous. Taking a couple of deep breaths, I focused, calming my racing pulse, then I grabbed my keys and walked purposefully down the stairs to my front door. A couple more deep breaths here and then I twisted the lock, pulled the door open and stepped out.

The noise assaulted my ears as much as the flashes firing in the dull gloom of the winter's day attacked my eyes. I didn't address any of them but kept my eyes focused on my initial goal – to find Flora. I knew that whether I said anything or not, the photos being taken right now would be all over the internet within hours, and in the papers and gossip magazines before the end of the week. There was nothing I could do about that, so I focused on getting to my friend instead. Stood at her doorway, Flora was still trying to do battle with the motley bunch blocking her shop. Shoving my way through, I reached for her outstretched hand and took it gratefully as she hauled me inside before closing the door and giving the lock a definitive twist.

'The police got another call. He said they'd come back after if they can.'

Leaning back against the door, I met her eyes, preparing to launch into the speech I'd had running through my head ever since I'd made my decision. As I opened my mouth, Flora stopped me.

'Whatever it is you're going to say, you don't need to.'

'But—'

She shook her head. 'Nope. I don't want to hear it. I can see from your face, and the way you've battled through that pack of blood-thirsty lowlifes out there that you feel you need to explain something to me, but you don't.'

I let out a sigh. 'I really do, Flora. Not to mention apologising for all this happening quite literally on your doorstep and disrupting your business.'

She waved the apology away, the handful of bracelets on her wrist making a gentle tinkling noise as she did so.

'Oh, they'll be off soon enough, and don't you worry about that in the meantime. The main thing is, how are you?'

I glanced over my shoulder out of the window for a moment, before turning back to her. 'Honestly, I'm not sure. I suppose I should have known this would happen at some point. It was just a bit of a pipedream to think I could carry on as I was.'

'It's good to have dreams, Soph. Pipe or otherwise. It's what drives us. It's what brought you to us, even if you didn't know it.'

I gave the rabble outside another brief glance. 'I'm not sure everyone will be so thrilled about that right now.'

Flora gave another tinkling wave. 'Nonsense. You've been a wonderful addition to the village.' She tilted her head to one side, studying me for a moment. 'I hope all this doesn't mean you'll be leaving us.'

I lifted my head from where I'd been studying the toes of my boots. Flora read something in my expression and reached out, taking my hand and pulling me gently away from the window and out of the sight of the intrusive eyes and camera lenses.

'It doesn't matter to any of us what your title is, or why you chose not to share that with anyone. We love you for who you are, and even if you take that title back up, it won't change anything. "A rose by any other name" and all that,' she added.

'I still should have told you.'

'It doesn't make any difference. I know you will have had your reasons and we respect that, and anyone who cares about you will understand that.'

'I think it will make a difference to some people.'

Flora's look was kind, if a little sad. 'Have you heard from him?'

I shook my head. 'He made it very clear he didn't appreciate being kept in the dark about my background. Honesty is a rather sensitive subject for him these days, which I can understand after his experience with Serena.' I thought of her possessive stance and Nate's cold look. 'Although he looked like he was about to forgive her all that from what I saw when I went to the house yesterday.'

'You didn't lie, love.'

'I lied by omission in Nate's eyes. And maybe that's true.'

'You did what was right for you, and that's what matters. You had your reasons and it's up to you whether you choose to share those. And if you do, it's got to be when you're ready and only because you want to. Not because of some misplaced sense of duty.'

I gave an automatic eyeroll Flora smiled. 'Something tells me you've had more than your share of "duty-calls" experiences.'

I gave a watery smile. 'Something like that.'

'That's what I thought. So, don't go putting any extra pressure on yourself now when you don't need to. We're all here for you, whatever you decide to do. Whatever you need, just let us know.' I gave her a hug then ran a hand back over my hair, smoothing it automatically, unwilling to give the gossip mongers any fodder about me 'looking dishevelled'.

Maybe Flora was right. I wasn't any different now that the whole village knew my real name, and probably my entire blood-line, if the gossip merchants had been as thorough as they usually were. Getting the facts correct, however, was often far further down their list. For those I was lucky enough to call friends, I could only hope that it wouldn't matter. That, as Flora said, they cared enough about me not to be bothered by any of it. I would still be the same old Sophia to them. Of course, it mattered to people like Corinne and Serena, but their motives were different. They were in it for what they could get out of it. I'd met enough of those sort of people to last a lifetime and, although Wishington Bay was pretty close to perfect, there was always going to be the odd blot on the landscape. In this instance, it had been Corinne, helping my world implode.

And then there was Nate McKinley. Clearly, I'd made a rather spectacular error of judgement in that area. I'd been swept up enough by him to think he really cared. But he hadn't. Not really. At least not enough, or as much as I'd thought he had. Maybe he was really just a lonely man looking for a soft touch and a warm bed.

So why hadn't he followed through with Corinne?

Having now seen Serena in the flesh, that was a pretty easy question to answer. Corinne and Serena were two sides of the same coin. Nate had been looking to try something different – maybe he even believed that was what he wanted. What he needed at the time. But, in the end, he'd returned to what he knew. What, somewhere inside, he truly wanted. I tried to tell myself he had cared about me at some point, in some way. Just not enough.

I'd given my messages a quick scan before deleting them wholesale earlier today but there'd been nothing from Nate – not that I'd really expected there to be. His expression and body language the day before had spoken volumes. Any thought that things might go somewhere with him had been a ridiculous flight of fancy. I'd got caught up in the excitement of someone actually wanting me – and me wanting them – and my romantic fantasies, kept in sensible check for so many years, had run on unhindered. As I moved, still feeling the ache in my body from what had turned out to be a rather active weekend, I knew I needed to ignore those physical reminders and put Nate out of my mind. It was over. Pushing my shoulders back and adjusting my coat, I tried to focus on that thought. The only trouble was, it didn't stop me missing him. Being with Nate, right from the beginning, before anything remotely romantic had begun to form, had been about so much more than just romance. It had been about fulfilling a need to be with someone who listened, who laughed, who had his own opinions but who also respected mine and, most of all, about being with someone who I could finally be myself with. Unfortunately, as far as Nate was concerned, I hadn't been myself at all.

The door handle gave another rattle and Flora strode back to the front of the shop, yanking the blind down on the door.

'Honestly, what's wrong with these people?' She shook her head as she headed back towards me.

I gave a shrug. I'd never been one for gossip, either in print or real life, but I knew some thrived on it. There was probably some psychology in there somewhere but I'd never had enough interest to look into it.

'People clearly have far too much time on their hands, clamouring after gossip about people they don't even know!' Flora's observation was probably as good an explanation as any. Outside, the mob clamoured and chattered and occasionally peered in the window.

'I need to get rid of this lot somehow. They're blocking the shop and ruining your trade.'

Flora gave another airy wave. 'Don't you worry about me, love. They'll move on soon enough. It's you I'm worried about.'

I returned the wave with a lightness I didn't exactly feel as I prepared to leave. By the look on her face, Flora wasn't buying it. In my pocket, my phone vibrated again. I'd turned the ringer off but apparently that wasn't enough. Changing my number was rapidly being moved to the top of my to do list. I pulled out the phone, readying to switch it off entirely when I saw that it was Ned calling.

'Hi,' I answered.

'Hi.'

'Before you say anything else, I just want to apologise for—'

'Soph,' he cut across me.

'Yes?'

'There's nothing to apologise for. So, you've got a slightly fancier name than we thought. Big deal. Other than that, you're still one of my best waitresses for as long as you want the job.'

'Oh Ned.' I felt the tears prickle my eyes. 'Thank you.'

'Nothing to thank me for. But it might be an idea for you to take the next couple of days off.'

'Oh,' I felt the colour draining from my face. Was this Ned's way of letting me down gently after all?

'And don't take that the wrong way. I literally only mean for a couple of days. It's not a prelude to anything. It's just that there's a whole pack of press camped outside the restaurant. I heard they're outside your place too. So, it's probably best you just keep your distance from this lot, at least for now. Obviously, no one is talking to them so they're not getting anything from here.' He paused. 'Not now anyway. I know Corinne had a pretty large hand in all this, and I'm sorry about that.'

'That's not your fault, Ned.'

He made a sound that suggested he didn't entirely agree but carried on. 'Anyway, she's been sent packing now. She was on her last warning anyway – and she'd had far more of those than she had a right to. I only ever hired her as a favour and she only did it because her mother insisted.'

'So, you're already short?' I said, thinking of the shift I was supposed to do.

'Not at all. There's a couple of university students home for the holidays and they're happy to fill in for as long as we need them for, so don't worry. And when you're ready, if you still want it, the job will still be here waiting for you.'

'Thanks, Ned. I really appreciate that, and I'm sorry if the press are causing you problems.'

'Don't worry about that. If they want food, they've got a limited choice with most of the other restaurants closed for the season.'

'I hope you're charging them double.'

'At least.' I could hear the cheeky smile in his reply.

'Glad to hear it.'

There was a pause and for a moment I thought the connection had dropped but then Ned spoke again.

'Nate was in here last night, with a woman. One of the kitchen staff said it was his wife.' The laughing tone of a moment before had been replaced by one of confusion.

'Yes. They were right. She flew in yesterday morning from what I understand. I guess she wants to give it another try.'

'And Nate's taking her back?' Ned asked, the surprise in his voice unmistakable. He and Gabe were close, and he had obviously heard various tales of Serena's behaviour from her frustrated brother-in-law. And Ned, like the rest of us, had also witnessed the change in Nate since he'd been here. On one hand it was hard not to be surprised. But on the other, you only had to look at Serena for the surprise to lessen.

'It rather looks that way.' At least it had yesterday, I thought, remembering Serena's possessive stance, her eyes warning me off, telling me Nate was hers.

Ned let out a sigh. 'Gabe always did say his brother was nuts about her, and I guess, on the face of it, I can see why. Even Carrie let out a small "wow" when she poked her head in.'

I made a faint sound of agreement.

'But he was so different, Soph. It's almost like he was back to where he was when he first got here. Like he'd retreated back inside himself. It was kind of sad to witness.'

The words, Ned's tone, all of it, settled in my stomach and twisted round, making me feel something I didn't want to. I shoved it away. I had enough going on right now – I couldn't take on Nate's pain too – if that's what it was. Maybe it was just discomfort going to Ned's with Serena, knowing that they all knew he'd spent the weekend with me. It was hard to keep a secret in this village, especially when that secret involved someone as drop-dead gorgeous as Nate. Not to mention that the 'married man' the papers had happily harped on about was, clearly, Nate, even if the media hadn't mentioned him by name. Why Corinne had kept that little nugget back, I didn't know. I assumed it was just to ingratiate herself with her new pal, Serena. Either way, I was glad for his sake he hadn't been identified. Whatever else had gone on, he didn't deserve to be dragged into my mess any more than he needed to be. I suddenly realised Ned was still speaking.

'He didn't laugh or even smile once. It was kind of sad.'

I squashed back down the feelings threatening to rise up. 'I'm sure they had a lot of serious things to discuss.'

'If they did, they weren't doing it last night. Nate barely spoke a word from what anyone saw.'

An extra commotion from outside the shop caused me to turn

and peer through the shop window's display. Great. This was just what I needed.

'Ned, I have to go. Thanks so much for ringing, and I'm really sorry about the disruption.'

'No apology needed. Just look after yourself, Soph, and keep in touch.'

'I will. I promise.'

'Now who's this?' Flora said, coming to stand next to me as the cameras now focused on the silver Bentley that had double parked on the pavement opposite. The door was flung open and Jeremy, looking more red-faced than ever, hauled himself out.

'That,' I said, letting out a sigh, 'is my ex-husband.'

27

I bent and kissed Flora on the cheek before hugging her close. 'You know where I am,' she said, as I began to pull away. I nodded against her, afraid that replying verbally to her kindness might fracture the fragile dam I had built to stem my emotions. Stepping back, I smoothed my hair again, took a deep breath and unlocked the shop door, heading back out into the fray.

For a moment the cameras and shouted questions remained focused on Jeremy. He was dressed far too casually for his own comfort, in clothes at least two decades too young for him. This was a man who had dressed his entire life like he'd stepped out from the covers of *Horse and Hound*. I was pretty sure even his nappies had been tweed. And yet, here he was, attempting to discreetly adjust his too-tight jeans and looking as out of place in the clothes as he did in the village. For a moment I felt a pang of something akin to pity for him. Perhaps being without anyone was better than pretending to be something, and someone you weren't, just to make a person like you, and want to be with you. I knew from experience that pretence wasn't a sustainable way of living. It only took you so far – and yes, you could carry on like that for years – but it didn't make you happy. And at some point, when you least expect it, everything falls to pieces anyway. Thoughts of Nate filtered through, and I had a feeling that he could testify to the same experience. But I was done with pretence. That had been my path for far too long and never would be again.

Jeremy was now blustering his way through the pack of media clustered round my front door, before beginning to hammer on it with the side of his fist. Suddenly one of them noticed my exit from the shop and the lenses swung towards me, clicking maddeningly. My ex looked round at this sudden flurry of activity, his eyes narrowing as he saw me. I took my time heading back to the flat, politely asking those in the way to move. Eager to see the showdown they obviously expected to happen, justifiably considering the fetching shade of plum Jeremy had now turned thanks to his exertions, they parted to let me through.

'I can't believe you'd do this to me!' Jeremy hissed as I reached the door, and pushed the key I had ready in my hand into the lock.

I kept my eyes averted from his and said nothing. I didn't want to discuss things outside where the press waited, craving gossip, and although I wanted to silence him with a look, I didn't want to give them the opportunity to grab a shot of that look which they would then write their own caption to accompany. Besides, for all his expensive education, Jeremy could be stunningly obtuse sometimes, so probably would have entirely missed the message anyway. I twisted the key and Jeremy made to barge in the door first.

This wasn't anything new but my time away from him had heightened my awareness of these attributes. I'd got used to them before. Just let them happen. It was too much hassle to argue and wouldn't have done any good anyway. Money could only buy so much. If Jeremy's parents had paid for manners at that ostentatiously expensive school they'd sent their prodigy to all those years ago, then they really ought to get a refund.

I kept my hand on the key for a few moments as Jeremy huffed and puffed beside me. Finally, he took the hint and made a small step back. I finished the turn of the key and stepped first inside my own property. Turning, I met his eyes, holding the gaze for a moment, before opening the door a little more to allow him to enter. The flicker I saw in his expression told me that even he'd got the message this time. This is my house. You're not in charge any more.

I walked steadily up the stairs, hearing him puff and bluster behind me, clearly in a rush to get on with whatever it was he'd driven down here to say. Unlocking the interior door, I stepped through before facing him, making sure my point was made.

'Please come in.'

He shot me a look and stepped through. His eyes took in the small, tidy flat before landing back on me.

'This is where you live?'

'It is.'

His brows knitted for a moment before a sardonic smirk slipped onto his face. 'Some of the servants' quarters are bigger than this.'

I didn't flicker. 'That is true. Some of those rooms are quite generous. Would you like tea, or coffee, perhaps?' I asked, moving towards the kitchen.

'No, I don't want bloody tea or coffee. This isn't a social visit.'

I gave him a quick glance. 'No. I have to say, it's rather a surprise to see you.'

'Even you can't be that stupid, Sophia.'

I gripped the jar containing the tea bags a little tighter. Had I liked it less, there was every chance it would now be sailing through the air towards Jeremy's head.

'Don't speak to me that way, Jeremy.'

'I'll speak to you any bloody way I please!'

'No,' I said, turning slowly and hitting him with a direct, self-possessed stare. 'You won't. You'll either speak to me respectfully or you will leave this moment. The choice is yours.'

His eyes widened a little. This was not the wife he'd been used to. The one who'd kept quiet for what she'd hoped would be an easier life – when in fact all it had been was a lonelier one.

'Believe me, I'll be leaving as soon as I can.'

'I'm glad to hear it,' I said, evenly, turning back to my teacup and finishing the process. 'So, why are you actually here at all?' I asked as I carried the delicate china over to the coffee table, set it down and took a seat.

'Why do you think I'm here?' he shouted. 'Because of all this!' He pointed towards the window. 'I can't believe you've done this to me!'

I took a sip of my tea before placing the cup back on the saucer and standing. Jeremy wasn't an especially tall man and now we were on a more even level. 'This may come as a surprise to you, Jeremy. In fact, having known you as long as I have, I'm certain that it does, and is perhaps something I should have made you aware of a long time ago – but not everything is about you.'

For a moment, he stared back at me, his mouth opening and closing a few times like a koi carp at feeding time, shock registering in his eyes. It was hard to tell whether this was due to him being genuinely flabbergasted at the news I had just imparted, or the fact I had dared to impart it at all. For so many years I had said nothing, letting him prattle on about things, allowing him to believe what he wanted because frankly it was too much effort for too little result to do anything other than that. But that was the old Sophia. And she was long gone.

'Of course this is about me!'

I gave a small shake of my head and reached again for my tea while Jeremy blustered on.

'You're doing all of this just to try and humiliate me and ruin my upcoming wedding!'

'So, firstly, I haven't done anything but try to take care of myself, ensuring I had a place to live, and employment enough to cover all my expenses. I didn't have a big exit plan, Jeremy. I just got to a point that I knew if I didn't leave, I would be irrevocably broken, so I took what money I had and left. I didn't spend months putting funds aside, preparing, so I had to be careful and sensible, which is why I got a job.'

'Waitressing? Cleaning?'

'Let's face it, Jeremy. A Swiss finishing school doesn't really provide you with a lot of skills for the world at large, so I took what I could get.'

'Since when did you know anything about cleaning?'

'The truth was, I didn't. But I had to learn, so I did.'

'Did you have to set up a bloody Instagram account about it? Honestly, it's mortifying! Of all the things!'

'Don't be such a bloody snob, Jeremy. I wasn't qualified for anything and I only had so much money. I was married to you for long enough to know how damn sneaky you can be when it comes to money and deals and I knew you wouldn't want to make the divorce easy. As my so-called friends and family also made themselves scarce the moment I left, I was on my own and I did what I needed to, to keep a roof over my head and food on my table. I'd say that I'm sorry it doesn't meet with your approval, but I'm not. I stopped trying to get approval from you a long time ago and I certainly don't give a fig about it now.'

He opened his mouth to say something but I held up my hand. 'I'm not finished.'

Surprisingly, he closed his mouth again. I'm not sure which one of us was the most startled by that particular turn of events.

'As for your other accusation,' I continued. 'As I said, none of this is about you and as I had absolutely no idea you were even getting married again, it was certainly not in my mind to try and cause any sort of disruption to that.' I gave him a glance. 'That does, however, explain this new look you're sporting.'

He gave me a glare and yanked at the crotch of his jeans.

'Of course you knew. You had to! Why would you pick now to let the world know about your fall from grace if it wasn't to upstage me?'

'Oh, for the love of God, Jeremy!' I slammed the teacup I'd just picked up back into the saucer, its contents spilling over. 'Get your head out of your backside for two minutes and see some light! If I never had to think about you again, it would have suited me. You are welcome to go and marry whomever you want, so long as I have what I need, and what I deserve from our marriage. I signed the papers and I hoped that would be the last time I'd ever have to think about that life again! All of this,' I jabbed at the window with a finger, 'was brought about by someone else looking to be unkind and to make money. I was more than happy living here, having put my old life behind me. This is not about you! It's about me and it's my life that's out there for everyone to gawp at. Me that people like you are sneering at for no good reason other than they think they are somehow better than people that do any sort of manual labour.'

'That's because we are!' His voice had a tone of surprise that I could consider things to be otherwise.

'No, you're not! We're all the same people, Jeremy. Just some of us landed, by luck of birth, higher up the financial tree which meant we were afforded opportunities not open to others. But the people who clean your house are just as good and valuable members of society as you are. In fact,' I gave him a look, 'possibly more so as they actually contribute something other than hot air to the world.'

'Oh, you're "one of the people" now. Is that it? I know what the divorce settlement was, Sophia, and there's no way you'll be staying in this pokey place now. You're just the same as me.'

I spun at him. 'I am not the same as you. I have never been like you. God knows it probably would have made my life a lot easier if I had been, but I'm not, and I'm incredibly thankful for that.'

'You've humiliated me in the eyes of my friends and in the media! Do you know what people are saying?'

'I don't care what they're saying, Jeremy! And don't you dare speak to me about humiliation.' He shifted his weight, looking a little unsure as I advanced on him. 'Not very pleasant, is it? But maybe now you'll have an iota of an idea how I spent years of my life, thanks to the person who'd vowed to honour me, cherish me, and respect me.'

'Sophi—'

'You spent our entire married life humiliating me in one way or another. Putting me down in front of people, laughing at me, having one bimbo affair after another. Sleeping with one of my so-called best friends!' I stepped up to him, fury sparking in my eyes now, 'So don't you dare speak to me about humiliation because whatever misplaced embarrassment you think you're feeling now, it's an absolute fraction of what you caused me during our marriage.' I was inches from his face and I saw, for the first time, him realising that he was no longer able to intimidate me.

He stepped back and made a small, dismissive sound but I'd

seen the look in his eyes and that had said far more than anything he could do now. Snatching his phone out of his jacket pocket, he glared at the screen. There was clearly not enough room in the trouser pocket for it. By the looks of things, there wasn't enough room for a lot at all in those, and sadly, I knew there wasn't even that much for them to accommodate.

His phone bleeped again seconds before my doorbell rang.

'You should get that.'

I looked at him in shock. The bell rang again.

'I beg your pardon?'

'I said,' he repeated slowly, the sneer back on his face, 'that you should get that.'

'I am not your maid, Jeremy, and I do not need to be told who I should and shouldn't answer my own front door to. That lot have been banging on it all morning.'

He turned the phone screen towards me briefly, showing me the text he'd just received, instructing him to open the door. 'This time it's your mother.'

28

I crossed to the window to see a current model Range Rover bumped up on the kerb behind Jeremy's Bentley. The window was down and I recognised my mother's driver at the wheel. I let out a breath slowly between my teeth. Today was just one surprise after another. I closed my eyes briefly as the doorbell rang again, this time more persistently. Opening them again, my gaze was caught by something on Jeremy's windscreen, flapping slightly in the stiff breeze. He always did think rules were for other people. However, parking on the kerb violations in Wishington Bay applied to everyone, no matter how titled you were, or how entitled you thought you were. A small smile crept on to my lips. It disappeared just as quickly when the door rang again.

'Are you going to let her in?' Jeremy puffed at me, his cheeks a vivid shade of plum.

'No. I didn't invite her, and I have no wish to see her.'

'Oh, for God's sake,' he said, before trailing a string of expletives behind as he yanked the top door open and stomped down the stairs. I leant on the door jamb. Even I knew my mother was going to have to come in at some point, but I was in less of a rush than Jeremy was. He was now staring at the exterior door. A grin slid on to my face as he stared at it. Jeremy hadn't been born with a silver spoon in his mouth – he'd had the whole cutlery canteen. Right now was probably one of the rare times he'd ever had to open a door for himself. Even his student accommodation had had Louis XIV furniture, a butler, valet and several other staff. After a few moments, he worked it out and opened the door. I left them to it, avoiding the intruding camera lenses trying to peer their way up the stairs, before I heard the noise muffle again as, I assume, Jeremy closed the door. My mother was even less likely than him to do any simple or menial task herself.

Her disdain seemed to enter the room before she did. I didn't bother to stand as she made her entrance. She'd made her position clear when I'd contacted her to tell her I'd left. People like me didn't do things like that. There had been no understanding, no support, no offer of comfort. Like Jeremy, she was only concerned about how it would reflect on her and what ripples it would cause within the family and her social set. Her daughter was crumbling into pieces, had no home and no idea what to do and the only thing my mother was worried about was how it would all look up at the country club. She'd told me to stop being so selfish and get back to my place and hope that Jeremy hadn't noticed I'd gone. To be fair, she probably had had a point there – I suspected it had taken him a little while to realise I'd actually left. But it had shown me where she stood – and it was firmly the other side of the fence to me. And now, here she was, in front of me.

She glanced round. 'So, this is where you've been hiding out all this time.' The disapproval laced itself through her words but, after years of cringing at it, doing everything I could to make it disappear, I realised that now, it didn't bother me. I no longer cared whether my mother disapproved of me, my home, or anything else. I knew what mattered to me now and, after so many years of trying to earn it, her good opinion was no longer one of those things.

'No, Mother. This is where I've been living, very happily – until now.'

'It's very small.'

I didn't reply.

'Thàt's what I said,' Jeremy butted in. 'Very pokey.' Had his tone always been that ingratiating towards her?

She turned away from him without acknowledgement.

'Living happily cleaning other people's bathrooms and sleeping with other people's husbands?' Her tone was cool, in contrast to my face which flamed at her last comment.

'Yes, I have been doing some cleaning to help supplement my income and also to help out a friend. I actually quite enjoy it.' My mother paled at the comment. 'It can be very calming.'

'This friend you're helping out. Is it her husband you're sleeping with?' I'd tried to move past her original comment, but she knew she'd hit a mark and continued to twist the verbal knife.

'What I do with my life is none of your business. You made it quite clear you had no interest in it when I needed you. However, as I think it's best that before you leave, which I'm sure you will be doing very shortly, you have your facts straight and get your information from a more reliable source than the *Daily Mail*'s column of shame, I will clarify a couple of points for you. Yes, I was seeing someone briefly, but he was separated, and had been for some time.'

'But his wife is here in the village with him now, so I understand.'

She really had had someone on the case, or at least someone scouring the internet for her information.

'Yes, that's correct. But at the time they were separated with no intention of any reconciliation.'

'So you threw him back in to the arms of his ex?' Jeremy snorted, apparently amused.

'It would appear those ridiculous trousers are letting even less oxygen up to your brain than usual,' I returned, keeping my tone cool.

Jeremy narrowed his eyes at me, before turning away and giving his clothing another surreptitious pull. I glanced at my mother. There was the slightest glimmer of amusement in her eyes.

'Talking of reconciliation, I don't suppose there's any chance of that happening here?'

My ex-husband turned his nose up as if a bad smell had just wafted there. 'Hardly! After all she's put me through?'

Even my mother had the wherewithal to briefly raise her eyes to the ceiling at this, letting out a sigh as she did so.

'Don't be so stupid, Jeremy. Everyone knows you were the problem in this relationship.' She gave him another cool glance, her eyes travelling up and down briefly. 'And at least Sophia didn't have you lose all scrap of dignity by making you wear those absurd clothes.'

I watched them both for a moment. Jeremy was practically vibrating with fury. If he exploded then and there, I wouldn't have been surprised.

'I don't have time for all this,' he snapped. 'See if you can talk some damn sense into her!' With that, he stormed out of the room and thundered down the stairs in a manner that suggested a herd of wildebeest had just left my living room. There was a brief surge of noise as the door opened and then closed with such force that a couple of my ornaments shook.

Standing, I crossed to the window, careful to remain in the shadow of the curtains. Jeremy was pushing past the reporters, his mouth making shapes that, if his puce coloured skin was anything to go by, weren't pleasant well wishes. He jerked the car door open and got in. Within seconds he was out again, snatching the ticket off the windscreen and staring at it for a moment before throwing it forcefully inside the car as he got back in. Slamming the door, he revved the engine and sped off down the narrow road in a manner that, if he wasn't careful, would add a dangerous driving ticket to his collection.

* * *

I returned to my seat and said nothing. My mother gave a glance over the armchair, as if seeing whether it was worthy of her gracing it with her backside. Apparently it met her standards, and she sat.

'He's making an absolute fool of himself, marrying that girl.'

'Well, lucky for me, all the final paperwork has now been signed so I really don't care what he does. I have what I need which is all I ever wanted.'

'It's his fault you're in all this mess now. I do know that, of course. Everyone does.'

I sat up a little straighter. 'I'm not in any "mess", Mother. I made my own decision to leave that house and that marriage and my only regret is that I didn't do it sooner.'

'Well, why would you?' she asked, incredulous. 'You had everything you could ever want. A beautiful house, car, clothes and a title. Not to mention more money than you could ever need.'

'I also had a husband who didn't love me and had countless, and sometimes very public, affairs.'

My mother shrugged. 'Often that's just part of the deal.'

I shot up out of the chair. 'Well, that wasn't the deal I signed up for. And it wasn't part of the deal for you!'

My mother looked up at me for a moment before looking away. 'No, it wasn't. You are right, of course. I was exceptionally lucky with your father. He was a very special man. There aren't many like him.'

'I miss him.' My voice was soft. I'd planned to do my best to keep my emotions below the surface when Jeremy and then my mother had shown up. I'd once been very good at that, but it seemed that particular talent was one I'd lost my edge at.

As I looked back at her, I saw, for the briefest moment, a softening in my mother's face and when she spoke, her voice was also softer, the normally hard edges of it rounded and gentle. 'So do I.'

But then the moment was gone and her cool, assessing gaze landed back upon me.

'So, I've devised a plan that will have all this cleared up as soon as possible.' I opened my mouth to speak but she continued on. 'You'll come back with me today. Forget all this nonsense down here.' She gave a brief flick of her wrist and the huge emerald ring she wore on her right hand caught the low winter sunlight, now streaming in through the window, and flashed.

'Obviously, you must get rid of that Instagram account immediately. Honestly, Sophia, whatever were you thinking? I'll put out a statement about you having some sort of mental breakdown as a result of your husband's continued infidelities. Is that the right term? Mental breakdown? I can't keep up with all this political correctness. It seems to change by the day.' She let out an irritated sigh. 'Anyway. My secretary can find out that day's correct term and we'll issue the announcement. Jeremy's already known as rather a louse when it comes to that side of things so it will gain us some sympathy and take the focus off the rest of it, and goodness knows he doesn't deserve to be spared if we can garner some benefit. What's that look for?'

I shook my head. 'This "nonsense", as you call it, is my life. And I happen to like it. A lot! Coming here has allowed me to finally be myself and do the things I want to do instead of spending my entire life trying to please someone else – even though I never could. First it was you, and then it was Jeremy and you. But you were both impossible. Nothing I did was good enough and I finally realised that it never would be. I may have had all the things you mentioned but what does any of that mean if one doesn't really have a life? I was merely existing. Now, here, I know what it means to really live! I've not had a nervous break-down and, should you dare issue any sort of statement to that effect, or any other with respect to my life, I will contact the media myself.'

My mother was watching me now. It was pretty hard to tell, due to all the fillers and Botox, but I guessed there was something akin to surprise on her face. This was, after all, probably the most I had said to her in one go since I was a child. And certainly the first time I'd dared to really defy her.

'What I have now is clarity. I'm happy, Mother. I know you probably don't think I'm right about that, but the importance of your opinion is something I've also gained some clarity on since I left, and that's actually been incredibly freeing.'

I gave another glance out of the window. The crowd were still milling around but their enthusiasm seemed to have waned a little, and I could see a few of them heading off in the direction of the chippy. The warmth of the sun through the glass was deceiving, as outside I knew a cold wind blew straight in off the sea and chilled those unprepared for it right through to their unmentionables. Of course, I had very little sympathy for the press pack and wouldn't have been too upset to learn that some of those unmentionables had got frostbite. When I turned back, my mother was watching me.

There was no wariness in her eyes as there had been with Jeremy. For all her faults, she'd always had more balls than my ex-husband. But there was something in her gaze. As though she were seeing me for the first time. And I suppose, in a way, she was. She was seeing a new and, I liked to think, vastly improved, version of me.

'Do you know how hard it was to be constantly criticised by you? I don't remember a time when I wasn't always striving to please you.'

'I think you're being rather overdramatic, Sophia.' Her tone had a touch of boredom to it now, but I didn't care. She'd barged into to my home, into my new life, so she could damn well sit and listen.

'No, Mother, I'm not. And I think, maybe deep down,' I looked over at her, 'incredibly deep down,' she looked up at my tone, 'I think you know it too.' She opened her mouth to speak.

'Daddy knew it.' She flinched slightly at that and I realised I'd finally touched a nerve. 'But even when he discussed it with you, you couldn't help yourself, could you?' I sat down, suddenly exhausted. 'I did everything I could to try and please you. Even more so when Daddy had gone. I know you were hurting and lonely and I wanted to be there for you. For us to be there for each other. But you didn't want that, did you?'

'It was a very difficult time, Sophia. I'd lost my husband.' Her voice was even but I'd now abandoned all hope of keeping the calm, collected exterior of my past.

'And I'd lost my father! The one person I could be myself with. The one person who loved me for what I was, who I was! And then he was gone and any love that had managed to live in that house withered overnight, just like the roses on his grave. I could have been there for you if you'd let me. But even that wasn't enough of a jolt for you, was it?'

'You know nothing about what losing your father did to me!' My mother snapped suddenly.

'No, because you wouldn't tell me! And you know nothing about what losing him did to me because you didn't bloody well care enough to find out.'

The atmosphere in the snug room was charged, as though one spark would ignite everything.

'That's not true.'

'Isn't it?'

'No. But it's a bit late for all that now, Sophia. You're a grown woman.'

'You're right. I am. But I'm still your child. Which is why I did so much to try to please you. For God's sake, Mother! I even married the "right" man,' I cried, making the punctuation shapes in the air. 'The one you said would be right for me. Would treat me well and who already had a, what was it you called it now, oh yes, a fondness for me.'

'He did.'

'He had a fondness for my title and my money. That's all.'

A shadow of distaste flitted across her features.

'I admit, I may have overestimated Jeremy's character. But it was all meant to be for the best.'

'The best for whom?'

'For everyone.'

'For "The Family"? For you? For the bloodline? Well that bit certainly didn't work out, did it?'

She cleared her throat. 'No, apparently not. Although from what I understand, that particular issue lies with Jeremy, and not you.'

I sat down, heavily. 'Is that all you can say?'

She looked round at me for a moment before standing and

walking to the window, sweeping her gaze up and down the street outside.

'What do you want me to say, Sophia?' she asked on a sigh. 'Unlike you, I haven't had some hippy makeover.'

I shook my head. 'You'll never get it, will you?'

'Get what, exactly?'

'Do you even understand how hurtful the casual comments you'd drop over dinners whenever one of your friends became a grandparent could be?'

'It was just conversation. Don't be so sensitive about everything.'

'I'm not being sensitive, Mother! I'm being a normal human being. With feelings and emotions and all the other things that seem to have completely passed you by!'

'Oh, really,' she muttered, exasperation in her tone.

'Do you not remember sitting at the table, making digs about how you were still waiting for your grandchildren? How you couldn't understand how things could take so long? How Jeremy's mother was likely to become a grandmother before you did, the way he carried on sometimes? Do you remember that?'

She didn't reply, which I took as a yes.

'Have you any idea how upsetting all that was? How humiliating? Laughing with your so-called friends about my husband's affairs in front of me? My inability to get pregnant?'

'You obviously took it far more to heart than you needed to. Like I said, I was just making conversation.'

'It shouldn't have been conversation! And I would have thought that so-called good breeding you're so damn proud of would have taught you that. It was cruel and hurtful and absolutely the last thing any mother should do to their child if they have one speck of humanity about them.' I swiped at my cheek with the back of my hand, surprised to find it damp. I'd been so caught up in my memories, the tears of now and years past had begun to flow unnoticed. My mother held out a delicate handkerchief towards me wordlessly. For a moment, I considered refusing it, but there had been enough pettiness in my life already, and I was disinclined to add to it.

'Thank you.'

'It was never my intention to purposely hurt you, Sophia. I suppose...' she cleared her throat. 'I suppose I can see now that those comments, although made in jest, could have been taken in a way they were not meant.'

It was the nearest I'd ever get to an apology from her, but I wasn't going to thank her for it.

'What did you mean about knowing the problems with conceiving lay on Jeremy's side?'

I tried to hand back the damp handkerchief but she waved it away before retaking her seat in the armchair and looking across at me.

'His fiancée is neither the brightest nor the most discreet of women. A couple of gin and tonics and out it all flows. She forced him to go and see some Harley Street chap and get things tested. Incredibly low sperm count as it turns out. Though why anyone should be surprised, I don't know. We all know Jeremy has a lazy streak. Apparently, that even extends to his little swimmers.'

I crossed my arms over my middle and hugged myself. All those years of him blaming me for not getting pregnant, for not providing him with a son and heir, like one of his bloody brood mares. And all the time it was him. I'd had an idea about that, of course, once I'd taken matters into my own hands and visited specialists and had an assortment of tests. So far as they could tell, there was no reason I shouldn't get pregnant. Now it all made a lot more sense. I felt the emotions tumble within me. Rage, hurt, grief. I wasn't sure which I felt the most of and perhaps, right now, that was a good thing. That information, however long suspected, would be something that I'd need to process, and right now definitely wasn't the most conducive time to do that.

'Why didn't you contact me? Tell me where you were? Instead I had to find out through some convoluted game of Chinese Whispers!'

I looked up, matching her cool gaze with one of my own. 'It's been over eighteen months, Mother. And you've only bothered to find out where I am now because it affects you. Because I might have embarrassed you by living my own life and taking on work that you feel is beneath you and your family. If none of this had been made public, you'd still be happily ensconced back in Surrey in your cosseted life, with all your country club friends, sipping G&Ts and sneering at all those around you. Life as usual.'

She tilted her head a little higher, her chin jutting out just a tad more. 'Is that what you think of me?'

I paused momentarily before answering. 'Yes.'

'I see.'

The air was still between us. For a moment she looked as though she were about to say something, when all of a sudden there was a flurry of commotion downstairs and I heard the front door opening. The only other person with a key to the flat was Flora for emergencies. Quickly, I rushed to the interior door and pulled it open. Flora's head was peering round the door to the street downstairs.

'You all right, love?'

I nodded, trying to find a smile amongst all the emotions swirling round me. 'Is everything—'

The door opened further and Nate stepped in, pushing it closed behind them both.

'I'm sorry.' She gave a small shrug. 'He's been in the shop for the last half an hour begging me to help him see you.'

29

I moved quickly down the stairs and patted Flora's arm, eager to assuage the concern on her face. 'It's all right. He shouldn't have put you in that position in the first place,' I said, throwing Nate a look. He looked pained and I saw his Adam's apple bob as he swallowed.

'I needed to see you. I left you a bunch of voicemails and you're not answering your phone.'

'I'll leave you to it.' Flora hugged me hard, before casting a glance up the stairs at where my mother was now stood at the top, watching our little tableau. Flora gave my hand a final squeeze then slipped back out of the front door, leaving Nate to close it behind her.

'That was very unfair on Flora.'

'I know. And believe me, I'm not proud of it and I'll do whatever I can to make it up to her, but I didn't know what else to do. I needed to see how you were, especially once I heard about this lot.' He jabbed his thumb behind him towards the street. 'And to apologise.' He took a step towards me and I immediately took a step back. A muscle flickered in a jaw that clearly hadn't seen a razor for a few days. I tried not to remember that part of that reason was because he'd been here, with me, and him being clean shaven was the last thing on either of our minds.

'It's of little consequence now,' I said, attempting to make the words sound truthful. From the corner of my eye, I caught the look on Nate's face and realised that strategy clearly hadn't worked. Time for a more direct approach. 'You should probably get back to your wife.' I turned away from him and made to return up the stairs. Nate caught my arm.

'Soph, please. I—' He stopped, suddenly becoming aware that we had an audience. I took the opportunity to slide my wrist from where his hand still gently circled it and made my way up the stairs. My mother made no attempt to move as I re- entered the flat until she finally took the hint my glare conveyed. She stepped out of the way, and I made to push the internal door closed.

'Soph, wait!' Nate, who had followed me up the stairs, grabbed the side of the door. 'Please!'

Had it been Jeremy, there was every chance I'd have consid- ered, if not actually acted on, closing it anyway but I pulled the door open a little more, staying at the threshold, thereby keeping Nate out. He looked down at me and I gripped the door tighter, hating the tension now back in his body, the dark circles under his eyes that suggested there'd been little, if any, sleep last night. Having seen his wife in her clingy bandage dress, that particular fact wasn't exactly a shock. However, that didn't mean I needed it rubbed in my face.

'You should go,' I said, struggling to keep my voice strong.

'Not until we've talked.'

'There's nothing to say.'

'Yes, there is!' He ran a hand back over his hair, his jaw tense with frustration. His other hand was still on the door, as if in readiness for me slamming it closed. The silence hung between us, heavy, and almost tangible.

'I'll be going now.' My mother's educated tones broke in as she approached us. 'There's obviously nothing I can say that's going to make you see sense and come home with me.'

'I am home, Mother.'

She gave the flat a cursory glance before her gaze landed on Nate, and lingered there for a few moments, curiosity clearly burning through her.

'So. You must be the married man.'

'Mother!'

Nate cleared his throat. 'Not that I believe this is any of your business, but for the sole reason of Sophia not deserving the tone, or implication of that statement, I am separated. I've been so for nearly a year and divorce proceedings are progressing.'

My mother raised one eyebrow in interest before swinging her glance to me.

'Goodbye, Mother,' I said, before she could add anything else.

She held my gaze a moment and nodded. Nate stepped aside, and she made her way down the stairs and out into the street. I walked away from the door, leaving Nate to close it behind him whichever side he chose to be on. From the window I watched my mother return to her car, the door opened by her driver, before he returned to his place behind the wheel and drove off. Part of me wondered if I'd ever see her again. Another part wondered if I cared. Turning away from the window, I found that Nate had indeed stayed. He was studying me, concern written across his features.

'You OK?'

I nodded.

'So that's your mum, eh?'

It sounded strange to hear her referred to as 'mum'. She'd

never been anything but Mother. Mum seemed far too informal and warm for the relationship we had – if you could even call it a relationship.

'You shouldn't have come here,' I said, changing the subject, wanting to get this over with as soon as possible so that I could sit and work out exactly what it was I was supposed to do next. I'd told my mother I was home and that much was true but I wasn't sure I'd be able to stay after all this. I'd enjoyed my privacy and now that had been shattered and, worse, so had other people's. I didn't want that to be a lasting legacy of my time here.

'I needed to see you.'

'They'll have your photograph now too,' I said, waving my arm in the direction of the window. 'Don't you think I feel bad enough already?'

'That was my choice.'

'It wasn't up to you, Nate!'

That stopped him and I couldn't bear the pain on his face. I turned my own away and sat on the sofa. Hesitating a moment, he then sat next to me. Tentatively he touched my hand as it rested on my knee. Suddenly I was exhausted. All I wanted to do was to lean against his warm, solid body. Feel his arms wrap around me as they had at the weekend and sink down in the comfort and security – and what I knew now on my side was love – of that embrace. But I couldn't. The weekend had merely been a brief sojourn into what might have been. The reality was here, now and far, far different.

'I'm sorry. I didn't think that part through. I apologise if I've made any of this worse for you by coming here but I needed to see you were all right.'

What was the point of lying now?

'No, Nate. I'm not all right. Not at the moment. But I will be.' I took a deep breath and let it out. 'I will. My life here has been turned upside down and I made that worse because I didn't tell people the entire truth. At the time, I thought that was the best thing to do, and I had my reasons for that.'

'Because you were trying to leave that part of your life behind.'

I lifted my head from where I'd been staring at a faded patch on the knee of my jeans. My gaze connected with his and I felt a flip in my stomach that I'd hoped had been extinguished.

'Yes.'

'I'm sorry I didn't come and meet you from the restaurant,' he said, taking my hand in his own.

'It's fine. You had other things to do.' I pulled my hand away, gently but firmly and tried to ignore the ripple of pain that crossed his face as I did so. Maybe he had felt something for me but that was all done now. It was in the past and he had a future to build back with Serena.

'I should still have let you know I wasn't coming instead of standing you up.'

I tried to laugh it off. 'It was hardly being stood up.' Except that's exactly what it had felt like. Nate's face told me he knew that too.

'I shouldn't have let you find out Serena was here the way you did. I should have warned you. Tried to explain.'

'There's nothing to explain, Nate. Nothing to say.' I made to stand but he caught my hand again, not stopping me but almost as a question. A request. I sat down again.

'I think there is.' He paused, seeing if I would listen. When I made no further attempt to move, he continued. 'I had no idea Serena was coming. She'd sent a couple of emails, which I deleted, and a couple of texts, which got the same treatment. I wasn't interested in talking to her at all, let alone getting back together with her.'

I picked up on the past tense he used and felt something inside me crumble a little more.

'The solicitor handling the divorce knew the only contact I wanted was to be through them. Serena didn't even know where I was, and I knew none of my family would tell her and work are way too worried about privacy disclosures to let any information out, even to her.'

'Corinne told her.'

He let out a sigh. 'Yep. Man, those two are like peas in a pod.'

'Apparently they're very close Facebook friends now.'

'So I heard. Except that hasn't lasted very long.'

'Oh?'

'Yes. Things haven't exactly gone to the plan Serena had laid out and, not being someone ever to blame herself, part of the blame for it has been fired back at Corinne who apparently should have contacted Serena sooner so that she could "save her marriage". The fact it was already dead and buried is irrelevant. Corinne had no idea who she was getting mixed up with when she contacted Serena. I don't think she knows what's hit her. I could almost feel sorry for her if she hadn't been instrumental in setting all these collision courses in action and hurting you.'

'I'm fine.' The statement was automatic. Some habits died harder than others.

Nate looked at me and I felt as though he could see straight through me, to inside me, where things were very much not fine. But I didn't want him to see that. I needed that distance. But however much I didn't want it, by the unhappy look on his face, he'd already seen.

'I know there's no excuse for how I acted when you came to the house. Serena showed up just as I was getting back from your place and I was still spinning if I'm honest. She turns up saying she wants to come back and how she realises now how good we were...'

I put a hand to my forehead, a headache now beginning to thump a repeat around my temples and above my eye.

'Nate—'

'Sorry. I'm not making a very good job of this.'

'It doesn't matter.'

'It does.' His voice had a strength to it. I met his eyes. 'It really matters.'

I sat back.

His thumb made a gentle pass over my palm and I tried to ignore all the things it made me feel, concentrating instead on what he was saying.

'When I came here, when I met you first, I meant what I said. Gabe had been trying to get me to meet new people and so on, encourage me to go out but I really wasn't interested. When he offered me this place, I was sceptical as I clumsily showed, but, from the horrified look on your face, I realised that I'd been a little too paranoid about my brother attempting to match-make.'

'They just wanted to help you.'

'Yeah, I know that now. Coming here has given me clarity in all sorts of ways.'

I thought back to what I'd told my mother, about having clarity. From what I knew about Holly's experience coming here, she'd experienced something similar. It seemed that Wishington Bay had a very special, almost magical, quality.

'Of course, once I'd made this big song and dance about not wanting to meet anyone, and you'd firmly, and quite rightly, put me in my place, I couldn't get you out of my head. And the more I saw you, the more I wanted to see you, spend time with you. I finally began to feel like me again. The old me. All the knots began to unfurl, I began enjoying my work as well as appreciating my time here, and of course, I was loving Bryan's company!'

'Where is he?'

'Carrie's got him. I'm going back to collect him in a bit.'

I nodded.

'All of that, all this new-found enjoyment, was down to you.'

I shook my head but Nate gently squeezed the hand he still held. 'It was, Soph. You made me feel like me again. I'd forgotten what it was like to just be able to relax with someone, be myself, and feel that being myself was good enough. More than good enough.'

He shifted a little in his seat and turned towards me more. 'The weekend? That was amazing. I mean, all of it. Working in Flora's shop, sharing that time and that experience. It was wonderful. And if you'd have told me six months ago, I'd be dressing up like some Victorian gentleman, I'd have thought you were nuts. That's really not my style.'

'It suited you,' I smiled a little sadly, thinking back to how good he had looked.

'I liked it. It was fun. But then, everything was fun with you. It was easy. I never felt like I had to try. Leaving here that morning was so hard. I just wanted to be with you, and I couldn't wait to see you again after your shift.' His face darkened then, tension filling it. 'And then, as I walked down the drive, a taxi pulled up and there was Serena. I had no idea she was coming and I didn't want her here, tainting this place. Tainting all the good memories I was making.'

'But you were too polite to tell her to leave.'

He flicked his startling blue gaze up from where he was gently running the pad of one finger over my thumbnail.

'I was so shocked to see her, I don't even remember what I said. But Serena has a tendency to take over, and before I knew it she was in the house, making herself at home. Telling me that she missed me, that the fling with the tennis guy was all over and it had only been a,' he paused. 'Now, how did she put it? "A desperate, selfless attempt to get you to notice me again".'

'Wow.'

'Yeah. I know.'

'From what I saw, she's pretty hard not to notice.'

'I bent over backwards for that woman. And I didn't care. I just wanted to make her happy. But I realise now that nothing would. And that our whole marriage, our whole relationship, had been about me making her happy, us doing things she wanted to do. There was no give and take. I was so crazy about her I didn't see it, but everyone else did. But I definitely see it now.'

'Maybe she did feel you weren't noticing her? It can feel like that once you've been in a relationship or married for a while.'

'Serena always made a point of being noticed. It was nothing to do with that, trust me. She just liked the attention and her tennis coach is pretty charismatic, which, as you've noticed, isn't exactly one of my top qualities.' He did a half smile and I knew he wasn't just fishing for compliments.

'You do yourself an injustice.'

Our eyes met and tenderly he leant his head against mine for a moment.

'Tennis Guy just got fed up with her constant demands. The sheen had worn off for him and he broke it off. Of course, then she panicked and thought she'd come back to me. I'd always taken her back before. Why not this time?'

'She'd done this before?'

'A few times. Never actually shacked up with a bloke before, but stormed off, saying she was leaving. Anyway, she just assumed that's how it would be and came here, and started acting as if she owned the place, and told me about all these plans she had for us to do this, that and the other. None of which, I have to say, appealed to me. There was no discussion. There wasn't even an apology. She just slotted herself right back into position as if she'd never left.'

I swallowed. That was exactly how it had seemed when I'd called on Nate that day as the snow fell round me. Serena had stood there, her arm possessively around his waist, dictating what I should and shouldn't cook and looking for all the world like she owned the place.

'Except she didn't fit any longer.'

I met Nate's eyes.

'It didn't feel right. I knew as soon as she got out of the taxi I wouldn't take her back this time. Other times, I'd always been partly relieved to see her back. But this time, I felt... nothing.'

'But when I came... she looked... I mean, you looked...'

He let out a sigh. 'Serena's pretty sharp in a lot of ways. And I'm sure Corinne had filled her in to some extent too. I'm a bank account and an easy life to Serena, and she wasn't about to let that go easily so she steamrollered her way through, just like she always does. And fool that I am, I've always just laid down and let it happen before. But this time it was different. This time I knew what love should feel like and this was nothing like it.'

'Love?' I asked, the word breaking as I said it.

His hand cupped my cheek. 'Yes. Love.'

'But when I came...' My stomach was performing backward flips but I was still confused.

'I know. I was so caught up with telling Serena that it was definitely over, and her screaming back at me that it wasn't and nobody but her decides things are over, and how dare I – you get the picture. Then when she saw that wasn't working, she tried the charm tactic.' He raised a brow. 'Sadly for her, that charm had long worn off for me. But just trying to get her to listen and, more importantly, leave was stressing me out. And then you arrived.'

'I hadn't meant to interrupt anything.'

'I know. Like I said, I should have messaged you, but I was still trying to find which way was up. All I wanted to do was pull you to me and hold you and wish the rest of it away but I know how devious Serena can be. I had to hold back because I didn't want you drawn into things any more than was necessary. Of course, I didn't know Corinne had told her I was seeing someone then. But the way she spoke to you, ordering you about, I couldn't take it and I was just about to say something when she recognised you.'

'I had planned to tell you. I promise.'

He nodded.

'With everything else spinning in my head, it threw me. All of a sudden, I felt like maybe I'd been stupid again. That what we'd had was a lie too. That you'd kept secrets from me and the woman I'd fallen in love with wasn't who I thought she was.'

The tears had welled in my eyes at his words, and my throat felt sore and tight. 'The only difference is that my real name is a bit longer than I originally said. I'm sorry I didn't tell you before.'

His hand rose again to my face, his thumb brushing away a stray tear. 'I know that now. I reacted badly, and for that I'll never forgive myself. My relationship with Serena had made me jump to the wrong conclusions about everything, and I am so worried I've ruined what we had by acting like I did. There's no excuse.'

'The way you looked at me...' I swallowed. 'It hurt so much...' The pain in his eyes showed me he knew that. And that he cared deeply that he had. 'But I understand too. When we're in a difficult situation we don't always act in the most rational way.'

He dropped his hand and shook his head. 'Don't forgive me.'

'What?'

'You can't just forgive me like that. That easily. You're supposed to stamp and scream and, I don't know, do something.'

I frowned, half laughing, half crying. 'That's not really my style. And why shouldn't I forgive you? You apologised and explained and even faced an unruly mob of reporters to come to me.'

'But I'm not sure I deserve it.' He tilted his head, then leant it against mine. 'I'm not sure I deserve you.'

I pushed him back gently. 'Both of us have had bad relationships and those leave scars. All we can do is try to learn and heal from those. We're bound to muck up sometimes. That's human nature. But if we're truly sorry, and we grow from it, there's no reason to keep being made to pay for it.'

'What did I ever do to deserve meeting you?'

I lowered my eyes and concentrated on his large, strong hand holding mine.

'Where's Serena now?'

'On a plane back home, I imagine. Although I screwed it up, seeing you at that moment was the best thing that could have happened. It gave me that clarity I was talking about. I told Serena it was over once and for all and that I'd pay for her flight back home and call her a cab. A mate of mine is the divorce lawyer. I spoke to him straight after, asking him to gee things along a bit. The fact that he'd said "about time" when I rang him initially about all this probably gives you some idea of what the few friends I've managed to hang on to thought about my marriage.'

'No one can really judge anyone else's relationship properly. It's all relative to how they see it, and that can sometimes be quite different to how those involved see it.'

'That's true. Although, on this occasion, I have to concede he was right.'

I smiled, but my stomach was still in knots. There was a question to ask and, although it was gnawing at me, I wasn't sure if I wanted to know the answer. Still, I had to ask.

'So, what happens now?'

'That depends on you.'

'Me?'

'Yes.'

'Why?'

Nate let out a sigh. 'Because if all this has shown me one thing, apart from how I can act like a complete idiot at times, it's that somewhere along the line, I've fallen completely, head over heels, absolutely madly in love with you. And right now, I'm not entirely sure what to do about it.'

'Oh,' I replied. Good to see that my expensive education was coming into its own right now.

'When I told Serena to leave, she started harping on about how you'd lied to me and that you would again. The fact that she could say all that with a straight face amazed me but still... But you never lied to me. I realised that almost as soon as I'd shut the door and possibly messed up the best thing that's ever happened to me. You never lied to any of us. You just kept certain things private, and that's your prerogative. Those things don't make any difference to who you are, or who you've been to everyone here.'

'How did she know who I was?'

'She's always been obsessed by English aristocracy for some reason. Reads all the gossip and magazines and all the who's who stuff. It's always been a thing of hers. I think ideally she'd have loved to land a duke or something.'

'I guess that explains things. It's a shame she wasn't nicer to me. I know a few I could have introduced her to.'

The smile I loved appeared then. 'God, how I'd love to tell her that.'

I giggled and he continued. 'Anyway, she's banging on about this and she starts pulling up all these photos of you. The thing is, all she did by that was strengthen my resolve to see you, apologise and try and do everything I could to fix this.'

'Why? I mean, why did the photos help?'

His hand stroked gently back over my hair, his eyes momentarily following its track before they focused back on me.

'Because one of the first things I fell in love with, apart from your spark, was your smile. And in not one of those photos she showed me were you really smiling. I mean, not properly. You looked absolutely perfect and your gorgeous mouth was in the right shape. But there was nothing here.' Gently he laid both his hands on my temples, the thumbs settling beside my eyes. 'There was no sparkle.'

'That's because I don't think I found it until I came here.'

'I know the feeling.' He let out a sigh, shaking his head gently. 'Can you forgive me?'

The answer to that one was easy. 'I already said I did.'

He grinned. 'I was just double checking.'

I met his eyes. 'But I live here. I love it here.' I knew now I wanted to stay, whatever happened with the press. I'd deal with them and move on and, in time, they'd forget about me as they moved on to the next person to hound. I'd built a life here. One I loved and one I wanted to continue to build on. I also knew that I wanted Nate in it. But there was the small matter of thousands of miles between our respective homes...

'I know. I love it here too. And I've done some research, and because of my heritage, and some work opportunities, staying here won't be a problem. But only if you want me to.'

'Oh, Nate... of course I want you to!' Emotion cracked my voice as he pulled me towards him, his embrace so tight I had to make an effort to breathe, but I didn't want him to let go. Not now. Not ever.

'I don't know how all this will work out. All I know is that I want it to.' His voice softened as he pulled back and looked at me. 'God, Soph. I want this to work out more than I've ever wanted anything in my entire life.'

I smiled through the haze of tears, my expression telling him I felt the same.

His kiss was soft, tender and as he wrapped me back in his arms, and I leant against his chest, I could feel the steady beat of his heart. It was soothing and I knew I was exactly where I needed to be. And with the man I was supposed to be there with.

'So, what can I do about those hounds out there?' he asked as I eventually sat back.

'Nothing,' I said, feeling a surge of love for him because he wanted to. 'But don't worry about that. I've had an idea.'

30

'This is fabulous!' Flora said, beaming as she flapped the glossy magazine at me as I stepped into the cosiness of her shop, shutting out the bitter January wind behind me.

'Oh, you got a copy?'

'Of course I did!' she laughed, coming over to give me a hug. 'And my granddaughter's been telling all her friends about it too. I think they're all a bit jealous of her having a grandmother who's so "in" with all the celebrities.'

I laughed and she winked.

'Do you think it sounds all right then?'

'It's perfect. Your contact at that magazine did a great job, and, I have to say, I think this was a very classy way of dealing with it. Not that I'd ever have expected anything less from you.'

I reached out and squeezed her hand, thankful as ever for her friendship and her stalwart support through what had been a bumpy time.

'Thanks, Flora.'

'So, where's your hunk today?'

'He's upstairs on a video conference thing about something or other. I didn't want to be seen flitting back and forth on it so thought I'd come and say hi to you and get some bits in the village.'

Flora grinned. 'Going OK then?'

I grinned back. 'It seems to be. It's a little snug up there, I have to admit. I'd got used to my own space and Nate isn't the smallest guy around so the flat definitely feels a bit different with him there.'

'But in a good way.'

'Definitely in a good way,' I confirmed.

'Have his parents gone back now?'

'Yes, we took them back to the airport yesterday but they promised they'd be over again soon.'

'They seem to really like you if what I saw when you were all in here is anything to go by.'

I rested my elbows on the shop's counter. 'Oh, Flora. They're so lovely. I have to admit I was rather nervous when Nate said they'd decided to come back with Gabe and Holly and have a family Christmas after he'd told them he'd decided to stay on a bit longer.'

'Had he told them why?'

'Apparently so. Although, from what his mum said, she'd already guessed something had happened just from when he called them on Skype. She said his whole demeanour was different, and that it was like she had her old Nate back.'

'Ah, Soph, that's lovely.'

'I know. I burst into tears when she said it, which was all a bit mortifying.'

Flora laughed. 'I'm sure she didn't think it was mortifying at all.'

'She wasn't the one crying!' I laughed. 'Well, not initially anyway. I think I set her off.'

'I'm so glad it's all working out for you, love. You definitely deserve it.'

'Thanks, Flora. I'd have been thrilled to just be with Nate. He's more than I could ever need. But the fact he seems to have come as package deal with his family, and by extension Holly and her family...' I stopped, feeling tears prickling at my eyes again.

Flora leant over, kissed my cheek and then laid her hand there. 'Like I said, you deserve it.'

I smiled, and made an effort to get my emotions back in check.

'How's the Instagram?'

I laughed. 'Crazy!'

When I'd made contact with the old schoolfriend who worked at *Chic*, one of the best-selling glossies, and asked if she'd be interested in an exclusive, she'd been incredibly keen. Having followed the story in the papers, she'd immediately wanted to reach out but more as a support than anything else. I wasn't naïve enough to misunderstand that if she could get a story, she would, but I also knew that this was my best chance at getting the right story out there and cutting off the heads of the other tales emerging.

Once I'd explained everything, answering her questions over a long, lazy lunch at a private table in an exclusive London restaurant, my friend had turned to the matter of the Instagram account. I'd told her I'd probably just delete it, but she'd suggested doing the opposite. The account had now been renamed 'Lady S' and, although I was no longer cleaning for other people, I still loved trying out new tips in my flat, and sharing them on my account, along with other little bits of my day. Unlike before, I also now featured on my own account. I didn't have to hide any more – not there. Not anywhere.

'I've nearly finished my first column for *Chic*. I have to admit I'm a bit nervous about it, but hopefully they'll like it. I can't believe I'm writing for them.'

'It's so exciting! I've already put my order in at the newsagents to save me a copy.'

'Oh, Flora, you are so sweet.'

She waved it away. 'And what about the book?'

'I've got a meeting on Friday up in town with my agent and a couple of publishers to see which deal we prefer.'

Flora was beaming, and, I soon realised, so was I. I shook my head. 'It's all rather crazy, isn't it?'

'It's wonderful is what it is,' she smiled, nodding behind me as the bell over the door tinkled. I turned to see Nate enter, ducking so that the little bell didn't clank him on the head. Some parts of Wishington Bay weren't built with men like Nate in mind but, like his brother, he'd still found it the perfect fit.

'Hi Flora. How's you?'

'All the better for seeing my two favourite love birds,' she teased as he bent and kissed her cheek.

I shook my head, laughing, as Nate came to stand behind me, wrapping his arms around me.

'Hello.'

'Hello,' I said, twisting my head a little to see him as he leant forwards. 'Conference call done?'

'Yep. All good.'

'I was just going to get some fish from Mac down on the front for dinner.'

'Want some company?'

'That would be lovely.'

He grinned, kissed my cheek and stood back.

'Do you need anything while we're out?' I asked Flora as I bundled the scarf I'd taken off in the warm shop back round my neck.

'No, I'm all right, love. Thanks for asking though.'

'OK, just ring me if you think of anything.'

'Will do,' she said, smiling with a look of indulgence at us both.

'Stop looking like that,' I laughed.

'What?' she asked, innocently.

'You know what.'

She gave me a shrug, still grinning, and we headed out of the shop with a wave and set off down to the seafront to see what delights Mac had on his fresh fish stall. I loved this aspect of living here. Being house-proud wasn't the only thing I'd discovered I liked since moving here. Cooking had also been another revelation to me, as Nate had experienced in his first days of staying in Wishington Bay. And as he still was now. The difference now was that it was often a joint affair. Having spent months living off ready meals, the dishes I'd cooked for him had reawakened his love of food. I knew his mum was a good cook but, over the years, his enjoyment of it had become sidelined. Serena had never cooked so they'd either had takeaway or eaten out, but, more often or not, she'd already eaten by the time he came in, having lunched with friends and, forever counting the calories, would be uninterested in having anything more. The fact that her husband may have only had time to grab a sandwich all day seemed neither here nor there to her.

Nate had not only rediscovered his love of eating good food but had also begun to learn to cook, remembering lessons from his childhood when his mother had ensured both of her boys had at least known one end of a saucepan from the other. And he was already getting pretty good, never afraid to experiment and happily going off-piste from the recipe book – something I never did! It had become another shared enjoyment. Just as our life together now was. And, finally, after both having been so alone for so long, together was a very special place to be.

EPILOGUE

Through the open window, the sound of the waves made a gentle shooshing sound, soothing and restful, as the sea washed the sand, ready for what looked to be another beautiful summer's day in Wishington Bay. I pushed myself up the bed as the door to the bedroom opened, Nate nudging it with one broad, bare shoulder. My stomach did a little flip. I'd thought that feeling would eventually lessen, but apparently not. He was still the sexiest man I'd ever met, and when he gave me that grin, as he so often did, a whole flutter of butterflies set loose within me.

'Good morning.' His softly accented words added to the butterflies.

'Good morning. What's all this?' I asked, accepting the kiss he placed lightly on my lips as he set the tray down on the bed.

'Breakfast in bed.'

'Did I forget something? Is it my birthday?' I asked, laughing.

He shook his head, smiling as he settled himself next to me in the bed and leant over to take a piece of warm, buttered toast.

'I didn't think there had to be a special occasion to make my fiancée breakfast in bed.' He turned to me, his smile widening before he stole another kiss along my collarbone. I felt the smile on my own face, so wide it almost hurt. It wouldn't have surprised me to learn I'd had a bloody great grin on my face all night. Admittedly, part of the night I'd been otherwise occupied, hence the slightly late hour of my rising, although those exploits had only added to the pleasure.

Getting married again was something I had been sure I would never do, and I guess I'd assumed that, because his own experience of the institution hadn't exactly all been roses and sunshine, Nate felt the same way. But apparently he didn't. And when it came to it, I realised I didn't either.

Last night, as we'd strolled barefoot on the sand in the bright moonlight beside the ebbing tide, Nate had stopped, got down on one knee and presented me with the most beautiful ring I'd ever seen. And, with my background, I'd seen a lot. Moonbeams caught it, causing it to sparkle brightly as it rested on a midnight blue cushion of velvet. I'd hesitated for a moment, not because I was unsure of my answer but because I was so sure. So immediately, entirely sure, that it had taken me by surprise.

The moment Nate had slid that ring on my finger, it felt as though everything I had gone through to get me to here had been worth it. Without all the heartbreak, I wouldn't have the overwhelming joy my heart was struggling to contain and that, I felt, was worth anything. The man in front of me on the beach last night. The man sat relaxed, at home, beside me in the bed right now was worth all of it.

'Have you told Gabe, yet?' I asked.

He nodded, swallowing a mouthful of strong, rich coffee. 'His reply came back so fast, I'm pretty sure him and Holly were practically sat on top of the phone waiting to hear what you said.'

As he spoke, his phone bleeped and he lazily put an arm out to reach it. Waking the screen, he smiled. 'Talk of the devil.'

I waited, munching on some toast as he read it. 'Apparently we're invited next door for a celebratory barbecue. Want to go?'

I laughed. 'Of course!'

Buying the other semi from Holly had been one of our best decisions last year as, with the help of connections she'd built up, we set about transforming it from the dated, dark place it had been when Gabe first rented it from Gigi, to the beautiful light and airy place we now called home. I loved having become closer to Holly and Gabe, and it was wonderful to see the two brothers build on and enjoy a relationship they'd missed out on, thanks to a combination of Nate's ex, and distance.

Their parents, now having both their sons living here, had also bought a little flat in the city so that they could spend more time close by. It was unlikely they'd leave the sunshine of Australia permanently, but we all loved it when they were over, laughing and chatting and sharing good food and wine.

I was still writing for *Chic* and the first household book had done so well that there was already another in the works. And, as the various posts I'd put up about our house renovation on my 'Lady S' Instagram account had proved incredibly popular, there'd been interest in a book on this aspect too. I'd suggested bringing Holly in on that project as she now had a wealth of expertise on the subject and would be able to add a lot of veracity and depth to it that I couldn't. The publisher had been hugely enthusiastic about this, loving the family aspect, and the project had received its green light on Friday. I couldn't wait to start working with Holly on it, although I'd be keeping an eye on her to make sure she didn't go overboard with work. She'd got better at that aspect of her life, with help from both Washington Bay and her husband and family, but there was still a spark of it left in her and, with an ever-growing bump to manage, it was important she not let that tendency take hold.

I looked over at Nate, who now had his eyes closed, resting against the luxuriously padded headboard. The weekend had certainly brought with it plenty of good things. And, as I looked at the man I was to marry, this time for love, I knew that Wishington Bay had once again sprinkled some of its magic over two broken people, making them whole again. And making them one.

ACKNOWLEDGMENTS

As always, thank you to James. Without your continual support and belief in both me and my writing, there is no way I'd now be sending my tenth (!) novel out into the world. I couldn't have done any of this without you. Thank you for everything you are and do.

A huge thank you to the amazing team at Boldwood Books, including Amanda, Megan and the amazing Nia. Special thanks go to Sarah Ritherdon, my editor, for her support, belief and guidance. Thanks also to the brilliant copy editor, Cecily and proof reader, Susan Lamprell, who both did excellent jobs tidying up the whoops moments.

Part of this book was written during the Covid-19 lockdown and, as for many people, it's been a very weird and anxious time. I know a lot of my writer pals have struggled with finding creativity and concentration during this time, as I have, and I'd like to send extra thanks here to Rachel Dove for all the fun veggie growing/gardening chats which proved a great distraction. Thanks, lovely! Hope you and the family (and, of course, Speedy) enjoy the fruits of your labours.

A big thank you to those special people who have provided

friendship and support, especially during the last several months, including Darren U who also kindly provided the seed of inspiration, and information, for Nate's occupation.

Extra thanks to Jo P for taking me to the wreath making workshop last year (even though we never ended up making a wreath!) Not only was it a good giggle but ended up becoming a very handy inspiration for Sophia and co in this book.

As usual, I'd also like to send a big thank you to the bloggers who help spread the word about my books. Your time, reviews and support are very much appreciated.

And last, but not least, thank you to you, the reader. There are so many wonderful books out there so I am always honoured when you choose one of mine on which to spend some of your precious time. Hearing that it's made you laugh, cry, or kept you up reading way beyond your bedtime (and hopefully all three!) truly fills my heart. Thank you.

MORE FROM MAXINE MORREY

We hope you enjoyed reading *Winter at Wishington Bay*. If you did, please leave a review.

If you'd like to gift a copy, this book is also available as an ebook, digital audio download and audiobook CD.

Sign up to Maxine Morrey's mailing list for news, competitions and updates on future books.

http://bit.ly/MaxineMorreyNewsletter

If you'd like to read more from Maxine Morrey, *#No Filter* is available to buy now.

ABOUT THE AUTHOR

Maxine has wanted to be a writer for as long as she can remember and wrote her first (very short) book for school when she was ten.

As time went by, she continued to write, but 'normal' work often got in the way. She has written articles on a variety of subjects, as well as a local history book on Brighton. However, novels are her first love.

In August 2015, she won Harper Collins/Carina UK's 'Write Christmas' competition with her first romantic comedy, 'Winter's Fairytale'.

Maxine lives on the south coast of England, and when not wrangling with words loves to read, sew and listen to podcasts and audio books. Being a fan of tea and cake, she can (should!) also be found out on a walk (although preferably one without too many hills).

Instagram: @scribbler_maxi (This is where she is to be found most)
Twitter: @Scribbler_Maxi
Facebook: www.Facebook.com/MaxineMorreyAuthor
Pinterest: ScribblerMaxi
Website: www.scribblermaxi.co.uk
Email: scribblermaxi@outlook.com

AUTHOR'S NOTE

If you have enjoyed this book, could I ask for a moment of your time to pop a review on Amazon. One line is plenty! Every single one really does make a difference, helping my books to have a much greater chance of being noticed by more readers. Thank you so much!

Love, Maxine

ABOUT BOLDWOOD BOOKS

Boldwood Books is a fiction publishing company seeking out the best stories from around the world.

Find out more at www.boldwoodbooks.com

Sign up to the Book and Tonic newsletter for news, offers and competitions from Boldwood Books!

http://www.bit.ly/bookandtonic

We'd love to hear from you, follow us on social media:

facebook.com/BookandTonic

twitter.com/BoldwoodBooks

instagram.com/BookandTonic

Printed in Great Britain
by Amazon

84458474R00190